CONSTANTINE CAPERS

The Veil of Death

CONSTANTINE CAPERS

The Veil of Death

NATALIE BRIANNE

Searose Press

MMXXV

To those who carry what they cannot say—
I hope a friend finds you in the dark and will listen,
so you might finally set your secrets free.

When the friend shows his inmost heart to his friend; the lover to his best beloved; when man does not vainly shrink from the eye of his Creator, loathsomely treasuring up the secret of his sin; then deem me a monster, for the symbol beneath which I have lived, and die! I look around me, and, lo! on every visage a Black Veil!

Nathaniel Hawthorne

January 7, 1889: Morning

*S*MOKE. NO, IRON. THAT METALLIC TASTE ON her tongue and the suffocating, smothering flame within her throat. The handkerchief was soaking through. She needed to press harder. Her hands were warm, too warm. But the darkness pressed in and sucked the heat away. Keep the pressure. Don't look at the face. The shadows curled towards her, hot breath in her ear. And that smoke again. The blistering heat. She had to get out.

"*Mira!*"

Byron? Where was he? He wasn't supposed to be there. Durant would kill him. Was it his blood on her hands? No, he came with the fire. But if she just kept holding the handkerchief—

A hand touched her shoulder and she jolted.

"Mira, are you with me?"

Her heart raced and she looked up at him, blinking. Concerned blue eyes stared back at her. The carriage jostled beneath them. She shook her head and took a shallow breath.

"Sorry. I-I was just considering what you said."

She closed her eyes, forcing a deeper breath. What had they been talking about? She couldn't remember. Opening her eyes, she took in the view outside the window, the buildings slipping past in the haze. They were on their way to the police prefecture for her to give her statement. That's what they had been discussing. She still tasted iron. Bringing her hand up to her mouth, she found a split in her lip.

"Are you certain that you're up to this?" Byron asked.

Was she? Her heart raced, the fear she had felt weeks prior pulsing wildly in her veins as if she were captive all over again. But no, she was with Byron. Safe. And he was still waiting for an answer.

"I'll have to be." She brought her gaze to her lap, tugging at each finger of her glove.

He reached over and took her hand. "What is worrying you?"

"We've settled on the story. I know the facts." She paused a moment. "What if they ask about something I can't explain? Or what if I give too much away?" She looked up at him. "I hate lying."

"You don't need to lie, outright. As long as you avoid mentioning Circe by name and don't bring up the Charger, it will be fine."

Her chest tightened. "How can I not mention Professor Burke? He's at the very center of everything."

"Oh, you can mention Professor Burke, certainly. Doting godfather, hero at midnight, drowned in the Seine." There was a flippancy to his tone with an edge of derision.

Mira swallowed. "And leader of a criminal organization."

Byron softened and squeezed her hand. "One of the leaders, yes. But it isn't safe to speak of his role as the Charger. Until we can determine how deep Circe goes in the Parisian government and justice system, we need to be careful of who we talk to about the organization. The more people who know that we know, the greater the danger." He tucked a stray bit of hair behind her ear. "And right now, I think it's best to avoid the danger."

"Says the man who means to steal from the police prefect."

Byron chuckled. "I won't be taking anything. And Prefect Lozé did tell me to do what was necessary to investigate his men."

"I doubt he planned for us to investigate *him*." Mira furrowed her brow. "I know that we have to be vigilant but I find it difficult to picture him as a member of Circe."

He tipped his head to the side, drumming his fingers on his leg. "We don't have enough proof, one way or the other. Though I can't imagine that someone in his position would be unaware of certain corruptions."

"Yes, but you said when you were searching for me in the catacombs, Lozé was surprised when that police officer turned on you."

"Ah yes, Officer . . . something or other."

"Tremblay." She forced a smile. His memory had been improving, but things still slipped through the cracks.

"Yes. Thank you." He cleared his throat. "Tremblay is exactly the issue. Because I was privy to that insubordination, Lozé is allowing me to investigate the prefecture. But he hasn't made any attempt to audit his men himself. Nor has he given me access to the records directly. Perhaps it is due to the language barrier, but I find it difficult to read his intentions."

He sat back in his seat. "On one hand, he may be giving me permission because he knows of the corruption but wants to keep it quiet so that those involved don't spook. On the other, he may be covering his own tracks."

She fidgeted with her gloves again. "If Lozé knows anything at all about Circe, then surely he will know that I am lying."

Byron shook his head. "He doesn't know that you know. That puts us at the advantage. Especially since he'll be underestimating you."

She took a deep breath, a wry smile crossing her lips. "I'm to play the damsel in distress then, am I?"

"If you're up to it. You do play the role so beautifully. Except, of course, when it comes to letting the dashing hero come to the rescue."

"Is he dashing, then?" She laughed in spite of herself.

"Rather," he smiled. "If you play it right, I believe you'll learn more from Lozé than he'll ever learn from you."

"He won't be alone though."

"No. He won't. From what I understand, there will be three people in the interview. Prefect Lozé, a judge, and a constable. I'd be most curious about the judge, personally. We aren't certain how far the corruption goes."

"I'll see what I can learn about each of them, then," she said. "How long will you need?"

"Ten to fifteen minutes. That's about how long Lozé's secretary takes his breaks. As long as Lozé doesn't come back during that time, I believe we'll have everything that we need. Do you think you can manage that?"

She smiled. "I'll give you twenty."

"WHAT IS YOUR RELATIONSHIP WITH EACH OF *the deceased, Miss Blayse?*" Lozé asked.

A bitter taste came to her mouth. "*Edward Burke was my godfather. Selene Vermielle was an acquaintance.*"

She sat in an armchair in one of the interrogation rooms. A fireplace stood behind her, the heat from the flames causing sweat to trickle down the back of her neck. Across from her sat Prefect Lozé, Judge Auclair, and a constable named Chabot who scribbled on a pad of paper. It seemed that Byron was correct in his assumption.

"You were acquainted with a thief?" The judge leaned forward, his wiry brow knitting together.

Even if she weren't being interrogated in French, it would be difficult to explain how she came to know Selene. The truth was simple enough, but would it be enough to not rouse suspicion?

"I work with Detective Constantine as his secretary. As such, we cross paths with all sorts of people."

Chabot's pen scratched over the paper. Lozé cleared his throat.

"Please explain the events that led up to your imprisonment in the catacombs."

Her gaze flicked over each of them in turn. Lozé's mustache twitched, as he sat, hands in his lap. Judge Auclair was an older man with more wrinkles than forehead. He removed his spectacles and wiped at the smudges with a handkerchief. Chabot worried at his lip as his hand muddied the ink on the page.

If she were simply a witness with no ulterior motive, she wouldn't have found anything suspicious about any of them. One could hope that none of them were the type of person to be swayed with promises of power, money, or influence, but one couldn't be certain. Their mannerisms betrayed nothing.

To cover for her initial lack of response, she sniffed a few times and let her breath catch as she pulled a handkerchief from her purse.

"I'm so sorry. I just . . . it was such an ordeal."

Chabot squirmed a little in his chair, clearly uncomfortable with her slight emotional outburst. He seemed a nervous sort, but she didn't know if it was because he had something to hide or because it was his nature.

"*Take your time, Miss,*" Lozé said.

With a couple of dabs to her eyes and a few measured breaths she composed herself again. "*We came to Paris to track down Alexander Durant. At least, that is the alias he has been using with us. He murdered a man named Vincent Sutherland in England, and his movements showed that he would be coming to France.*"

She wrung her handkerchief in her hands, her anxiety creeping up again. "*We discovered that he would be attending the masquerade at Trocadero Palace last month. We found him there but he ran from the scene to the bridge. My godfather was assisting with the investigation and was shot during the altercation. He fell into the Seine.*"

She swallowed, a bout of real emotion threatening to bubble to the surface. Regardless of what really happened with the professor, the godfather she knew and loved was dead. Taking a deep breath, she continued.

"*The next day, we discovered that Durant had likely fled to the quarries beneath Paris. That night, around midnight, Selene Vermielle came to the boarding house where I am staying, explaining that Detective Constantine had gone into the tunnels.*"

"*And you believed her?*" Lozé asked.

She froze. It was a question she had asked herself multiple times since her imprisonment. If only she had recognized the deception. So much hurt could have been avoided. And yet—

"*I had no reason not to, given the circumstances. Detective Constantine had told me that he had some investigations of his own to attend to before leaving me. And we had consulted Vermielle several days previous about Durant's whereabouts. She led me to an entrance to the tunnels. But it was a trap. Durant intended to use me as bait to kill Detective Constantine, thus stopping any threat of being arrested.*"

She bit her lip, trying to remember the exact words Byron had used for the cover story. "*Durant was leading a group of smugglers beneath the city. Once Selene had led me to him, he killed her.*"

"*She was part of the smuggling ring?*" Auclair asked.

"*F-from what I understand, she used to be.*"

"*Why did she work with him, if she had left?*" Lozé asked.

Her stomach twisted as she told another half-truth. "*She wanted to leave the smuggling ring. He promised if she helped him one last time . . . she should have known. Any promise from Alexander Durant is only a delayed lie. After he shot . . .*" She paused, the image coming back to her, the stench of iron. She curled her fingers into her dress. Soft silk. The men were looking at her expectantly. "*I-I was imprisoned in a section of the tunnels until Byron came with the search party. In an attempt to escape, Durant set fire to the tunnels.*"

"*What can you tell us of the smuggling organization?*" Auclair asked.

She swallowed. "*I'm afraid I don't know.*"

Chabot scoffed and they all looked at him.

"*Did you have something to add, constable?*" Lozé asked.

Chabot tensed up his shoulders, gaze flicking between each of them in turn. "*She was kept there for several days. Surely she knows something.*"

Judge Auclair narrowed his eyes at her. "*If you have anything else to tell us, I would suggest you do so.*"

"*I-I'm sorry. They kept me in a cell away from everything. There's nothing else that I remember.*"

"*If you knew nothing, why would Durant take you?*" Chabot asked, leaning forward.

Mira noted the force behind his words. Was his interest simple suspicion or something else?

"*Watch your tone.*" Lozé said, terse. "*This is not an interrogation,*"

"*But he makes a point,*" Auclair said. "*Why does the head of a smuggling ring have interest in you, Miss Blayse?*"

She knew they were referring to Alexander, but her thoughts trailed back to her godfather. After all, he was the true leader of the Crossroads, one of the heads of Circe. She closed her eyes, trying not to think of her discovering the professor within the tunnels and the realization that he had been working with Circe all along. She pushed back the thought that he had killed her parents, that everything had been a lie. Her breath hitched. He'd been prepared to kill her too. The walls seemed to close in, and she was back in that alcove, listening to her beloved godfather discuss poisons and toxins with that French scientist before the police had arrived.

"*Miss Blayse?*" Lozé said.

She took in a ragged breath, coming back to herself. She couldn't keep getting lost in the memories. Why couldn't she keep them at bay?

"*What was the question?*" she asked, voice shaking.

"*What did Durant want with you? Was it personal?*" Auclair asked.

The flames behind her grew hotter, and for a moment it felt like breath on her neck. She forced herself to look up at the judge.

"*As I said before, he knew of my relationship to Detective Constantine and believed he could use me to disrupt the investigation against him. I'm afraid I know nothing more of his plans.*"

Except she did. She knew that he had attempted to usurp the Charger and become the head of the Crossroads. She knew that his burning of the catacombs destroyed the evidence that Circe aimed to start a war in Europe. Her pulse quickened.

"*If you do remember something, please let us know,*" Lozé said. "*I believe anything you have to offer will help during the trial.*"

Mira swallowed, heart heavy. "*When will the trial be held?*"

The judge sat back in his chair. "*With the amount of evi-*

dence against Durant, it would be remiss for us to put it off. I believe, at the latest, March."

Mira's stomach sank. That was much too far away. Why couldn't it just be over already?

Lozé stood and offered her a hand up. *"Thank you for coming in today. May I walk you out?"*

Mira opened her purse, fiddling with the contents as a ruse to glance at her watch. It had only been twelve minutes. Was that enough time? She smiled at him. *"Yes, thank you."*

He opened the door to the interrogation room and escorted her out. *"I apologize for Chabot's behavior. He is fairly new and doesn't know the difference between a statement and an interrogation."*

"I understand." If he was a new constable, was it more likely for him to be a member of Circe?

"Also, I *recognize that you will likely be unable to stay in Paris until March. As long as you return to give your testimony at the time of the trial, you may return to London in the interim. Just be sure to give us your address so we can contact you."*

"Thank you. As it stands, my family intends to stay in Paris, at least for the remainder of January."

A constable approached at a quick pace, folder in hand.

"Sir, I'm sorry to interrupt, but we just received a message from General Boulanger. He's been sent another death threat."

Lozé gave a deep, nasally sigh. *"Give it here."*

He took the folder from the constable and glanced over the contents.

"My apologies, Miss Blayse, I believe I ought to assign this immediately. Do you know the way out?"

Of course she did. She knew the Paris prefecture almost as well as Scotland Yard at this point. And she knew that Lozé would head directly to his office if she didn't do something.

"I-I . . ." she let her voice wobble and placed a trembling hand to her forehead, hesitating near the stairs.

"*Miss Blayse?*" Lozé froze, mid step.

She let herself teeter in place. When Lozé stepped closer, she allowed herself to fall and his arms came to catch her, folder forgotten.

A flurry of movement and noise happened all at once.

"*Cartier, call for Doctor Ogier.*"

"*Ogier is at the conference in Lyon, sir. I could get Doctor Moreau?*"

Lozé sighed again. "*Moreau is at La Santé today. Just fetch some water.*"

She kept herself limp as Lozé carefully laid her on the ground.

"*Godot, I believe Inspector Lafayette has some smelling salts in his office. Can you fetch them?*"

Mira resisted the urge to preemptively scrunch her nose. She'd prefer that the smelling salts never came, but how long could she pretend to be in a dead faint?

"What's happened?"

Her heart leapt.

Lozé switched to English. "I think all the stress was too much for her. She may have overheated. I noticed that the fire was bothering her."

A cold hand came to her forehead. "She is a little feverish."

"I've sent for smelling salts and water. We're just waiting on them."

A strong arm came underneath her, sitting her up. Mira drew a larger breath than usual, fluttering her eyes.

"B-Byron?" she said, as his face came into focus.

"Yes, my love. How are you feeling?"

Strangely, she felt a little dizzy. She looked around. "Did I faint? I don't remember . . ."

"That's my job," he teased, but a flicker of worry remained. "Do you think you can stand?"

She nodded and let him help her up and to a nearby bench.

Byron kept his arm around her. Cartier returned with the water, which she took gratefully. Lozé retrieved the strewn papers and folder.

"I'm so sorry, Monsieur Lozé," Mira said. "I didn't mean to keep you from your work. After all, it seems that you all are quite occupied. Did I hear mention of death threats?"

"It isn't anything to worry about. We wouldn't be half as busy if the politicians would keep their scandals to themselves. But then most of us would be out of a job," Lozé said, chuckling. "Do you need anything else?"

"No, thank you."

He nodded. "Good day, then." He stepped down the hall towards his office.

Byron tightened his hold around her shoulders. "If I had known you were unwell, I would have put off the appointment."

Mira shook her head, suppressing a laugh. "I am perfectly well, thank you. But he was about to go to his office and I didn't know where you were."

Byron's eyes widened. "You didn't actually faint?"

"Heavens no."

"You were so pale!"

"Were you worried, Mr. Constantine?" She tried to hide her smile.

"I always worry." He stood and offered his arm. "How did it go?"

She set her hand on his wrist and let him lead her out of the police prefecture. "It felt wrong." She lowered her voice. "But I think you were right."

"Who was in there with you?" He opened the door and the cold wind swept over them.

"Lozé, Judge Auclair, and a constable named Chabot."

Byron hummed. "I haven't heard of Auclair, but the name Chabot seems familiar. Maybe he was with us in the catacombs."

"I'm not sure about either of them. Chabot spoke out of turn several times, asking what I knew about the organization."

"That could be because of his own involvement or because he heard the name Circe in the tunnels. Anything else?"

She tightened her hold on his arm, stepping around a particularly icy spot on the pavement. "Auclair also questioned me about why Durant would have interest in me, but I think it was because Chabot roused his suspicions."

"And Lozé?"

"He kept trying to divert their questioning. Really, I'm not sure I learned much of anything from any of them. Did you find anything?"

"There were a few gaps in the employment records and I found a couple of unusual letters, but nothing concrete that would tie the police prefecture to Circe. I did find a book of finances, but I didn't have time to check for irregularities. I did manage to get this." He opened his coat and pulled out a folder.

"What's that?"

"A list of individuals who work closely with the police, their addresses, and positions." He tucked it back into his coat.

"I thought you weren't going to take anything."

"I wasn't. But this particular file had dust piling on it. I don't think they'll miss it while I borrow it."

She narrowed her eyes. "Byron . . ."

"Yes, love?"

She sighed. "I suppose since you have it we ought to make the best of it."

"Exactly. For the time being, we carry on as usual continuing to work with the police while keeping our secrets." He waved down a carriage.

"But what of the professor?" She stepped back as the horse came trotting next to them, nostrils steaming. "We can't possibly track him down on our own and if we're the only ones who know that he's alive, he can do whatever he wants with no consequences."

She gave the driver the address of the boarding house. Byron helped her up into the carriage and she settled in as they began to move down the road.

"I doubt that he's still in France," Byron said. "Even if he is, I would expect that the Crossroads and their Charger will lie low for a little while. Whether or not we have allies, we'll have to wait for him to make a move."

"In the meantime," he continued, "it's safer to keep our knowledge of Circe limited to those we know we can trust, don't you think?"

"I suppose." She worried at her lip, the split stinging. "Aside from the two of us, we have Fred, of course, Thatcher, but he's back in London . . ." she trailed off. "Is that it?"

"I've been thinking about the prospect of telling some of your family. Cyrus and Walker—perhaps even Loretta."

Nausea came over her at the thought. "No," she whispered. "They don't need to know."

He frowned. "Why not? They've more than proved themselves. And it would be good for you to have that kind of support."

"They are already mourning the man they thought he was. I wouldn't want to add to that." She shook her head. "It would break my uncle to know about everything."

Byron removed his hat, running a hand through his hair. "I suppose I can see your point there. I just don't want you to have to shoulder this secret alone."

"I'm not alone," she forced a smile, not wanting him to worry. "I have you."

January 7, 1889: Afternoon

*T*HEY REACHED THE LAVIGNE BOARDING HOUSE JUST before dinner. Mira hung her coat on the hook in the hall and rubbed at her arms as Byron closed the door behind them. The clattering of dishes and overlapping voices echoed down the hall from the dining room. Byron offered his arm, and they moved in the direction of the noise. Her cousins, Jean-Marie and Clarisse, were rushing about setting the table.

"*I want the little spoon, Jean-Marie!*" Clarisse shrieked, dashing after her older brother. Jean-Marie laughed and dodged out of the way, narrowly missing Mira in his attempt to escape.

Mira half expected Loretta to pop her head out of the kitchen to admonish them, but the kitchen door didn't sway.

"*Give it back!*" Clarisse said.

"*You'll have to catch me first!*" he bumped against the table, jostling the flatware as he came around the corner.

"Should we do something?" Byron whispered to Mira.

Before she could answer, her Uncle Cyrus came in the side door. "What is all this racket?"

The children stopped in their tracks, Jean-Marie tucking the spoon behind his back.

"He w-was . . ." Clarisse paused, trying to parse the English. "Teasing me!"

"Is that so?" Cyrus said, turning to Jean-Marie.

"I thought she was having fun!" he said.

Cyrus gave him a look. "Make it right."

With a sigh, Jean-Marie passed the spoon over to his little sister, who laughed with delight and moved to place it next to her bowl.

Mira moved over to her uncle and pressed a kiss to his cheek. "Good evening, Uncle."

"Good evening, my dear."

He seemed to be in a good mood, which was hardly a surprise. It had been just about two weeks since Cyrus had proposed to Loretta. They would have run off to be married the day after Christmas if their children, niece, and nephew hadn't insisted on them doing it properly. The last two weeks had been a whirlwind of chaos as they prepared everything for the wedding. Mira almost wished that they would wait for the spring, but the two lovebirds had waited for almost thirty years before finding one another again. They certainly didn't want to waste any more time.

"Have you seen Walker around?" Byron asked. "I had a question for him."

Cyrus shook his head, furrowing his brow. "I haven't seen hide or hair of him since lunch."

"What sort of question?" Mira asked.

"Fred's been itching for company, and seeing as they got on so well I'd hoped that Walker—"

"Talking about me behind my back, are you?" Walker said, clapping Byron on the shoulder.

Byron jolted, turning with a laugh. "Not intentionally, by any means. I was just looking for you."

"Oh, I went for a walk with Georges. Trying to bond with each of my new cousins and all that." He gestured across the room. Georges was helping Clarisse to fold the napkins into little swans. "What can I do for you, though? Did I hear something about dear old Fred?"

Byron straightened. "He's going stir crazy. His wound's almost healed up, but the doctor still has him on bed rest."

"Poor chap. I'd be happy to drop in and liven things up."

The kitchen door opened and Loretta came in with a tureen of soup. "Dinner is ready. Will someone let Klasha and the Allards know?"

"I can!" Clarisse jumped up and down before running from the room. Mira was grateful that most of the boarders had left after Christmas. With all the chaos of wedding planning, she didn't think that Loretta could handle much more stress.

Loretta wiped her hands on her apron. "I really ought to get back on a schedule with things."

"There will be time enough for that in a few days," Cyrus said, moving to pull her chair out for her. "And when we move back to London, you won't need a schedule."

"London?" Loretta furrowed her brow, looking up at him, but did not sit down. "What do you mean?"

Cyrus elaborated. "After the wedding, I thought we'd return to Swan Walk."

"You never mentioned this before."

He paused, a confused look on his face. "I hadn't?"

"No." Her shoulders tightened. "You hadn't."

"Well," Cyrus cleared his throat. "It wouldn't be a permanent move, of course. But there are some things with the business that need to be attended to."

"What about the boarding house? And the—" She cut herself off mid-sentence, realizing that they had an audience. She took Cyrus by the arm and the two disappeared into the kitchen.

A tension was left in their wake. Had her uncle really not thought to discuss his plans with Loretta? Byron reached over and took Mira's hand, giving it a squeeze. She looked up at him, and her unease slowly melted away.

Walker rocked back on his heels. "I think our uncle needs to learn a thing or two about being married."

"Because you have so much experience," Mira teased, moving around to her spot at the table with Byron close behind. The Allards came in soon after. They were an older French couple who had checked in a few days after Christmas and Mira didn't know them very well. Cyrus and Loretta emerged from the kitchen, but Mira couldn't tell if they had worked things out or not. She was about to ask when Clarisse returned, pulling Klasha Ivonovna into the room.

"Slow down, little one. Let the old bones creak a little." Klasha complained, but there was a twinkle in her eye.

"You can sit between Emilie and . . ." Clarisse trailed off. "Emilie not back yet?"

"*Is* Emilie not back yet," Loretta corrected, before frowning. "She was meant to get off at four. Has anyone seen her?"

When no one answered in the affirmative, Loretta shook her head. "Something must have come up. Georges, can you say grace?"

Once everyone was settled, and a prayer said, dinner commenced with the usual talk and bother. Walker spoke up over the low din.

"How did things with the police work out?"

"As well as they could have," Mira said, glancing at Byron. "Durant's trial won't be for another few months."

"Unfortunate," Cyrus said. "But at least he's locked up. We

won't need to worry about this Circe business anymore. Will you need to be there for it?"

Mira swallowed, her muscles tightening. "Yes. They said it would probably be in March, but we don't have to stay in France."

Walker nodded. "Maybe by that time it will be warm enough. We could hold the funeral at the same time."

A rare quiet fell over the dining room. Mira's stomach churned, cold guilt spreading over her as if the soup were ice. Byron took her hand again, grounding her.

The door to the dining room opened and Emilie rushed in. "I'm so sorry." She moved to her mother and gave her a quick hug around the shoulders before taking her seat next to Klasha. "Madame needed me a bit longer today."

"But you'll be . . ." Clarisse frowned and looked at her mother. "Be home tomorrow?"

"That's right, dear," Loretta said.

"Won't you?" Clarisse looked back at her sister.

"Not exactly," Emilie said, serving herself some soup. "Madame needs me as much as possible in the next few days."

Loretta furrowed her brow. "She isn't having you work during the civil ceremony is she?"

"I still can't believe France requires that before getting married in a church," Walker muttered to Mira.

Emilie shook her head. "I can come, but I'll need to return in the afternoon. And Madame is giving me the whole of next week off for the proper wedding."

"My offer still stands," Cyrus said. "You could quit tomorrow if you like."

"I know, but Madame has asked me to stay at least until the end of the election, if not the end of the month. I owe her that much after everything she's done for me. And to make up for it, I have some news!"

"Good news, I hope?" Loretta asked.

Emilie grinned. "As an apology for taking me away, Madame has insisted that she pay for your wedding dress."

Loretta's eyes widened. "W-what?"

"When I asked for the ninth off, she asked me why and when I mentioned that you were getting married, she became so excited. I couldn't talk her down. Not only is she paying for it, but she insisted on it being a Worth gown."

Walker leaned over. "She does realize that the wedding is next week, yes?"

"She does. Which is why she arranged with Worth to have Maman fitted with one of her old dresses tomorrow. Isn't it wonderful?"

Loretta sat there, open mouthed and speechless. Cyrus cleared his throat.

"That is very generous of her."

"More than generous," Loretta said. "We can't possibly accept."

"She won't take no for an answer," Emilie said. "Believe me, I tried."

"Take it as a good omen for your future," Klasha said. "And do not look too closely at the fortune."

"Well . . . I suppose," Loretta said. "The House of Worth . . . that's on Rue de la Paix?"

"Number seven, if I remember correctly," Emilie said.

"That reminds me," Walker said. "Georges and I ran into a little political demonstration around that area on our walk today. Something about revenge?" He buttered a hunk of bread.

Loretta sighed. "The revanchists, yes. They support General Boulanger."

Mira touched Byron's hand. "Didn't he give a speech at the masquerade last month?"

Byron opened his mouth and closed it again, brow furrowing. "I . . . erm . . . I don't quite remember."

"Oh." She flushed. "Sorry."

He shrugged. "I'm afraid my memory thinks there were more important things to pay attention to."

"Who exactly is General Boulanger?" Walker asked.

Monsieur Allard spoke up from down the table.

"He's a politician like the rest of them, with a bit more spirit, I'll grant you. Has this idea of restoring France's glory after we lost Alsace-Lorraine to the Prussians. That's why they call him General Revenge. I call him a coward."

"That's enough, Henri," his wife said.

"No, please continue. I find this all quite fascinating." Walker leaned over the table. "Why is he a coward?"

Mira's stomach churned. It was just like her brother to lean into politics.

"He is all talk and no work. His supporters say that he'll save the country. Save us from what? Peace? If he comes to power, we'll head straight into another war with Prussia, and he'll stay safe in the Elysée while good men die. And if he doesn't come to power, it is because he will be too spineless to take it."

"So he is a coward regardless of the outcome of the election?" Emilie said, her words clipped.

"His true character exists outside of any current events," Henri stated with a nod.

"Have you met him?" Emilie asked.

"No. But I have seen him speak. That tells me enough."

Emilie remained silent. Mira frowned. She didn't take her cousin to be political. Although she had only met Emilie a few weeks before. Perhaps there were things she didn't know about her.

"When is the election?" Byron asked.

"The twenty-seventh of this month," Loretta said. "All I can hope is that it will be peaceful. There's been talk of a coup d'état."

"Why would he stage a coup if he is up for election?" Walker asked.

Henri Allard spoke up. "The current government would rather he stay out of office. If he wins and does not take power immediately, there would be time to find some way of being rid of him. If he wants to guarantee his position as Deputy of Paris, he will need to march on the Elysée the night of the election."

"I hope he has the sense not to. Heaven knows we don't need another Bonaparte," Cyrus muttered.

"I like his mustache!" Clarisse said. "And the hat he wears in pictures."

Mira suppressed a laugh, the tension and discomfort around the table dispersing as others did the same. She decided to use the little girl's outburst as a means to change the course of the conversation.

"If he was the one I remember from the masquerade, I think you would have liked his costume too. He looked like the sun." She turned to Emilie. "Actually, I think I met Madame de Bonnemains there as well. She was dressed as the moon, with silver stars on her cape."

"Yes!" Emilie said. "I remember that dress. It had such a wonderful full skirt that swooshed around the ankles as you turned. And the cape was made of this wonderful crepe."

"Will your wedding dress swoosh, Maman?" Clarisse asked.

"I suppose we'll all find out tomorrow," Loretta said. "Georges, help me with those dishes, won't you?"

January 8, 1889

THE COLD WIND RUSHED PAST THE CARRIAGE as Mira and Loretta trundled their way towards Rue de la Paix. Emilie had asked Mira to take her place and ensure her mother didn't back out of the fitting. Loretta fidgeted with her gloves, staring out the window in silence as she had for most of the ride. Mira could tell that she was anxious, but didn't know quite how to break the tension. It seemed her cousin had been right to worry.

"This is ridiculous," Loretta said, finally. "I don't have time to be playing princess. There's so much to do."

"And it will all get done," Mira said, setting a hand on her soon-to-be aunt's. "The church is reserved, the flowers are ordered, and I'm sure my uncle is overseeing the full scrub of the boarding house as we speak. Everything is ready for tomorrow and once we've baked everything for the celebration next week, everything will be sorted. The only thing missing is your dress."

"The dress I chose was perfectly fine."

"The one you're wearing to the civil ceremony?" Mira raised an eyebrow.

Loretta pulled at a loose thread on her coat. "You forget that I've already had two wedding dresses before. I don't need anything fancy."

"Perhaps. But this wedding is different than the last two."

"Is it?"

"When you first eloped, you married the man you loved, but didn't have family to support you. The second wedding was exactly the opposite. This time, you'll have both. And so this wedding ought to be the best of the three."

A small smile came to Loretta's face. "You do have a point."

"And besides, we don't want to get on the bad side of Madame de Bonnemains, now do we?"

Loretta laughed. "No, I suppose we don't."

THE HOUSE OF WORTH WAS MUCH THE way Mira remembered it from the first time she had visited. She had accompanied Emilie to complete a fitting for the madame, and had spoken with Worth himself about one of his old coworkers. The main difference was the amount of activity. When she had been there before, it was just before Christmas and there weren't many people milling about. Now, there were tailors and customers flitting in and out of the foyer, their steps clicking on the checkered floor. Enormous double doors led to either side, and a grand staircase sat at the back of the space, leading up to additional sewing and fitting rooms. The rhythmic sound of sewing machine pedals reverberated through the space.

Mira led Loretta to the front desk. After the receptionist confirmed their appointment, he called for an attendant to lead them to the fitting room. The attendant introduced herself as Sandrine.

"*If you have any questions at all during your appointment, feel free to ask any of the staff,*" she said. Her blue dress had a very small bustle and puffed sleeves that were so large they reached her ears. "*And of course, if you have any requests for the fitting, be sure to tell the tailor.*"

"*Thank you,*" Loretta said, her gaze trailing up the marble columns.

Sandrine nodded to a few other tailor's assistants and attendants as she led them up the stairs. Most of the attendants had dresses of a similar style to Sandrine's. It was almost comical in comparison to the enormous bustles their clients wore. But if the cuts of the attendants' dresses were any indication, it would seem a great migration of fabric was in the future of women's fashion—from bustle to sleeve.

"*If you would please wait here.*" Sandrine directed them towards a sofa. "*I will inform your tailor of your arrival.*" She curtsied and left the room.

Loretta followed her directions, gaping at the opulence around her. The walls were paneled with boiserie molding and carved frames in a baroque style. Heavy, damask drapery with tassels lined the windows at each side, with thin, voile sheers flowing between. A large mirror stood before them with a screen off to the side.

"I still think this is all too much," Loretta said, smoothing down her skirts. "I can accept that Madame de Bonnemains wishes to lend me her dress, but I could just as easily make the adjustments myself."

"Yes, but it is lovely for her to offer the fitting as well," Mira sat next to her. "You shouldn't have to be the one fussing over all the details."

"It's in my nature to fuss." Loretta's eyes brightened. "I ought to have the right to do it."

Mira laughed. "You and my uncle certainly are meant for one another, aren't you?"

Loretta fell quiet and Mira sobered immediately.

"Is something wrong?"

A flicker of unease crossed her aunt's face before Loretta smoothed out her expression.

"Of course not. I'm just nervous, that's all."

Mira was about to press further, when the door to the room opened again. Two figures stepped in. The first was a man with a light blue vest and grey suit. He had a pencil-thin mustache and thinning black hair that was slicked back. He held a sketchbook under one arm and held the door open for his assistant with the other.

His assistant carried a large parcel in her arms. Her deep red walking dress fluttered about her ankles as she crossed the room, the color contrasting with her deathly pale complexion. She walked in a strict manner, and held herself as if she were much older than she was. That being said, Mira couldn't imagine that the woman was older than thirty-five.

"*Which one of you is here for the fitting?*" the man asked.

Loretta stood. "*I am she.*"

He gave a sharp nod and stepped forward. "*I am Pierre Marchand and this is my assistant, Liliane Aguillard.*"

As he gestured towards her, Liliane set the parcel on the table and began unwrapping the tissue paper and string that held the dress. Strands of her dark, brown hair fell into her face and she brushed them behind her ears as she unfolded the skirt and lifted it up for them to see.

The fabric was a light rose colored silk—appropriate for a widow remarrying—with embroidered flowers, swirls, and lace in a wide strip along the hem. Several more embroidered flowers were scattered along the full length of the skirt. The center of each flower was beaded with pearls. Liliane draped the skirt over her arm and picked up the bodice. The sleeves were made of the same kind of lace and embroidery, while the rest of the bodice was modest in its decoration.

"*If you would follow her behind the screen, she will help you into the garment,*" Marchand said.

Loretta hesitated only a moment before following the tailor's assistant out of sight.

"*What was your name, miss?*" Marchand asked.

"*Samira Blayse. I'm her niece.*"

He nodded. "*I am to understand that she is to be married in a few days?*"

"*Tomorrow is the civil ceremony. Their wedding is next week. Thank you for accommodating us at short notice.*"

"*You are certainly cutting it fine,*" he tutted and consulted his sketchbook. "*It is usually not our custom to refit a gown that was previously worn by a client, but for Madame de Bonnemains, we seem to always make exceptions.*" He spoke under his breath, but Mira was certain he meant for her to hear.

Loretta emerged from behind the screen, Liliane helping her with the short train as they moved to the platform and mirrors. Based on the cut of the dress, it was meant for evening wear, but Loretta looked every bit a bride, even without a veil. She seemed to glow, a true joy exuding from her as she turned from one side to the other, looking in the mirror. Her worry lines faded away and she carried herself with a lighter air. Mira smiled at the transformation. It felt like she was privy to a glimpse of a past Loretta, one without the hurt and heartache.

"*I think there will need to be a slight adjustment in the neckline, and we will want to bring up the hem,*" Liliane said, producing a pin cushion and setting to work on tacking things in place, her pale hands working quickly. Marchand made a note in his sketchbook and stepped forward.

"*Stop. You are turning the hem unevenly.*" He paused, a sheepish smile crossing his face. "*Apologies, ladies. Liliane is still in training.*"

He stooped to the level of the hem and modeled the method of pinning. The rest of the fitting followed after the same manner, with Liliane attempting to follow the proper pattern, and inevitably failing to fall in line with Marchand's strict methodology.

When Loretta emerged once again from behind the screen in her own clothes, Liliane's eyes were wet and her gaze avoidant as she took the dress and left the room.

"*How long has she been your assistant?*" Mira asked.

"*A few months,*" he sighed. "*She came highly recommended, but I do not see why.*"

"*Perhaps you are too hard on her,*" Loretta said. "*She will learn with time.*"

He straightened. "*The House of Worth is not the place to learn such skills, but rather to improve them.*" He opened the door. "*If you ladies would care to wait in the foyer, Liliane will bring you the information for picking up the dress.*"

Loretta and Mira found their way down the stairs to the foyer. The receptionist looked up at them as they approached.

"*Will you be requiring a follow-up appointment?*"

"*No, thank you,*" Loretta said.

They sat on the bench by the far wall and Mira grinned.

"You were a vision, Loretta. Absolutely beautiful."

Loretta ducked her head. "It was rather marvelous, wasn't it? Now I only need to figure out the rest of the ensemble."

"Well, I believe you have the 'something borrowed' sorted, as you are borrowing the gown from Madame de Bonnemains."

Loretta let out a surprised laugh. "That's right! And the amethyst ring your uncle gave me can count for something new."

Liliane came down the steps, and the two of them stood to meet her.

"*The alterations will be finished in a few days. If you'll write down your current address, we'll send a note when it is finished.*"

Loretta took the paper and pen from her, jotted down the address and handed it back. "*Thank you so much for your help.*"

"*It was my pleasure. I apologize for the difficulties in fitting, Madame de Bonnemains.*"

Loretta shook her head. *"Oh, no. My name is Lavigne. I am only here at the madame's behest."*

Liliane's eyes widened, *"I'm sorry, I didn't realize."*

"It is perfectly all right. You did a wonderful job, Liliane," Loretta said. *"Do not let him get to you."*

"Thank you, Madame. You are too good."

As they left the House of Worth, Loretta took Mira's.

"He really was too harsh with her," Loretta said. "Nothing she did compromised the garment. And she only pricked me once. Why, when I work on my own children's clothes, I tend to draw more blood."

"He seemed to be a very unhappy man," Mira said, looking back over her shoulder.

"Well, I can't worry another minute about him," Loretta said. "There is far too much to do."

WHEN THEY RETURNED TO THE BOARDING HOUSE, the place was spotless. Loretta kissed Cyrus on the cheek and headed off to the kitchen to work on dinner. Mira smiled and headed up the stairs to the room she shared with Emilie. Of course, it had been her cousin's all along. When Mira had first come to stay at the boarding house, it had been one of the only rooms available. While several tenants had moved out since then, Emilie still insisted on sharing when she was home from Madame de Bonnemains. Emilie had said, "It's not worth the fuss of you moving everything. And besides, we're going to be sisters in a way. We ought to act like it."

Mira smiled at the memory and set to work on hemming Jean Marie's suit (handed down from Georges) and Clarisse's new dress. They'd already taken the proper measurements the night before, so it was a simple—if tedious—process. She sat near the fire and let herself get lost in the repetitive motions. Her thoughts wandered.

Byron would probably be back at Rue Geoffroy. He'd mentioned that he wanted to visit La Santé prison to see if he could interrogate any of the men from the catacombs. Would he have met with Durant? She shivered and rethreaded her needle. Better to think of something else.

About halfway through the alterations, the door opened and Emilie came in. Her cousin took off her coat and hat and threw them over an armchair with a sigh.

"Is everything alright, Em?" Mira said.

"Oh!" Emilie jolted, turning in place. "Yes, everything is fine." Her shoulders slumped as she kicked off her shoes.

Mira raised an eyebrow. Emilie sighed again, sitting on the bed.

"Don't look at me like that. I'm tired, that's all." She adjusted her skirt. "Nothing that a bit of rest can't fix."

Mira hummed and tied off her stitch.

Emilie pulled her feet up under her. "Really, I think the hardest bit, today, was handling Madame's cat," she teased.

Mira frowned. She didn't remember there being a cat when she visited Madame de Bonnemains with Emilie a few weeks prior. She said as much.

"The little thing was a Christmas gift. It's a kitten, and it seems to want to get its claws on everything, myself included." She rubbed at her arm.

Mira leaned over and caught sight of a line of scratches along Emilie's wrist. "It seems both you and your mother were stuck with needles today."

Emilie's eyes brightened a bit. "What happened with the dress? Did Maman like it?"

"Once I finally convinced her that she deserved it, she did. She was fussing up until she went behind the screen. But when she came out well, it was incredible, Em."

"It should have been. I helped to pick it out." Emilie slumped back with a laugh.

"Well yes, the dress was gorgeous. But . . ." Mira paused in rethreading the needle. "She seemed to carry herself like a different person. As if all of the stress had melted away. She looked . . . younger. As beautiful as ever, but happier."

Emilie's expression softened. "I wish I could have been there."

"I wish you could have too."

The fire crackled in the hearth and Mira managed to thread the needle to start on a new section.

"Am I a good person?" Emilie said after a moment, breaking the silence.

Mira frowned at the abrupt change in subject. "What sort of a question is that? Of course you're a good person."

"How can you be so sure?" Emilie sat up. "You've only known me for a month or so."

"Why are you asking?" Mira studied her cousin's face. There was a weariness to her gaze that didn't come from physical exhaustion.

Emilie fell silent for a moment, considering the question. "I was fifteen when Père died. He left so many debts. We've been paying them all this time. Maman has had to work so hard, all of us have."

She sniffed, a few tears coming to the surface. Mira set her sewing aside and moved next to her on the bed.

"This is so silly."

"No, it's alright." Mira pulled a handkerchief from her pocket and handed it over.

Emilie dabbed at her eyes. "I never knew that Père wasn't my father. And now your uncle has come—my real father. He's paid off everything all at once. Maman will never have to work again. He's offered to take care of me as well. I'm terrible, Mira." She sobbed.

Mira put an arm around her, pulling her close. "No, Em. You're not."

"But I'm so angry! Why couldn't he have come sooner? Or not at all?" She cried into Mira's shoulder, shudders going through her body.

A creak on the floor brought Mira's gaze up to the open doorway. Walker stood there, eyes wide. She motioned for him to leave and he nodded, closing the door softly behind him.

Emilie pulled back, taking a breath and wiping her eyes. "I was going to pay it all off this year."

"You saved enough?"

She wrung the handkerchief in her hands. "Madame de Bonnemains was going to help." She bit her lip. "And maybe it's just as well that everything has happened the way it has. I know it isn't his fault that he had to leave."

"No. If he could have stayed, he never would have left you."

Emilie's eyes brimmed with tears again. "I do love him. And I'm so happy for Maman. But I'm still so angry."

"So am I."

Emilie froze, looking at her. "You are?"

Mira lay back, closing her eyes. So much of her life had been dictated by Circe, without her even knowing. Her parents' deaths, Cyrus and Loretta being forced to separate, her investigations with Byron. And at the heart of it all, her godfather. A burning heat spread through her, tears coming to the surface.

"Mira?" Emilie squeezed her hand.

She opened her eyes, letting the tears fall. "We've lost so much time."

"I know. I hate it." Emilie passed the handkerchief back.

Mira laughed, sitting up and dabbing at the tears. "Then can we be angry for a little while longer?"

Her cousin considered the question a moment and nodded. "But we'd best be done with it by tomorrow. We wouldn't want to ruin the ceremony."

"I think I can manage that," Mira smiled.

January 9, 1889

THE MOONLIGHT WAS STILL TRICKLING THROUGH THE
window with no sign of the sun when Mira woke the
next morning. It wasn't because she wanted to be awake, but
rather that she couldn't fall back asleep. The particulars of the
nightmare had left her the moment she opened her eyes, but
she couldn't shake the sense of unease in its wake. After lying
in bed for a few minutes, she did something that she hadn't
done since she was small. She left her room and went to find
her uncle.

His room was just down the hall from hers. Coldness seeped
into her bare feet from the floor as she pressed down the hall.
She hesitated outside his door. Did she want to disturb him?
After all, it was only a dream.

A hand came to her shoulder and she jolted, a scream
tearing up her throat. Another hand came to her mouth as she
turned to find the darkened form of her brother standing there.

Scream muffled, he let go of her and she took a few measured breaths.

He held his hands out in defense as she whacked him on the shoulder.

"What are you doing?" she whispered.

"I was coming to check on you, when I saw you coming down the hall. And I knew when you saw me, you'd scream. Didn't want you to wake everyone up." His voice was soft but alert.

"Why were you checking on me?" She folded her arms across her chest.

"I heard you call out. Nightmare?"

She gave a short nod. "What were you doing up?"

"Same reason as you, I expect."

They both looked towards their uncle's door.

"Everything is going to change tomorrow, isn't it?" Mira said.

Walker took her hand. "It feels like it, doesn't it?"

It was only the civil ceremony. The church wedding wouldn't be for a week. But regardless, Cyrus would be married. What a strange thought that was.

The door opened, letting out a line of flickering light and both of them startled. Cyrus stood on the threshold, a lit candle in hand, his eyes wide at the sight of them.

"What are you two standing in the dark for?" he hissed.

The twins looked at each other and then at him.

"Where are you going?" Walker said, eyebrow raised.

Blustering, Cyrus took a step back. "I . . ."

"Yes?" Mira said.

Taking a breath, he said, "I was coming to look in on the two of you, actually." He looked down the hall. "Why don't you both come in?"

He brought his arm back so that the candle was out of the way, and the twins stepped into the room. Door closed, Cyrus moved to each of the gas lamps and coaxed them up into a small flame.

"Will you answer my question now?" he asked.

"We both couldn't sleep," Mira said.

"Do you . . ." Walker started, rubbing the back of his neck.

" . . . check on us often?" Mira finished.

Cyrus sighed, settling onto the foot of the bed. "When either of you are at home, yes. Usually when I can't sleep it's because I'm anxious. Seeing the two of you safe calms me enough that I can get some rest."

"Are you anxious, Uncle?" Walker teased.

"Yes," Cyrus said, without hesitation.

Mira sat next to him on the bed. "What about?"

He ran a hand over his face. "Quite a few things, to be honest."

Walker came to sit on his other side and the trio sat in silence for a few minutes.

Finally, Cyrus said, "It's been the three of us for so long."

"Four, if you count Landon," Walker said.

Cyrus chuckled. "Four, then."

"Oh, and there's the cat," Walker said, counting it out on his fingers. "That would make five. Although he's only been around for a year."

Mira swatted at him behind their uncle's back. "Would you stop teasing?"

Cyrus laughed, a round full laugh that had them all falling into giggles. He took both of their hands in his and squeezed them. "It was six, until . . ."

Their mirth slipped away in an instant, leaving a cold silence in its wake. Mira's shoulders tightened, as if her guilt was a crushing serpent wrapping its body around her neck.

"He would have been the best man," Walker said.

Mira closed her eyes. They wouldn't be speaking so fondly if they knew the truth. Mira's father could have been the best man if they had never known the professor. In fact, Cyrus and Loretta might have lived a happy life together already if Edward Burke had been a stranger instead of a so-called friend. As if such a man could ever be considered "best."

Cyrus put his arm around her shoulder, bringing her closer, even as her insides roiled with unspoken truths.

"I'm sure he'll be watching," he said, as if the thought were comforting.

They sat in silence for several moments, until Walker said, "I will miss this."

Cyrus chuckled, putting his other arm around his nephew. "As will I."

"It doesn't have to change," she whispered.

"Oh, but it does," Cyrus said. "It already has. So much has changed in just a few short months." He squeezed Mira's hand again. "And the future is uncertain."

"We'll sort it out," Walker said. "We always do."

"Yes, we do." Cyrus released their hands.

"This is just adding to our family," Mira said.

"Adding to the chaos, more like," Walker laughed. "But I've always wanted brothers, and it's not as if Liza has any to spare. Although, if you and Constantine ever figure things out, that's three."

Mira blushed a little, but smiled. "I've always wanted sisters."

"Three for each of us. I'd say that's fair," Walker said. "And an aunt to boot!"

Cyrus laughed. "What silly children I've raised." He kissed each of their foreheads. "And what a privilege."

Mira settled her head onto her uncle's shoulder again. For a moment, it felt as if time had stopped and if she didn't move they could stay that way forever. She held her breath as long as she could, but the unrelenting sun came creeping over the windowsill, just the same.

MIRA HAD NEVER ATTENDED A WEDDING BEFORE. She'd always thought the first one she'd attend would be hers or Walker's. Or, as a much younger Mira hoped, both of them getting married on the same day. She'd had great daydreams of what the ceremony would be like.

The civil ceremony was not at all what she imagined. When their family arrived at the town hall at fifteen minutes to noon, they were ushered upstairs into one of the marriage rooms. They waited there for several minutes under the watchful eye of a stone bust that stood off to the side. Clarisse kicked her feet on the red carpet, and though the group whispered, their voices still echoed in the space. Eventually the deputy mayor came in with the paperwork. Mira translated for those who didn't speak French (mainly her uncle), and Walker and Emilie were witnesses.

It was a rather quiet affair with only the family of either side in attendance. Her uncle and new aunt signed the marriage certificate and that was that. In truth, it took longer to take the photograph after the fact than it did to actually marry the two of them, and that was mostly due to trying to figure out how to arrange everyone. In the end, Cyrus and Loretta sat in front with Clarisse on her mother's lap, Emilie, Georges, and Jean-Marie stood behind her, and Walker and Mira stood behind Cyrus.

By quarter past one, they were all back at the boarding house, shaking off their wet things from the rain that had descended in the interim. Klasha had prepared tea and hot chocolate for the group, which everyone was grateful for.

Cyrus stood by the fireplace and held out a hand towards Loretta, beckoning her to join him. If Mira had been asked a month before how she would describe her uncle, she would have said he was a melancholy and grim man, caught up in years of grief. The man who raised her looked barely recognizable as he took Loretta's hand in his and turned to face their little family. Both of them were younger, happier, and—most importantly—at peace.

"Was that all?" Clarisse asked, brow furrowed. "You are married?"

"In the eyes of the law," Loretta said. "But it won't be official until we're married in the sight of God."

Cyrus smiled, "We are at least half-married."

"And you were married before." Walker said. "So that counts for at least another quarter."

"Good point, my boy," Cyrus said. "And three quarters of a marriage is practically a whole one. Which I believe, gives me the right to kiss you."

Loretta shook her head, laughing, and kissed him first.

"Can we have the . . ." Clarisse scrunched up her nose and switched to French. "*Are we going to have the party now?*"

"No, love," Loretta said, "We'll celebrate next week."

"And good thing too," Emilie said, setting her teacup to the side and standing. "Because I need to return to Madame."

"Already?" Cyrus said.

"Couldn't you stay a little while longer?" Loretta said.

"I've already stayed longer than I should have," Emilie said. "Just a few more days, and then I'll be off for a whole week."

"*And we will play games?*" Clarisse said.

"*As many as you like,*" Emilie said. She turned to her parents, taking one of their hands in each of hers. "I'm so happy for the two of you." She kissed them both on the cheek.

Cyrus pulled her into a hug. "I'm happy for all of us. I only wish it could have happened sooner."

THAT AFTERNOON, MIRA SAT IN HER ROOM and pulled out her sketchbook for the first time in weeks. Oh, how she missed it! Her hands were quickly covered in graphite smudges as a crude sketch of the wedding party took shape beneath her pencil.

A knock came at the door and before she could say, "Come in," her brother crossed the threshold.

"You have a visitor downstairs," he said,

She furrowed her brow. "Byron?"

"Are you expecting any other gentlemen?" He widened his eyes in mock surprise.

She ignored his teasing and set her sketchbook to the side, glancing in the mirror to tuck some stray strands of hair behind her ear.

"Before you get too excited," Walker said as they walked down the stairs. "Cyrus called for Klasha. The dreaded chaperone strikes again!" Walker set a hand to his forehead in a dramatic fashion.

She rolled her eyes and parted ways with him, Walker heading to the kitchen and Mira moving into the sitting room. Byron stood as she came in.

"Good morning, Miss Blayse," he nodded to her.

"Good morning, Mr. Constantine," she nodded back. They hadn't seen one another in two days and she wanted nothing more than to pull him into a hug.

Klasha snorted from where she sat in her chair by the fire, needlework in hand. She worked deftly with her red threads. "Do not have the formalities on my account."

Both of them laughed a little and Mira moved over. "Hello, Byron."

He took her hand and kissed the back of it. He glanced down at it as he led her to the sofa. "You've been sketching again?"

"I thought I'd memorialize the wedding. Although in a few weeks we'll have a photograph."

Byron sat as close as he dared to her, and she could feel his warmth.

"How was the wedding?" he asked.

Mira paused, trying to find the words. "It was rather abrupt, all told."

"A rare case of efficient bureaucracy?" Byron teased.

She laughed a little. "You could call it that. It certainly wasn't romantic."

"And what sort of wedding would you say is?" He tapped his finger on the top of her hand.

A flush came to her cheeks and she ducked her head with a smile. "Oh, I don't know . . ."

"I'm sure you have some idea." He leaned closer, with one eye on their chaperone. Klasha, for her part, didn't seem to notice.

Mira gently pushed him back. "The sort that has more flowers and music and significantly less paperwork."

"The French do love their paperwork, don't they?"

"I'm sure you know better than I do. How did things go with Lozé?"

That sobered Byron up immediately, and Mira regretted asking.

He lowered his voice. "He gave me a pass to visit La Santé yesterday, but when I arrived they would only allow me to see a few of the prisoners."

"Durant?" Mira asked, pulse quickening.

He shook his head. "He was meeting with the police physician at the time. I said I would wait, but they didn't trust me enough to speak with him. I did meet with a few of the lesser members. Rousselot, Astier, and Cordonnier if I remember their names correctly. Every one of them was obstinate. I'm afraid we won't get much out of them about the whereabouts of the pro—" He glanced up at Klasha and amended his statement "—the Charger."

"I doubt they would know even if they did talk. So few people know the identity of any of the leaders of Circe." She sat back.

Klasha cleared her throat. "It would seem I am out of blue thread. Can I trust you two to continue speaking of business while I step out to find some?"

"Of course," Mira said, glancing at her all red crewel work.

Klasha nodded and stood, leaving her needlework on her chair as she left the room.

"I think she's my favorite chaperone," Byron said.

"She doesn't have much in the way of competition," Mira sighed, blowing some hair from her face. "Seeing as the last one was the Charger and was quite willing to kill both of us."

"If only they would let me talk to Durant," Byron said. "He's our only lead at the moment."

"I don't think he'd talk to you even if the police let you in." She slumped back. "And we can't exactly negotiate with him, as there's nothing we can offer."

"Yes. His freedom isn't exactly on the table." Byron drummed his fingers on his leg.

"You're right though. He might know where the professor is hiding. And he knows the identity of the Hound. If he would only do something decent for once."

Byron put an arm around her. "Whether he helps us or not, at least he can't hurt anyone else."

She leaned into his shoulder, an involuntary shudder running through her at the thought of Alexander escaping. If there was corruption in the police force, would it extend to the prisons as well? The fire crackled in the hearth, much too warm. But she smelled sandalwood instead of smoke and heard Byron's heart beating, steady and calm.

January 10, 1889: Morning

*T*HE NEXT MORNING, EVERYONE WENT ABOUT THEIR business as if a wedding hadn't happened at all. Georges and Jean-Marie went to work. Klasha was assigned to keep Clarisse entertained for the day. In the library, Loretta and Cyrus discussed the final particulars for their wedding at the church. Thus, Mira and Walker were left to be bored in the sitting room.

It rather reminded her of a winter when they were twelve. There was no snow to play in, no lessons to be done, and they'd grown bored of their usual games. They'd spent some time telling each other secrets and coming up with new ones to keep from their uncle. By the end of one particular day, they'd ended up laying backwards on the armchairs to see who could stand being upside down the longest. They never found out, because

Landon or their uncle came in to chide them for having their feet on the furniture.

The scene was almost the same, in terms of boredom, but with their feet planted on the ground. They were making a good show of staving off ennui. Mira was working on a scrap quilt while Walker read from Middlemarch.

"'Certainly those determining acts of her life were not ideally beautiful,'" he read. "'They were the mixed result of young and novel impulse struggling amidst the conditions of an imperfect social state, in which great feelings will often take the aspect of error, and great faith the aspect of illusion.'"

They'd been reading it on and off since Christmas, and truly she'd only heard half of it. Walker's voice inevitably became background noise to her thoughts about Byron, Circe, and the professor. She wished she could forget it all for a little while, that her mind would not be so occupied with such terrible things. Not that Byron was terrible, mind you. He was the bright spark in everything. But part of her wished that she never knew about Circe, or Durant, or any of the sordid things she knew because of her acquaintance with him.

Although, perhaps it had always been her fate to be thus entangled. Professor Burke was so involved with her family, practically another uncle, that even if she wasn't consciously aware of Circe and their dealings, they would always be affecting her. Was it better to know the truth or to be kept in ignorance? A silly thought to have, seeing as she couldn't very well throw her knowledge to the wayside and skip back into the soft embrace of inexperience. She was burdened with knowledge and secrets and unable to do anything with them.

"Mira?" Walker said.

She blinked and looked up at him. "Yes?"

He held up the book. "We've finished. I just asked what you thought of it."

She opened her mouth and closed it again. What did she

think of it? Nothing. Nothing at all. Once, she would have told her brother anything and everything about her life. They had no secrets between them. Now, she wasn't even being truthful about listening to him.

"It was rather long," she said, trying to remember anything of the plot she could use in conversation.

A knock came at the door, and Mira let out a short sigh of relief. "Just a moment." She stood, heading for the entryway. Perhaps by the time the visitor had left, Walker would have forgotten about Middlemarch. And if it was Byron, all the better. Although, he'd promised to stop by in the afternoon, so it was a little early.

When she opened the door, she found a woman standing on the front step. Her eyes were rimmed with red and she shivered as she pulled a threadbare coat tighter around her shoulders. She seemed vaguely familiar, but Mira couldn't place her face.

"*Is this the Lavigne residence?*" she asked, in French.

"*Yes, it is,*" Mira said. "*Are you looking to board?*"

The woman shook her head, stepping closer. "*I must speak with Madame Lavigne, immediately.*"

Mira hesitated. "*I can find her for you. May I ask why?*"

"*No, I must speak with her alone.*"

Mira moved back so that the woman could enter and closed the door behind her. An uneasy feeling settled in her gut as she led the woman to the sitting room. "*What was your name?*"

"*Heloise Pichard.*" Her breath hitched and she seemed liable to cry at any moment.

"*Walker this is Heloise. Can you sit with her for a moment while I fetch Loretta?*" She tried to communicate silently for him to keep a close watch over her, just in case.

"*Of course.*" He pulled a handkerchief from his pocket and offered it to the woman as Mira left the room. Mira found her aunt and uncle still working in the library.

"Loretta, there is a woman to see you. Her name is Pichard. Do you know her?"

Her aunt frowned. "I'm afraid not. Did she say why she came?"

"No, although she seemed rather distressed." She worried her lip. "Something feels wrong about it all. She wants to speak with you alone."

Cyrus stood. "She'll have to settle for talking to both of us. Where is she?"

"In the sitting room. She's with Walker."

The three of them walked back down the hall and entered the sitting room.

"*You asked to see me?*" Loretta asked.

Heloise sat up straighter, her form quivering. "*Can I speak with you alone?*"

"*May my husband stay?*"

The woman's gaze flicked to Cyrus and she nodded.

Walker stood and moved with Mira into the foyer, closing the door behind them.

"I don't like this," Mira said, rubbing her arms.

"I'm sure there is a reasonable explanation," Walker said, leaning back on his heels. "She seemed incredibly upset."

So did Selene, Mira thought.

A weighted silence fell over them, punctured by a scream and something crashing behind the door. Mira's eyes widened as she rushed into the room, Walker right behind her. A vase had fallen from one of the side tables and lay in pieces on the floor. Loretta sat next to it, in a heap, sobbing, with Cyrus holding her. Heloise sat on the sofa, pale as anything and looking as if she wanted to bolt.

"What's happened?" Mira asked. Walker blocked the doorway.

"I don't know," Cyrus said. "I didn't understand what they were saying."

Mira turned to Heloise. "*What did you say to her?*"

"*I'm so sorry,*" Heloise said, eyes shining with tears as she repeated what she had told Loretta.

Mira froze.

"What did she say?" Cyrus asked.

Mira stepped back, a hand coming to her throat as she locked eyes with her uncle.

"She's dead." Her voice was hoarse. "Emilie is dead." She knew what each of the words meant individually, but somehow it didn't make sense together. A coldness spread over her, emanating from her core.

Cyrus blinked at her. "No . . . that isn't . . . how is it possible?" He looked back at Heloise, then his wife. "What happened?"

Mira repeated the question in French, stumbling over the words. Her own voice sounded foreign to her, as if it weren't connected with her at all. Her body was going through the motions but she couldn't feel anything. It was as if she was floating a pace off, watching it all. Walker came to stand next to her, placing a hand on her shoulder and while she was aware of it, she didn't feel it.

"*She was very sick last night. This morning she didn't come upstairs.*"

Mira relayed the story to her uncle, her breath hitching in her chest. Her lungs didn't seem to know how to work properly on their own.

"*I don't understand,*" Loretta said, finding the strength to compose herself. "*She was perfectly fine when she left us.*" The light from the window made her blonde hair seem white.

"*I wish I knew more,*" Heloise pulled at the cuffs of her coat. "*Madame wanted you to know as soon as possible. She sent me here straight away, and another of us to the police.*"

Loretta pulled away from Cyrus' hold and stood. "*Take me to her.*"

"*Yes madame, right away,*" Heloise said.

Despite the urgency of the statement, the group stayed frozen for a moment or so more before bursting into a flurry of movement. Walker moved directly to the stairs, citing a need to inform Klasha that she would be in charge of the boarding house. The rest of them tracked down coats and hats to leave as soon as possible.

In the hubbub, Cyrus stopped Mira with a hand on her arm, his eyes rimmed with red.

"I know you'd like to come with us, but I need you to fetch Byron. Regardless of how it happened, I'd feel better if he was there."

Her grief mixed with a strange warmth at his request. He'd been so against Byron when they'd first met, and yet he was so quick to ask for his help now.

Mira swallowed. "I'll bring him at once."

THE COLD BIT AT MIRA'S CHEEKS AS she trundled along the street in an open carriage towards Rue Geoffrey. She hardly noticed, as the cold inside her was far more bitter than anything nature could make. Even with a little time and distance from the scene in the sitting room, she still couldn't understand the words.

Emilie is dead.

The sentence repeated again and again, overlaid with memories of her cousin. Her wonderful, beautiful cousin. She had known her for such a short time. How would it be for her brothers and little Clarisse to find out?

A few tears escaped and she wiped them away with her gloved hand. Heloise could be mistaken, couldn't she? There could be some misunderstanding, some fault in her comprehension of the language. Except there was no mistaking the grief in Loretta's expression. Mira knew the pain of losing both parents. She had witnessed the grief of her uncle for his sister. This pain seemed far, far worse.

She wrapped her fingers around her mother's brooch, rubbing the cameo with her thumb. The carriage would soon approach Rue Geoffrey and Byron's flat. Could she get through an explanation without falling to pieces? This wasn't just her cousin. Emilie was her uncle's only child, one he didn't know about until recently. Her poor uncle. To lose his parents, his sister, his closest friend, and now his child. Somehow she felt greater grief for her uncle and aunt's loss than for her own.

She paid the driver and stepped onto the pavement, looking up at the building. If she was to be any use to Byron at all, she couldn't be fragile. He would need her to be alert and observant, and that was difficult to achieve through tears. She took a bracing, shuddery breath and wiped the remaining tears away. She could be a proper secretary, even on a case like this.

With another breath, Mira's emotions stacked themselves, waiting to be dealt with later. They sat together like sticks in a pile waiting to be burned, but the hearth remained unlit. She couldn't allow a single ember if she were to be successful. Just a few hours and she could let it go up in smoke in the secret security of her own room. Of Emilie's room. She tamped down that thought, stepped up to the door and let the knocker fall with a clang.

A moment or so later, Fred opened the door.

"Why if it isn't Miss Mira Blayse!" He called her name over his shoulder, announcing it into the house. The cheeriness of his tone was such a contrast to the scene she had come from, she almost wanted to cry. "What a pleasure to see you," he said, before frowning a little. "Are you alright? Your face is a bit red."

"It's just the cold," she said, giving a wan smile. "I'm surprised that you're up and about."

He pulled the door wider and allowed her into the entry-way. "Oh, I just wanted to make sure my feet still worked." He moved a bit stiffly as he brought her to their little sitting room. "Besides, it is boring sitting in bed all day."

"I know the feeling." The normality of the conversation was so dissonant to her true feelings, and yet she found herself falling into the familiar pattern. Her voice carried on as if it had a mind of its own. "I thought I'd never be free when I twisted my ankle. But that is a little different from being stabbed."

"Is it? I hadn't noticed," Fred teased.

She didn't laugh, even though she ought to have. She didn't have the energy to care.

Fred frowned. "I'll go fetch Byron. Won't be a minute!"

Mira stepped farther into the room, observing everything and yet only seeing the similarities between this sitting room and the one at the boarding house. The curtains hung like veils framing the window. She could almost see Heloise sitting in front of it. She turned away, choosing to sit on an adjoining sofa instead. But from there, she could envision Loretta sobbing on the floor. She closed her eyes, but it didn't help. The image of her aunt's grieving form was burned into her mind's eye and there was no escaping it.

A creak on the stairs above gave plenty of warning, so she pushed her emotions back yet again. A few more footsteps and Byron came into the room, journal in hand as if he had been referencing one of the pages.

"I thought I was visiting you today?" he asked.

"I'm afraid there's been a change of plans." She pulled at the fingers of her gloves, trying to determine the best way to explain the situation.

"How so?" Byron asked, coming closer.

She looked up at him. "Emilie is dead. We got the news this morning."

His eyes grew wide. "How did it happen?"

"I don't know. The messenger was one of the other maids. She came for Loretta."

He came and sat next to her, taking her hand. "How are you feeling?"

The phrase meted out a tiny spark that latched onto the grate in her heart, threatening to burn everything. In a moment she could be a mess of tears, blubbering about every past grief that weighed upon her soul. With a careful breath, she doused it.

"A bit shocked," she said, knowing he wouldn't allow her to ignore the question. "My uncle sent me to fetch you. I'm not sure, but I believe he wants us to investigate."

"He thinks it's murder?" His brows knit together, his hand tightening around hers.

"We don't know one way or the other. But I think we'd all feel better about it if you came."

"Let me grab my coat." He stood but paused after a step. "Do you need anything before we leave?"

She shook her head. "The sooner we get there, the better."

THEY REACHED THE RESIDENCE OF MADAME DE Bonnemains a little after noon. The house seemed quiet, with the exception of two police vehicles and an ambulance on the street. A man stood nearby, keeping an eye on the horses. The silent, looming dread had Mira hesitate on the pavement.

"What is it?" Byron asked, stopping beside her.

I'm terrified.

I can't see her.

I can't be strong.

"I'm not sure this is the right house," she lied. "I can't remember the number."

The double doors to the house opened and a group moved

down the stairs. Two of the men carried a stretcher covered in a white sheet. Every inch of Mira wanted to look away, to turn into Byron's chest. But she forced herself to watch as they slid the stretcher into the back of a horse-drawn ambulance and closed the doors. Her aunt and uncle came out next, Loretta sobbing into a handkerchief as Cyrus held her. Walker was last, but he moved ahead of them on the stairs.

"Do they know what happened?" she asked as she approached.

"The doctor said she had a seizure," Cyrus said, his voice hoarse. "It couldn't have been helped."

The ambulance pulled away, along with one of the police vehicles.

Byron frowned. "The police have finished their questioning, then?"

"For the most part. An inspector is still with Madame de Bonnemains," Cyrus said. "I'm sorry for calling you all this way. It seems there is nothing to investigate."

"Please, don't be," Byron said. "I will always come for your family, regardless of the circumstance."

Cyrus swallowed, a swell of emotion coming to his features. "Thank you."

Mira stepped back, a new sort of numbness spreading through her limbs as the ambulance drove out of view. Walker moved around the group, calling a carriage.

"Which inspector?" she asked.

"He said his name was Inspector Grandpierre," Cyrus said. "He came shortly after we did, with the police doctor."

Mira's stomach sank and she looked at Byron. "He was the inspector we worked with last month, wasn't he?"

"I don't recall," Byron said. "But I believe there is an easy way of finding out."

January 10, 1889: Afternoon

*A*FTER THE OTHERS HAD LEFT IN A carriage, Mira and Byron moved to the door and knocked. A tall, slight maid with blonde hair tied up in a neat bun opened the door.

"*I am sorry, but Madame is not taking visitors at this time,*" she said before they could make any explanation.

Mira fully intended to make a case for seeing the madame, but the words wouldn't come. Her mouth wouldn't cooperate. Finally, she managed to say, "*I'm Emilie's cousin.*"

The maid looked her over, nose wrinkling, but she stepped back nonetheless.

"*The sitting room is the first door on the right, up the stairs.*"

Mira thanked her and led Byron across the foyer. It was a little strange to not have an escort through the house, but in a way she was grateful for the moment to breathe. Besides, she knew the way. She had been here once before, when she and Emilie came to ask the madame a favor.

Only the day before Christmas.

And now Emilie was dead.

She pushed the thought aside.

They met the inspector at the top of the stairs, and sure enough, it was the same man that had made their investigation of Alexander Durant difficult.

"Detective Constantine." He gave a short nod. "I was unaware that you were coming. I will have you know that this investigation is under my jurisdiction."

Byron stood a little straighter. "I come as a family friend of the Lavigne's, nothing more."

"Be that as it may, I would prefer you keep your nose to yourself."

Byron tipped his head to the side. "I understand that Miss Lavigne died from a seizure?"

"The doctor established that, yes."

"In that case, why is the investigation considered open?"

The man bristled, his eyes narrowing. "Are you questioning my methods?"

"Not at all. However, I still intend to give my condolences to the lady of the house, if you will let us pass."

The inspector stepped out of the way, and the two of them moved past him without a second glance.

Once they were out of earshot, Mira said, "Why must he always be so troublesome?"

"I'm sure he is quite nice when he isn't intimidated. Or hiding something."

She frowned. "You think he's hiding something?"

"His tone seemed off." Byron paused in front of the sitting room door. "And he was the one we worked with?"

"Definitely."

Byron hummed.

"What are you thinking?" Mira asked.

"I think I need more facts." He knocked on the door.

"*Come in,*" Madame de Bonnemains said.

The sitting room was overrun with gauche floral wallpaper and lush green carpet. Spindly legged tables held lamps, a telephone, and ornate porcelain knickknacks of shepherds and the like. A soft light came in through sheer paneled curtains and rested on Marguerite de Bonnemains' delicate figure. She reclined on her tasseled chaise lounge in a feathered, wrap dress, with a dark veil covering her face. A white and orange kitten was curled up on her lap.

"*Oh, you are Emilie's cousin, are you not?*" the madame asked. "*Remind me of your name, won't you?*"

Mira blinked, not expecting to be remembered at all after so short a visit.

"*Mira Blayse. And this is Detective Constantine.*"

"*Ah, and here I thought that the police had all left. How do you do, Monsieur?*"

Mira glanced back at Byron and shook her head. "*Apologies, I didn't explain. He is from Scotland Yard, visiting Paris with me. Do you speak English?*"

"Of course I do," she switched over seamlessly as she stroked the cat.

Mira let out a relieved breath. She didn't fancy translating the conversation. In fact, the beginning of a headache gripped her neck at the thought of it.

"It is awfully convenient that you've traveled with a detective," Marguerite said. "Might I ask why?"

"We're courting," Byron said, without hesitation. "You are Madame de Bonnemains?"

"Yes. But under the circumstances, I would feel better if you both called me Marguerite." She sniffed and brought a handkerchief to her mouth.

"My condolences," Byron said. "It must be terribly frightening to have a member of your household pass away so suddenly."

Marguerite set the handkerchief beside her. "It's more than that. You might think me silly, but Emilie was my friend as much as she was my head maid."

"I know that you have likely already answered a great many questions, but would you be willing to answer some more?" Byron asked.

She gave a small nod. "Will you sit down? I'm sorry, I should have invited you in sooner."

Mira and Byron settled themselves in the armchairs across from her while Marguerite rang for some tea.

Byron pulled out his notebook. "Actually, I believe I need to start with you, Mira."

"Me?" Her heart rate spiked.

"When did you last see Emilie?"

She bit her lip, thinking back. "We'd just come back from city hall after the civil service. We had tea and then she told us she needed to return to work. That was around one or two."

"And then she left?"

Mira nodded.

He turned to Madame de Bonnemains. "Do you know when she arrived here?"

"I'm afraid I don't. Heloise or Angeline would know better. Or Dufresne. She's my cook."

"That's alright," Byron made his notes. "What happened yesterday afternoon and evening?"

Marguerite leaned back. "I'm afraid I don't remember much about the afternoon. It was all quite normal. I read for a while, and then Emilie brought me a light luncheon."

"Did you share any of it with her?" Byron looked up at her.

Marguerite paused, considering. "No. While we do eat together quite often, yesterday she told me she had already eaten."

"And what happened then?"

She continued to stroke the cat. "As it grew closer to evening, she helped me become ready for the opera. I left to meet a friend for dinner around five and did not return until close to midnight. Emilie had already retired to bed, so I didn't see her. Angeline told me that she had taken ill."

"And this morning?"

Marguerite shuddered. "I sent Heloise to check on her around eight. She was dead."

"You then called the police?"

"First, I sent Heloise for Mrs. Lavigne. I sent Angeline for the police afterwards."

"May I ask why you sent someone to the police when you could have called?" Byron gestured to the telephone with his pen.

Marguerite sat up a little. "While I don't have children, *monsieur*, I can imagine what it would be like to lose one. I wouldn't want to come to be with my daughter and be swarmed with police."

A knock came at the door and the maid from the foyer entered carrying the tea things. She set the tray on the table, gave a small curtsy and moved to leave.

"*Stay here a moment, won't you Angeline?*" Marguerite said, in French. "*This detective would like to ask you some questions.*"

Angeline moved to stand next to the chaise lounge, but betrayed no nervousness at having been asked to stay. "*What would you have me tell?*"

Mira spoke up. "*You told Madame de Bonnemains last evening that Emilie was unwell, is that correct?*"

"*Yes, miss. She told me she was feeling weak and had a headache. I brought her to bed and she mentioned how cold and numb she felt. I thought she might have a fever so I brought her a cold cloth to put on her head.*"

"*You didn't call for a doctor?*" Mira's jaw tightened.

"*I planned to do so in the morning after speaking with Madame.*"

Mira relayed the information to Byron. He tapped his pen against his cheek.

"Ask her if there were any other symptoms."

Mira did so and Angeline hesitated. "*I did wake up in the night and went to find some water. When I passed her room, her breathing sounded odd, but it was only for a moment. I stepped in to check on her and she seemed to settle.*" She averted her gaze. "*At the time I thought I had imagined it.*"

If Mira weren't in polite company she may have said something she regretted. Then again, if she were in the same situation, would she have done any differently? She sighed and continued to act as translator.

"I think that's all we need for now," Byron said.

"*Thank you, Angeline,*" Marguerite said.

Angeline curtsied and moved to leave the room. She paused near a sideboard that had a teapot and a single cup.

"*Would you like me to take these, Madame?*"

Marguerite sat up. "*Is that from last night?*"

"*Yes, Madame, I believe it is.*"

Marguerite glanced back at Mira and Byron and gave a short nod to the maid. Angeline poured the contents of the cup back into the teapot, then settled the handle on one finger. A few drops fell from the rim as she took it and the teapot out with her. The cat stood and stretched, padding after the maid.

"Did you have any other questions?" Marguerite asked.

"A few," Byron said, his gaze lingering on the door for a moment. "Was Emilie acting strange at all before you left for the opera? Any signs of sickness?"

"She seemed entirely normal, chattering on about her mother's wedding *et tout ça*. I didn't sense anything amiss." Marguerite furrowed her brow. "The doctor said she had a seizure. You don't suppose it was something else, do you?"

Mira's gaze darted back to the sideboard near the door. Something didn't sit well with her about it.

"We only want to understand the facts, Madame," Byron said. "Can you tell me more abo—"

The door to the sitting room burst open and a tall man in a dark suit came in, his mustache twitching. The entire party jolted at his entrance, Byron standing to shield Mira. She brought her hand over her heart as it raced again.

The man came immediately to the side of the chaise lounge. *"Marguerite, my love, you are all right?"*

Madame de Bonnemains looked between him and the detectives with wide eyes and gave a sigh. *"Yes, of course I am. Why would you think otherwise?"*

"I giving a speech when I heard there was a death here."

Mira frowned. Something in his voice and mannerisms was familiar, though she didn't meet a gentleman the last time she had visited.

The man said, *"Come, show me your face. Let me know it is you."*

"I have guests," Marguerite whispered, gesturing towards them.

The man seemed to notice them for the first time, standing, and brushing off his sleeves.

"My apologies. I did not realize."

Marguerite switched back to English. "Allow me to introduce General Georges Boulanger."

Mira studied his features and recognized him as the man who had spoken at the masquerade the month prior. Monsieur Allard had spoken ill of him only two days previous, reproaching his politics and describing the possibility of war with Prussia should the general take office. Mira frowned. This interaction did not paint him as the violent type.

Marguerite continued. "Georges, this is Mira Blayse and a Detective . . . Constance?"

"Constantine," Byron said, offering his hand.

The general shook it, "You are an Englishman?"

"Yes, sir."

"Forgive me, but you are not the one assigned to the death, are you?"

Byron shook his head. "No, sir, but I am a friend of the family."

Mira sat forward. "You see, we are courting, and Emilie . . . she was my cousin." Her stomach twisted. The more they spoke of it, the less she had a handle on her emotions.

Boulanger stepped back, looking towards Marguerite. "Emilie?"

Marguerite nodded, her veil shifting with the movement. "Yes, the poor thing."

"She was murdered? Last night?"

"The police believe it was natural," Byron said.

A small breath escaped Boulanger's lips before he moved over and took Mira's hand in both of his. "I am so very sorry for your loss. It is a terrible thing."

"Thank you, sir."

He made no response but drew away towards the window. She swallowed and looked back towards the door. The teapot. Could that be the answer?

"Would it be possible for us to speak with the rest of your staff?" Mira asked.

Marguerite hesitated. "Certainly. I can call Heloise to take you to the servant's quarters."

Mira shook her head. "I know the way," she said. Then, as an afterthought, "If that is more convenient."

"However you like," Marguerite said.

Mira stood. "Thank you for your hospitality."

"Of course," Marguerite said. "You may come whenever you like."

Mira inclined her head towards the general and the madame

and moved towards the door, Byron close behind her. She sped up, racing to the stairs. They needed to get to that teapot before it was cleaned. Byron caught her arm before she reached the landing.

"Mira, slow down. We have time."

"No, we don't. We have to get to the kitchens."

"All right," he said, linking his arm with hers and starting down the stairs. "Why?"

"Angeline said that that teapot was from last night. Why would they bring tea when they knew the madame was out?"

Byron hummed. "And if it was an oversight on the cook's part, why would there be tea in the cup?"

Relief flooded through her. "So you see why we need to hurry."

"While I may not know French, I do understand body language. There was something that bothered both you and Marguerite about that teapot. So I took the liberty of swiping this across the sideboard as I passed." He held up a tea-splotched handkerchief. "I expect that we have enough to test for arsenic, at least, if that is what you are thinking."

"It's the only thing that makes sense. And once we know what sort of poison we are dealing with, we can determine who did it."

"You suspect someone had reason to kill your cousin?"

"Well no, but—"

Her words petered off as he pulled her to a stop in the foyer. He tipped his head back, as if considering his words. "Mira, perhaps we should go home."

She shook her head. "No, I want to see this through."

"The police have already made their investigation. We could wait for the report."

She picked up her skirts and moved to the servant's stairs. "And let them have time to conceal the truth?"

"We still don't have definite proof of corruption." He followed after her.

"But you feel it, don't you?" She stopped on the third step, turning towards him. "You feel that something is wrong, the same way that I do. Otherwise you wouldn't have sopped up that tea."

She didn't wait for an answer as she continued down the stairs.

"I can't stand idly by if my cousin was murdered."

"And if it was natural?"

She picked up her pace. "It won't hurt anything to talk with the others."

January 10, 1889: Late Afternoon

THE KITCHENS WERE DOWN THE HALL FROM the servant's stairs and easily found using one's nose. Mira's mouth fell open upon entering. There, standing behind the table with her back to the door was her cousin, Emilie. Her blonde hair was tied up into a low bun with a bonnet over it and there was no mistaking her form. That is, until she came around the corner and revealed that she was at least eight months in the family way. The woman's belly protruded from underneath an apron dusted with flour and splotched with sauce. While her complexion was the same as Emilie's, her eyes were brown, not green, and her nose leaned off to the left.

Mira stood there, gaping like the fish that sat on the table-top. The woman held the teapot in her hands, drying it with a small rag. She looked up at them and cocked her head to the side.

"*May I help you?*"

The voice was different too. Mira shook herself out of her stupor. "*Yes. I'm sorry for the intrusion but may we ask you a few questions?*" She stepped farther into the kitchen and surveyed the space. It had a good amount of light from a rectangular window and smelled of herbs and spices. The little cat was in the corner lapping at a saucer of milk.

The cook narrowed her eyes. "*What sort of questions?*"

"*About Emilie and what happened last night.*"

"*You're with the police?*" She set the teapot on the table.

"*In a way, yes. What was your name?*"

"*Sorcha Dufresne.*"

Mira nodded. "*My name is Mira Blayse, and this is Detective Constantine. I'm his . . .*" she hesitated. "*I'm his translator.*"

"*I don't see what other questions you could have. I already answered for one set of police.*" Sorcha moved to the oven, checking on the contents.

"Excuse me," Byron said. "Do you speak English?"

The cook blinked. "I do."

"I had wondered."

"How did you know?" Sorcha wiped her hands on her apron. Her accent was a bit strange, but Mira couldn't place it.

"If I understood correctly, you said your name is Sorcha. A very uncommon name in France," Byron said.

"My mam was from Scotland."

"Ah." Byron smiled. "A union of the Auld Alliance?"

Sorcha grinned. "You could say that. Did you have some questions for me?"

"Yes." Byron pulled out his notebook. "We are trying to determine the exact events from yesterday afternoon and evening."

Sorcha frowned. "I don't think I would be much use to you. I was in here for most of the day."

"Do you know when Emilie returned?" Byron asked.

"Oh, around two. She was in time to serve a light luncheon."

"Could you tell us what you cooked for Madame?" Mira asked.

"Oh, certainly." She picked up the fish and a knife and set to work deboning it. The little cat darted over, mewing for a taste. "To start, she had a thin consommé, to prime her appetite. For the fish, Sole à la Meunière, followed by a salad. Since she planned to dine out in the evening, we left it at that."

"Did you see Emilie at all for the rest of the evening?" Byron asked.

She pursed her lips. "No, I did not. I think she may have been helping Heloise with something."

"One last question," Mira said. "Did you prepare tea for the madame yesterday evening?"

"I did." She dropped the fish skin to the floor and the cat was on it in an instant.

"Even though she was out?" Byron asked.

The cook narrowed her eyes and slapped the fish on the table, repositioning it so she could do the other side. "One falls into habits when you work for a viscountess. A little tea got cold, but nothing is harmed."

"And how long have you worked for her?" Byron finished a note.

"A little under a year. My husband was hired on at the same time. He's the coachman."

"Thank you for your time," Byron said.

THEY FOUND HELOISE DUSTING THE FRONT ENTRYWAY. Her

eyes were still puffy, but she seemed more composed than she had been at the boarding house that morning.

"*Excuse me,*" Mira said, in French. "*May we speak with you for a moment?*"

Heloise gave a nod. "*I will need to return to work soon, though. I do not want Angeline to see me idle.*"

"*Is she the head maid?*"

Heloise sighed. "*Now that Emilie is gone, yes.*"

Mira relayed the information to Byron. He tapped his cheek with his pen. "Did Emilie ever mention a rivalry?"

"Not that I remember." She turned back to Heloise. "*Did Angeline want that position?*"

"*I couldn't say.*" She shuffled from one foot to the other. "*But she is certainly making the most of it now.*"

"*How long has everyone worked here? Do you know?*"

"*Emilie was the first,*" Heloise said, considering. "*It was Angeline next, then me. I don't know how long they were with her, but I came on before Madame . . . er . . . separated from Viscount de Bonnemains.*"

"*Are they divorced?*"

"*Just last year.*"

"*Were you here yesterday afternoon when Emilie returned?*"

"*Yes, miss. I don't know what time it was, but she was in a hurry. She left me with her coat and hat and rushed upstairs immediately.*"

"*Does Madame de Bonnemains get angry when any of you are late?*"

"*Not exactly. But Emilie has been more careful to be punctual, especially since —*" She cut herself off.

Mira's heart rate picked up. "*Since when?*"

Heloise averted her gaze. "*Since Madame Dufresne was hired. She likes to stick to a schedule with meals.*"

"*I understand. What happened next?*"

"*I'm not sure. I'm assigned to the lower rooms, usually.*"

I was brushing the curtains, in there." She pointed towards a partially open door. Mira could make out a row of bookcases and a few armchairs beyond it.

"And when Madame de Bonnemains left for the opera?"

She twisted the feather duster in her hand. *"I don't really remember. I think I may have been polishing silverware down-stairs, but that might have been the day before."*

"With Emilie?"

"No. Emilie stayed upstairs. The last time I saw her was when I took her things at the door."

Mira turned to Byron and repeated everything she'd learned. "Have I missed anything?"

"Ask her about Boulanger. It might be helpful to know when he came into the picture."

Mira nodded. *"Do you remember when General Boulanger first came to visit?"*

Heloise shook her head. *"They were already friends when I came on."*

A door closed on the upper floor and Heloise jolted, turning back to her dusting. Angeline came down the stairs a moment later.

"Is there a problem?" she asked, eyeing the other maid.

"Not at all," Mira said. *"But I have a few more questions for you, if you'll allow me to ask."*

"Of course," Angeline said, folding her hands in front of her.

"After Madame de Bonnemains left for the opera last night, what did you do?"

Angeline stiffcncd, but smoothed her expression with a smile. *"I tidied the sitting room."*

"All evening?"

"It does take a bit of time."

Mira glanced up the stairs. *"Do you know what Emilie was doing?"*

"I'm not sure." She folded her arms.

"*And yet, you were the one who brought her to bed?*"

Angeline straightened. "*She came to me and asked if she felt warm. I don't know what she was doing before then.*"

Mira wanted to question further, but Byron took her hand. She looked towards him.

"Ask if we can see Emilie's room," he said.

And so she did.

FOUR PALE, BLUE WALLS. ONE WHITE BED, already remade. A small rectangular window at the top of the left wall. A dresser. A watercolor of a flower in a crooked frame below the window. The fashion of the room was so stark compared to the opulence two floors above, it made Mira sick.

In spite of this, she set to work. She checked the drawers of the dresser to find a few spare changes of clothes and some shoes. An inspection of the floor yielded nothing, although she never expected to find a hidden compartment. She knelt next to the bed to look under it, as Byron watched from the door.

She reached her hand this way and that under the bed frame until her fingers caught hold of something soft. Grasping it, she pulled out a dark veil. With a sigh, she tossed it onto a pile with the other clothes she found.

"There's no sign of a struggle," she said, sitting on the bed. "Nothing to indicate anything happened at all."

Byron sat next to her. "The police may have taken something as evidence. Although, it is strange that there aren't many personal effects."

Mira brushed some hair out of her face. "She kept most of her things back at the boarding house. The room I'm staying in is actually hers."

"Ah. That explains it." He drew his gaze across the sad, empty space. "Why do you think it was murder?"

"I never said—"

"You did. As we were coming down to the kitchen. And you did ask me to come investigate."

"My uncle asked you to come."

"When we arrived, he said there was nothing to look into. That the death wasn't suspicious."

She stood, moving to straighten the picture on the wall. "If you thought that, then why did you ask Marguerite all those questions?"

"Because I saw that look in your eye. It's the same one you get when you know you are right. Now answer my question. Why murder?"

"It was so sudden." She turned back towards him. "I don't trust the inspector. There was something odd about our whole interaction with the madame and the general. Then there's the tea. Even if the cook sent some up, why was there any in the teacup? And why is it that none of the staff know what Emilie was doing last night?"

Byron hummed. "Let's take each one individually, shall we? Working backwards. Do you know what everyone in the boarding house was up to last night?"

She sighed. "No, but I would expect that everyone would be accounted for by someone."

"But is it plausible that Emilie may have slipped through the cracks here? Especially considering that two of the three staff generally stay below stairs?"

"I see your point."

He shifted on the bed. "Now, the tea. Could it be that the madame poured herself a cup out of habit upon returning? And then realized it was cold?"

"The teacup didn't seem full, but I suppose."

"All right then. What struck you as odd about the conversation between Marguerite and the general?"

She frowned. "The last time I visited, Marguerite wasn't

wearing a veil. Yet now she seems almost reluctant to be seen without it. And I don't know if you noticed, but I thought Boulanger was relieved to discover that the police thought the death was natural."

"I did sense that, yes. Although it could have been a continued relief that Marguerite was unharmed. Do you know their relationship?"

"I'm afraid I don't know for certain. I remember Emilie mentioned that Marguerite was married to a viscount before her divorce. I assumed she was simply friends with the general, but with the way they acted . . ."

"Yes. It does speak to a deeper relationship. And if it is one that they would rather not have public, that could explain their conduct. Now what was next?"

"The inspector. I already didn't trust him because of his involvement, or lack thereof, in helping us track down Durant. And today he was rude altogether. You pointed out the inconsistency in his words. Why is the investigation still open when the death was natural?"

"Likely, it is because the death happened close to a person of public interest."

"I still don't like it." She rubbed at her arms and moved back to the dresser.

"Of course not." He stood and came to her side. "We're discussing the death of your cousin. The news of which you only received a few hours ago. It is certainly sudden, but so is a seizure."

"Are you saying you don't believe it was murder?"

He took her hand. "We still don't have enough facts. I agree that there is something suspicious about the whole set of circumstances. And if you want me to investigate the matter further, I will."

"But?" She looked up at him.

"I'm concerned for you. This is the closest a case has ever

come to you. Yes, the matter with Pennington was connected with your parents, but you were farther removed. I'm not sure it would be wise for you to help this time."

She shook her head. "I've been connected all along. With my godfather as the Charger, how could I not be?" She paced away, listing each point on her fingers. "He's the one who killed my parents. He's the reason my uncle was a suspect for murder and the reason why Alexander Durant pursued me. And now, here we are, investigating corruption with the police and looking for a connection to Circe, and my cousin is killed. It can't be a coincidence."

Byron stopped her in place, setting his hands on her shoulders as he studied her with his piercing blue eyes. "And what if it is?"

She pulled away, turning towards the window, but didn't answer.

He sighed. "I think I may have done you a disservice."

"What?"

"You used to see the beauty in everything. And now you only see the darkness."

A tightness formed in her chest. "The darkness was always there, Byron."

He came behind her, slipping his arms around her waist. "I know, love." He pressed a kiss into her hair. "I know."

She closed her eyes. "You'll help me, won't you?"

He tightened his hold. "Of course I will."

January 11, 1889:
Morning

THE WALLS WERE CLOSING IN AROUND HER with tunnels in every direction. Her torch flickered, the shadows dancing on the wall. Were they really shadows? Or was it something else? She held a handkerchief over her mouth to stop her lungs from choking with the dust and decay. She couldn't breathe. Was that a hand around her throat? She dropped the torch as she was pushed against the wall. Smoke rose, higher and higher, billowing into the space as the fingers tighte—

She sat up in bed, gasping for breath and clutching at her neck. Another nightmare. Although she remembered this one. She forced herself to take deep breaths. The moonlight filtered through the curtains onto the bed. She turned in place to see if she'd disturbed Emilie in her sleep. But as soon as the thought had come, the reality crashed into place.

Emilie is dead.

She pushed herself out of bed, pacing over to the window as her heart continued racing. The death could have been natural. Her passing was terrible enough without it being murder. And there wasn't exactly a motive for anyone to kill her. But she had the same sort of feeling about this as she had with her parents' so-called accident. Was Byron right? Was she seeing darkness because it was there or because she could see nothing else?

It was no use trying to go back to sleep. The nightmare would only shift from bones in the catacombs to bodies beneath white sheets. She moved over to the dressing table, lighting the lamps as she passed them. Pulling out her sketchbook, she flipped to a fresh page. If she could start a drawing, perhaps her hands would take over for her brain and the present thoughts could be pushed out of her mind.

The issue was getting started. The blank whiteness of the page stared up at her, daring her to sully it with a mark. There was a certain perfection in the emptiness of it. But the point wasn't to have an empty, perfect book.

She had pushed aside her woes and anxious thoughts for a moment or two, but they returned as she looked around the room for a subject. There was an ink stain on the desk, one that Mira hadn't left. Chairs strewn with clothes that Mira didn't own. A veil hung on the bedpost. She arranged some of the things on the dressing table into a still life. A cold, glass perfume bottle. A hairbrush, comb, and mirror. A buttonhook and some hatpins lying haphazard on the surface. Objects unwittingly left behind.

She pressed her pencil to the paper, creating several dark lines on the page. It was strange. The day before, she had told herself that she could grieve and cry and feel once she was alone. And here she was, quite alone, with everyone in the house asleep, and she couldn't get herself to feel much of anything. Certainly, there was the impression that she ought to feel something. The notion of sorrow. But there was no spark for the little hearth within her that she'd been so careful to keep cold.

Perhaps she was tired.

As she darkened one of the lines she wished to keep, the tip of the pencil shattered, sending lead dust scattering over the page. She brushed it away, inadvertently smudging what she had done. Perhaps if she had been more awake she would have been upset. As it was, she only sighed.

Her pencil box and supplies were clear across the room. Her mind went through the motions of standing and moving over to look for them, but she couldn't bring herself to leave her seat. Surely, there would be a pencil or other drawing implement among Emilie's things. But would it be a breach of etiquette?

She'd already rearranged the things on her desk without a second thought. Was this any different? With a sigh, she began looking through the drawers.

The first held nothing of interest. The second was much the same. When she came to the third, the drawer stuck fast about a finger's width open. She pulled harder, and with some effort, she took the drawer clean out, scattering half of the contents onto the floor.

At this point, she felt somewhat inclined to simply go back to bed and abandon the drawing, like half of the others in her current sketchbook. But as she moved to put the drawer back, she noticed that the bottom of the drawer was loose. Upon closer inspection, she found a small hole towards the back. Using her finger, she was able to pull the base up, revealing a hidden compartment full to the brim with papers.

Mira frowned. What would Emilie have to hide? She picked up the first paper. It was a letter from Marguerite to General Boulanger dated in 1887. Before Marguerite was divorced. Scanning the rest of the documents she found several more letters, a series of receipts for stays at a guest house in Royat, France, and a handwritten account of visits to Marguerite's flat complete with dates and times.

There were only two possibilities that came to mind. The first was that Madame de Bonnemains had given these papers to Emilie for safekeeping, to help maintain the secrecy of her relationship with the general. But she couldn't ignore the second: Emilie was blackmailing Marguerite.

Except Mira knew her cousin. She wasn't the type of person to be attracted by greed and opportunity. She turned in her seat, looking over at the bed. Just a few days previous she had sat there with Emilie and talked about whether or not her cousin was a good person. Hadn't Emilie mentioned that she intended to pay off all of her father's debts? Perhaps it wasn't personal selfishness that prompted her to take this action, but rather, a hope that she could free her family from a cruel shadow.

Oh, and how she hated the hope that sprung from the revelation. This was proof of motive! Marguerite had reason to want Emilie dead. And what better way to orchestrate it than when she had an alibi: the opera.

The morning sun was sending its first rays in through the window. Mira yawned. She hadn't intended to stay up for the rest of the night. She only wanted a distraction, some way to keep her mind off the so-called case. But now she had evidence that proved there truly was something to investigate.

Emilie was dead. No. She was murdered.

EVEN IF SHE HAD EVERY INCLINATION TO bring Byron the proof as soon as possible, she waited until her uncle would deem it a proper time for her to leave. Anxiety was her companion through breakfast. It continued to attend her as she finally hurried off to Rue Geoffrey, evidence in hand. Of course, she didn't take everything. Most of the blackmail was tucked safely back into its hiding spot in Emilie's room. She brought one example of each paper: a letter, a receipt, and a page of dates written in her cousin's hand.

All of this was hidden in the sketchbook tucked under her arm as she knocked on the door. Moments passed and once more the first face she saw was Fred's.

"Good morning," she said, her breath clouding in front of her.

"Hello, Miss Blayse. Lovely seeing you again." He stepped aside to let her in.

"Is Byron in?" she asked. "I have something of interest to the case."

"Ah, yes." Fred scratched the back of his neck, leading her to the sitting room once again. "I'm terribly sorry to hear about your cousin."

Mira swallowed. "Yes, well. It was quite a shock."

"Certainly." He glanced back towards the stairs. "You're early enough I don't think he's finished reading his journal."

She paused in taking off her coat. "Still?" It was almost nine o' clock, and from her experience as his secretary, she knew he was generally an early riser. Perhaps he had slept in.

"He has written a rather substantial amount since coming to Paris. It takes him a little longer to read it each day."

She sat on the sofa, a numbness coming over her. She couldn't remember the last time she saw him referencing his journal. Yes, there were things that he forgot from time to time. He tended to focus on more big picture things, so little details would get lost. He hadn't needed to read his journal thoroughly in months. At least since his memory loss improved at the end of October.

Although, it had been some time since she had seen him early in the morning. Could she have missed it? But if he were struggling again, why wouldn't he have told her? A lump formed in her throat. Perhaps she was overreacting.

Fred didn't seem to notice that she was in the middle of a rather startling realization, and continued his destruction of her understanding.

"And of course, he wouldn't want to miss any details about you," he said, as if to cheer her up. "Especially after what happened in Reading."

She frowned. "You mean the case with the sheep? Back in November?" She had stayed at Swan Walk with a sprained ankle when they'd gone off to solve the Sheep Panic. Byron had brought back flowers for her.

"That's the one. Can you believe the man left his journal in London thinking he could remember everything on his own?" He laughed a little. "Poor fellow couldn't remember anything about the case half the time we were there."

She forced a laugh. "Surely you're exaggerating. It couldn't have been that bad."

"On my honor, he had to rely on me to keep track of things, and even then he forgot something important." He cocked his head to the side. "Although he never told me what it was. Did he ever tell you?"

She furrowed her brow. "No. He didn't."

Fred scratched the back of his hand. "I'd hoped he had. Whatever it was, he was so terribly upset by it. I've been curious to know what it was." He stood. "Oh well. I'll go fetch him, shall I?"

As he left, Mira's mind traced over the familiar patterns she'd been ignoring for the last few months. He had been a little more forgetful than usual. Although he was never as bad as when she first met him. Was he pretending to remember for her sake? Did it matter?

Perhaps Fred was wrong. She knew Byron well enough. He would tell her if there was something wrong. A little voice in the back of her mind asked, *would he?*

The man himself came down the stairs, no journal in sight.

"Good morning, love," he said, pressing a kiss to her cheek. "I haven't quite set up the chemistry set to test the tea yet."

She blinked. "O-oh. Yes. We were going to do that today, weren't we?"

He furrowed his brow. "Did something else happen?"

"Nothing serious. I found something this morning in one of Emilie's drawers." She pulled out the packet of papers and handed them over.

As he scanned them, she said, "I recognize Emilie's hand in a few of them, but the letters . . ."

His eyes narrowed. "Those belong to Madame de Bonnemains, do they not?"

"They do, and there are dozens more back at the boarding house." Part of her hoped that he wouldn't see the awful possibility, but that hope was quickly snuffed.

"Blackmail, do you think?" He looked up at her.

"I'm not sure. She did mention the other day that Marguerite would help her pay off her family's debts. That would be a reason for her to do it, but I hate to think that my cousin would resort to such a thing."

Byron hummed. "And if she did?"

Mira let out a long breath. "Well, if she did, it gives Marguerite, and General Boulanger for that matter, motive for murder."

He scanned over one of the letters again, speaking slowly as he read. "Yes, these certainly prove that the two of them were having an affair before the divorce." He folded up the evidence and handed it back. "Quite a scandal for a political official, and potentially dangerous for Marguerite. She could be sent to prison for this if the Viscount wished to prosecute."

"Unfortunately, Marguerite had the perfect alibi at the time of the murder," Mira said, tucking the evidence back into her sketchbook. "But that doesn't mean she didn't find some way of arranging for Emilie to be killed in her absence."

"I suppose we ought to test the tea then." He turned and led the way into the kitchen. She followed, and soon they were well along in the meticulous process of arranging the chemistry set.

"I hate to disappoint you," Byron said as he twisted a little metal ring to fit around one of the glass vials, "but even if there is poison in the sample, we might not be able to detect it."

"Why not?" She continued to cut out the splotched parts of the handkerchief.

"There is only one reliable test for any poison, and that is for arsenic. While one can certainly narrow it down by looking at the symptoms and whether it was likely for a poison to be introduced, it is impossible to know for certain."

"So, if this test doesn't work . . ."

"It still doesn't rule out poison, but it also doesn't give us any definitive proof."

She pressed her lips tight, a weight coming over her.

"Can you hand me one of the samples?" he asked.

She passed over a piece of the handkerchief and he added it to a glass beaker with two chemicals and heated it up. He held a ceramic dish to the other side of the tube and waited. It remained clear.

"Well, it wasn't arsenic," he said. "Although I think we knew that from the symptoms."

"What poison would cause a doctor to think it was a seizure?"

Byron let out a breath, leaning against the counter. "Strychnine is most likely. Cyanide would have worked too quickly. Nightshade is a possibility. But without a test, it's impossible to know."

She slumped against the counter. "This really is hopeless, isn't it?"

"I wouldn't say that. We are one step closer to learning the truth, and there is always hope in that. And we have the potential blackmail as evidence now. I believe that might be enough to convince the police to reexamine the case."

"Then we mustn't waste any time." She set the remains of the handkerchief in a pile and headed to the entryway. He followed behind and helped her into her coat.

"Oh, did you need to fetch your journal?" she asked, trying to keep her tone nonchalant.

He considered the question a moment. "Good idea. We might want it as a reference."

As he headed up the stairs, she couldn't decide whether that was evidence for or against Fred's information. And she hated that she was questioning it at all.

January 11, 1889: Afternoon

*P*ERHAPS IT WAS MIRA'S OWN ANXIETY, BUT the atmosphere in the police prefecture seemed especially tense. She and Byron took their usual path to Prefect Lozé's office and found themselves speaking with the constable at the desk. Although, it wasn't the usual one.

"*How can I help you?*" he said.

"*We have evidence regarding a case.*" Mira held her sketchbook close to her chest. While she had plenty of other examples of the blackmail safely tucked away in Emilie's room, she didn't want to take any chances.

"*Which inspector?*"

Her stomach sank. "*I believe it would be best to bring it directly to Prefect Lozé.*"

The constable gave her a glare. "*Monsieur Lozé is too busy to be bothered with every case or detail. And aside from that, he's in a meeting with the interior minister.*"

"*The interior minister?*" That seemed serious.

The constable waved his hand. "*Which inspector was assigned to the case?*"

She sighed. "*Grandpierre.*"

The constable nodded and consulted a document. "*I believe he is free. His office is up the stairs, down the hall to the right, five doors down.*"

Mira cocked her head to the side. "*If I may ask, what happened to the previous constable on duty here?*"

A smirk graced the constable's lips. "*Something was stolen from Lozé's office while he was on watch. As such, he has been placed on probation.*"

"*I see. Thank you.*" She linked arms with Byron and headed towards the stairs.

"What's wrong?" he whispered.

"They won't let us see Lozé." She lowered her voice. "I think they may have noticed that you borrowed a file."

"Did I?" He frowned.

"It was a record of individuals who contract with the police. You have it back at Rue Geoffroy," she said, taking note of the additional evidence against his memory. "That's probably why everyone is on edge. In any case, I doubt that Grandpierre will be helpful."

"He might surprise us."

Mira shook her head. "Ever the optimist."

An old, dinged name plate was attached to the door of the office with Grandpierre's name etched onto it in cursive lettering. Byron knocked and a muffled call from inside bid them enter.

Grandpierre's office was much smaller than Lozé's. Files were stacked neatly on low shelves on either side of the room. A door stood to the back of the space. Grandpierre sat behind a large desk at the center of the room and looked up as they came in, a grimace coming over his features. He sighed and continued working.

Byron cleared his throat.

Grandpierre didn't look up again, but said, "What can I do for you Monsieur Constantine?"

"We have something that might be useful to your investigation."

Mira stepped forward, pulling the evidence from her sketchbook. "I found these in my cousin's room. I believe she was blackmailing Madame de Bonnemains." She handed the papers over.

Grandpierre gave the evidence a cursory glance and set it on the desk. "And?"

"It gives Madame de Bonnemains motive," Mira said.

The inspector let out a sharp nasally sound. "It would be motive if there was a murder. But the death was natural." He went back to his work. "I will add it to the file, but the investigation is officially closed. In fact . . ." He set his pen aside and looked up at them. "If you would be so kind as to let the family know, I would appreciate it." He handed over a sheet of paper. "Here is the permit. You may take the girl's body from the morgue whenever is convenient. Good day."

Mira clenched her fists. Would he not even consider the evidence? She stepped forward to say as much, but Byron grabbed her arm, stopping her. Upon her questioning glance, he opened the door and pulled her out into the hallway.

"I don't think antagonizing the inspector is going to help our cause."

"He didn't even look at it! How on earth did he ever become an inspector in the first place?" She folded her arms.

"It really isn't any of our business at this point. If the investigation is closed here at the prefecture, then we'll have to continue on our own."

Mira tucked some stray hair behind her ear, her stomach twisting. "I think I know where to go from here."

Byron nodded. "Yes. I believe we need to see Emilie."

THE PARIS MORGUE WAS ON THE EDGE of Île de la Cité behind Notre Dame. The street in front was crowded with people looking into a shop window. Mira approached, curious about what could bring such attention.

"*Excuse me,*" Mira asked one of the women closest to her. "*What are they looking at?*"

"*Not* what. *Who,*" she said.

A few people shuffled away allowing her to see. Nausea spread through her as she realized it wasn't a shop, but the morgue itself. A large, glazed window took up most of the wall. Metal slabs were set at an angle, propping up near-naked bodies. Some strips of fabric or leather provided a little modesty. Their clothes were hung above on a line, as if they were simply drying from a wash. Children stood, faces pressed against the glass, staring at the spectacle of death. Mira turned away almost immediately.

"*They say they do it for identifying the bodies,*" the woman said. "*But most everyone is here because it's free theatre. I know I am.*"

Mira swallowed. "*And the bodies that have already been identified?*"

"*The south wing. There's a gate around there.*"

"*Thank you.*"

Avoiding the front window, Mira led Byron to the southern side and slipped through the gate. Her chest tightened and she paused on the path.

"Are you all right?" Byron asked, coming to stand next to her.

"How could anyone . . ." she couldn't find the words to describe the scene occurring around the corner.

Byron grimaced. "Unfortunately, I've come to find that a fascination with death is quite a natural phenomenon."

"But to put people on display as if they were some side show." She shuddered. "Those people had lives, had families, once."

"Yes. They did." Byron looked towards the door of the morgue and back to her. "Do you want to wait out here?"

"No," she said, the word sharp and clipped. "I'll come in."

"It will be grim."

"It can be no worse than what they have on exhibition." She moved past him, taking the handle of the door and pulling hard.

Several doors led off of the small entry. One open door showed a desk with a red-headed clerk sitting at it. When Mira knocked on the doorframe, the man looked up and smiled.

"*How can I help you? Have you come to identify?*"

Mira shook her head, gesturing to Byron. "*This is Detective Constantine visiting from Scotland Yard. We were wondering if we could examine—*" She stopped, another wave of nausea passing over her. "*Emilie Lavigne.*"

The man stood and stepped around the desk. "*I presume that he speaks no French?*"

"*Yes, but only a little. I can translate.*"

"No need," the man said, switching to English. "I was hired in part because I speak English. The morgue has had quite a few tourists from Britain." He extended his hand for Byron to shake. "My name is Hugo Rousselle."

Byron shook his hand. "Byron Constantine, although I gather she already told you."

Rousselle laughed, and the sound seemed out of place. "Yes, but she didn't introduce herself."

"Mira Blayse. I'm Emilie Lavigne's cousin."

Rousselle sobered immediately. "Pardon me, *mademoiselle*. I am very sorry for your loss."

"Thank you." She handed the permit over. "May we see her?"

He looked over the paper and nodded, handing it back. "Everything seems to be in order. If you will follow me."

He opened the door across the hall. It was a heavy, steel door and it took some effort for him to open. Cold spilled out, much colder than the January air outside on the street.

The room resembled a large metal box. On the left wall were fifteen compartments, five across and three high. A pulley system hung from the ceiling with rigging. A machine stood in the corner, quietly humming, with a door in the wall next to it. A wheeled table sat at the center of the room. Strangely, there was no smell.

Rouselle led them into the room and used a hook to open a compartment on the second level. The hook was used again to pull out a large drawer. An iron plank was set on top of the drawer with a body lying on top of it. Three heavy, leather straps were wrapped around the body and the plank, and Rouselle attached the pulley system to four rings on either side of the plank. Pulling on the rigging, he lifted the plank off of the drawer and swung it gently onto the table. He unbuckled the straps, letting them fall to either side, and stepped back.

Emilie was naked, save for the two wide strips of leather providing modesty, and a tag with her name attached to her foot.

Mira kept her distance, her chest tight with grief. It was one thing to be told of her cousin's death and quite another to be witness to it.

Byron looked up at Rouselle. "Were you the one to examine her?"

"Officially, no. That was Doctor Moreau. However, I was the one to prepare her for burial."

"Did you see anything of note?"

Rouselle stepped closer to the body. "There are some bruises here along the legs, but those are common enough. A few small punctures on the arms and legs as well."

"Punctures?" Byron crouched to be at the same level as Emilie's arm.

"Yes. And a scratch mark here." Rouselle gestured to her wrist.

Mira found her voice. "Marguerite has a cat. Emilie complained about its claws."

"Ah, that would explain it," Rouselle said. "Aside from that, I haven't found anything amiss."

Byron hummed. "Any sign of poison?"

Rouselle furrowed his brow. "The death was natural by all accounts." He stepped back. "Are you wanting to take the body now?"

Mira shook her head. "My aunt will come for her."

The door on the opposite side of the room swung inward and a man entered, holding the door open behind him. Another followed, pulling a table bearing a corpse.

"*I think it's about time for that one to be iced, wouldn't you say Hugo?*" the first man said in French, gesturing to the new body.

"*Yes. Compartment three, if you would,*" Rouselle answered.

The man who spoke nodded, and moved past the group, opening a compartment level with the floor. The other wheeled the table around. The blood rushed from Mira's face, matching the pallor of this new corpse before her. A bitter taste filled her mouth.

"Mira, what's wrong?" Byron asked, coming to her side.

"It's D-Durant," she stammered. "Alexander Durant."

Byron looked closer at the body. "The resemblance is striking. But surely it must be someone else."

Mira shuddered, each encounter she had with the villain coming to mind. She would never forget that face. The last time she had seen Durant, his face had been lit with flames, his eyes wild and murderous, his skin coated in sweat, grime, and blood. Despite the cold surrounding her, she could almost feel the heat of the fire in the catacombs, could almost smell the smoke.

"Mira?" Byron said, concern lacing his tone.

His voice brought her back to the present moment and the dead man in front of her. She turned away, her stomach roiling. "I have no doubt that it is him."

Rouselle moved over and examined the tag on the man's foot. He nodded.

"Alexander Durant. You knew this man?"

"I-I did." She took a steadying breath and looked back again. "When did he die?"

Rouselle gestured to one of the other men. "*Do you remember when he came in?*"

"*The seventh. Or the eighth. I know it was early this week.*"

Rouselle repeated the information for Byron and said to both of them, "What was your relation?"

Byron answered this time, "I was the detective responsible for his arrest."

"Ah. Yes, he did come from La Santé. If his next of kin do not claim him in the next few days, he'll be sent to the university."

"H-how did he die?" Mira asked.

"A seizure, I believe."

Her breath hitched. "A seizure? You're certain?"

Rouselle nodded. "I remember thinking to myself, after learning of what his crimes were, that he could have died much worse."

Her gaze flicked between Durant and her cousin, a dizzying sensation coming over her. Byron took her arm, steadying her.

"Hopefully his next of kin are in contact with you soon,"

he said. "Speaking of which, might we be able to take Emilie's clothes with us?"

"Of course. This way."

He led them out of the chamber, through the large iron door, and back to his office.

"If you'll wait here, I'll retrieve her belongings."

Without another word he left them alone. Mira took a deep breath.

"It can't be a coincidence," she said. "It can't."

"I would agree. It doesn't seem probable that two people with ties to you would die in such close proximity and from the same cause." He paused a moment, tipping his head to the side. "Although, I'm not surprised that Durant is dead. After all, he knew quite a bit about the organization. I'd expect that Circe would want him out of the way before the trial."

"Yes, but what does that have to do with Emilie?" She rubbed at her arms. "I'm the only connection between them. Either Circe murdered my cousin to stop us from investigating and they just happened to use the same method or . . ." she trailed off.

"Or what?"

"You don't think that General Boulanger or Marguerite are part of Circe, do you?"

Byron hummed. "They are rather high up in their respective positions. And if Boulanger wins this election, he would have the power to declare war."

"Which is exactly what Circe wants! And if Emilie were to release the information about the affair, it would cause a scandal. Of course they would want her dead now."

Footsteps sounded down the hall as Rouselle returned with Emilie's personal effects.

"Here you are. When your aunt comes to retrieve the body, make sure that she brings fresh clothes. The permit requires her to take the body within three days' time."

Mira took the parcel from him. "Thank you."

"Of course. Let me know if I can do anything else for you."

Mira took a step towards the door, but Byron stilled her with a hand on her shoulder.

"One last question," he said. "Did you happen to examine that Durant fellow when he came in?"

"When I was preparing the body, yes."

"Anything of note?"

Hugo furrowed his brow. "A few faint scars, but no new injuries."

"Thank you." Byron took Mira's arm and led her out of the morgue.

The crowd loitering outside the window was much the same as it was before, the only difference being a man handing out pamphlets about the election and shouting about votes for Boulanger. Mira kept hold of Byron's arm as they moved away from the morgue and around the side of Notre Dame.

"We're on our own, aren't we?" she said. "Even if we did manage to meet with Lozé again, I doubt that he will see Durant's death as relevant to Emilie's."

"Especially since the case is considered closed. No, I believe that we ought to keep the police out of it until we find more concrete evidence. Yes, we know Emilie was blackmailing Marguerite, but that doesn't mean Marguerite killed her." He slowed to a stop at the center of a bridge, looking out over the water.

"What sort of evidence do we need?" Mira leaned against the balustrade.

"Well, I think I ought to look into Marguerite's alibi about the opera. And determine where Boulanger was at the time, as he also has motive."

"Don't you mean, we should?"

He turned towards her, his scrutinizing stare in full force. When he spoke there was a careful deliberation in his cadence, as if he were trying not to spook her.

"The last few days have been one terrible thing after another," he said. "I can't even begin to imagine how you are feeling after everything with your cousin, and then seeing Durant just now."

"I'm fine," she said, voice trembling.

"That is a lie and you know it. And you know that *I* know it." He squeezed her hand. "I'm used to this sort of thing and even I feel unsettled after being in that morgue. It was grim, absolutely grim."

A moment of silence passed between them before he continued. "I know we discussed this yesterday, but I feel that it is prudent to bring it up again. Perhaps it is unrealistic for me to ask you to leave the investigation to me. But I think, at least, that you need some time away from the case."

"No. The sooner we can solve this the—"

"Sooner you'll be able to grieve?" he interrupted her. "Mira, you can't put these sorts of things on a schedule. It's not a train you can delay." He placed his hand on top of hers. "And running from it won't stop it from coming."

Tears pricked in the corners of her eyes.

He squeezed her hand. "I can look into the alibis on my own. You ought to go home and be with your family, at least for a little while. They need you far more than I do right now. And I think you need them."

A few tears escaped, and she laughed a little. "You sound like Landon."

"He's a wise man," he said, brushing a tear from her cheek. "Come on, I'll walk you home."

ONCE BYRON BID HER FAREWELL AT THE door to go off to check the alibis, Mira found her aunt and uncle in the sitting room. It wasn't too late—the sun was still sending soft rays through the curtains—but the room seemed dim and gloomy all the same. Flames crackled in the fireplace. Loretta was embroidering Emilie's shroud. Cyrus was looking over some papers but stood and pulled her into a hug as she came in.

"Where have you been all day?" he asked.

"Byron asked me to come to the prefecture with him," she half lied. "Before we left they gave us this and asked us to go to the morgue." She handed the permit to her uncle and set the bundle of Emilie's clothes next to Loretta. "We can bring her home now."

Loretta stopped her work and pulled one of the articles of clothing out of the parcel. She ran her fingers over the fabric, her eyes rimmed with red. "We received the burial permit from the mayor this morning. He didn't give us a set day, since we didn't know when we could take her, but he told us she ought to be interred before Monday."

"When would you like to do it?" Cyrus said, moving to sit next to her on the sofa again.

"Tomorrow," Loretta said without hesitation. "She deserves the chance to rest now . . . now that—" she burst into tears again, sinking into Cyrus' side.

Mira stepped closer, unsure of what to do. Cyrus stretched his free hand towards her and she took it, letting her own tears flow as she came to rest at his other side. He held both of them tight as the fire raged on in the hearth.

January 12, 1889

*E*MILIE CAME HOME FOR THE LAST TIME early in the morning on Saturday. Cyrus was the one to bring her back from the morgue, in clothes prepared by Loretta. Each member of the family had a few minutes with her. Clarisse and the boys went first. Strangely, the little girl didn't cry much. She seemed too tired to cry. Klasha went in next. Then it was Mira's turn. She stepped into Loretta's room and found Emilie laying on the bed.

There was some comfort in seeing her in warm, familiar surroundings. She wore her nicest dress, and Loretta had curled her hair. Emilie's hands were up on her chest, the cat scratch and little scabs visible. Were it not for the deathly pallor to her cheeks, Mira would have thought she was sleeping. Unlike the morgue, there was a light stench in the air, but somehow it didn't bother Mira at all.

"Hello, Emilie," she said, coming to sit in a chair next to

the bed. There were so many things to say, and yet she didn't feel like saying any of them. She sat there for a few minutes in silence.

"I'll find out what happened to you," she said at last. "I promise."

FROM WHAT MIRA UNDERSTOOD, THE LAVIGNE FAMILY had never been particularly religious. Loretta's first husband, Charles, had been raised Catholic but didn't practice. Loretta kept her Anglican faith but refrained from attending church during his lifetime to keep the peace. Now, she wanted her daughter to be sent off in the sight of God, and felt it appropriate to hold the service in English so that Cyrus could understand.

Byron came, standing next to Mira in the pews. Madame de Bonnemains was there as well, still veiled in black, standing towards the back. There were a few others that Mira didn't recognize who must have been friends of the family.

The priest was reading from Psalms. "'I held my tongue, and spake nothing. I kept silence, yea, even from good words; but it was pain and grief to me.'"

It was the usual reading for an Anglican funeral, and yet Mira couldn't help but imagine Emilie saying the words. How much had she kept silent? There was now one great secret that Mira knew. Blackmail. Part of her couldn't believe that her cousin would resort to such a thing, but the facts told a different story: a tragedy anchored in years of grief and sorrow. And wasn't it only natural for her to want to escape the debt?

"'My heart was hot within me, and while I was thus musing the fire kindled: and at last I spake with my tongue.'"

Mira wished that Emilie could speak. There was so much missing in this case. If only they could ask her what had happened. What had she been doing that night before she took ill? Who was with her?

"'For man walketh in a vain shadow, and disquieteth himself in vain: he heapeth up riches, and cannot tell who shall gather them.'"

While she still didn't know the entire truth about how or why Emilie had been killed, Mira could still trace the events that led up to this moment back to Professor Edward Burke. Hot tears flowed down her cheeks at the realization.

If Professor Burke hadn't told Loretta's father about their elopement, Cyrus and Loretta might have been happy. They could have escaped to England and been far away from the influence of Circe. Loretta wouldn't have had to marry Lavigne or suffer because of his neglect and debts. Even if Mira and Walker's own parents had still died in that accident, they would have been raised with another mother and sister. With all of that, Emilie would never have worked for Madame de Bonnemains. And even if she did, she never would have felt the need to blackmail in order to pay off a debt that wasn't hers. That coffin would be empty.

Anger overtook her grief. Anger at her godfather and his selfishness. He cared more for money and power than his own humanity and morals. Anger at her cousin for turning to crime to resolve her family's debt. And most of all, anger at Marguerite de Bonnemains. She looked back at the woman. How dare she come to such a sacred space when it was her fault that her cousin was dead? Perhaps that was why she wore the veil. An outward expression of grief for her servant, certainly. But what expressions did it hide? Was the madame's smile hidden beneath the darkness?

Byron took her hand, giving it a squeeze. The action grounded her and she took a breath. They didn't know for certain that the madame had a hand in the murder. It was too soon to know. And besides, Emilie wouldn't want her to be angry. She turned to the front again, but as she did, some movement in the narthex of the church caught her eye. A shadow. She looked back again, but there was nothing.

When the priest finished his reading, Loretta stood, coming to the front of the church.

"I cannot express the grief that fills me at the loss of my Emilie. My first little one. But I also have so much hope and love. She has been released from the earthly burdens that are present in all of our lives and can finally rest." She paused, her emotions becoming too strong to continue. Once she found her words again, she said, voice wavering, "She was the best daughter, the best sister, the best friend, the best servant, and I am glad that she might find peace now, even if we are parted."

When the service concluded at the church, Cyrus, Georges, Jean-Marie, Byron, and a few family friends acted as pallbearers and brought the coffin out to the hearse. A procession followed from the Anglican Church to the cemetery. As they walked, Clarisse came up next to Mira and took her hand, resting her head on Mira's arm. Her face was red and splotchy.

The sun was shining when they reached the Lavigne crypt. Georges opened it, and the pallbearers descended the stairs, setting Emilie's coffin on top of the rest, like a brick in a wall. They closed the crypt door and Byron came to stand next to Mira again as the priest did another reading.

"How are you feeling?" Byron whispered,

Mira dabbed at her eyes. "A little wrung out, truth be told."

He put an arm around her. "Quite understandable, considering the circumstances."

"What did you find out about the opera?" Her gaze trailed over to Marguerite.

"I thought we agreed you would take some time before getting back into the case."

She leaned into his side. "How much time will appease you?"

"This isn't about appeasing me. It is about ensuring that you have the means to grieve."

The priest read, "'In the midst of life we are in death . . .'"

"What if this is my means to grieve?" she whispered. "What then?"

"Is it?" he asked.

She closed her eyes, the warmth of the sun resting on her eyelids as the chill, winter air stung her cheeks. She knew what Byron was trying to say. In spite of her efforts to keep her emotions hidden from him, she was certain that he had known from the beginning that she was struggling. Perhaps he didn't know the full extent—he couldn't know about the nightmares and memories—but he could read her better than just about anyone of her acquaintance. Quite a fantastic thing, considering how short a time they had known one another.

"'Thou knowest, Lord, the secrets of our hearts; shut not thy merciful ears to our prayer . . .'"

Did she even know all the secrets in her heart? There was such a falseness in living, in having to continue on, day by day. Perhaps falseness was the wrong word for it, because was one lying if you had forgotten the truth yourself?

Was she running from the past, from the pain, from the heartache? Or was she moving forward? Was she healing? What was the difference? How could she know?

And did it matter, when her cousin had been murdered and they were the only ones who could solve it? She couldn't just set aside the investigation, even if Byron wanted her to.

The priest prompted those congregated to speak the words of the Lord's prayer. Mira spoke along with the others, her gaze flicking to each member of the group. Her aunt, uncle, and cousins all mourning a daughter and a sister. Her brother, who barely knew Emilie at all. The friends who Mira had never met. The priest and clerks. Klasha. Byron, standing there, still waiting for an answer. And Marguerite, a little way off, with nothing in her posture to betray her thoughts.

"'Lead us not into temptation, but deliver us from evil.'"

They all said "Amen," and the priest began the final passage. When it was finished, Loretta placed a single, white rose on the latch of the crypt and a low murmur of voices sounded from the mourners.

Mira looked up at Byron. "I can grieve and solve a case at the same time. I've done it before."

He sighed. "That doesn't mean that you have to."

Off to the side, Madame de Bonnemains was making a quick retreat towards the gate of the cemetery. Mira stepped away from Byron, moving in that direction. After all, someone ought to thank her. And if Mira were able to glean any additional information, all the better. She reached the ex-viscountess just in time.

"Thank you so much for coming," Mira said.

Marguerite stilled, her whole form stiffening. After a moment she said, in French, "*It is so unfortunate what happened.*"

Mira frowned, but switched to French as well. "*I'm sure Emilie would be grateful to know that you were here.*"

"*It is nothing,*" Marguerite said, adjusting a green scarab brooch on her dress. "*Please excuse me, but I have another appointment.*"

She gave a slight bow with her head and turned, hurrying away towards a waiting carriage.

Byron came to stand next to Mira, but remained silent.

Mira sighed. "I know you worry for me, and in truth I wouldn't have it otherwise. But I really am all right. I would rather get to the bottom of everything than be stuck at home doing needlepoint. Not that I have anything against the craft, mind you. In fact my quilt is coming along quite nicely. The point is—"

He stopped her ramblings with a quick kiss on her forehead. "I'll stop bringing it up if you promise you'll tell me if anything is actually wrong."

"I thought you always knew."

"There are limits to my observations." He tucked a stray bit of hair behind her ear. "Do you promise?"

"Of course," she said, stomach twisting.

"I also think we should take the rest of the day off to spend with your family." He looped his arm with hers and they started back towards the Lavigne crypt.

"I can agree to that," she said. "After you tell me about the alibi."

He chuckled a little. "I really shouldn't be surprised." He helped her over a rocky part of the path. "It's watertight I'm afraid. Boulanger and Marguerite were seen at the opera together by several of the staff. They were in a private box."

"They must have had someone else—" she stopped talking as they rounded one of the mausoleums. There, ahead of them, was a figure, hiding in the shadows of an archway. For a moment, she thought it might be a statue, but then it moved and she caught a glimpse of his blue coat.

"Byron," she whispered. "Who is that?"

He followed her line of sight. "I'm not certain. Maybe it's someone come to mourn a relative." He pulled his arm free of hers. "Stay here. I'll go have a chat."

Byron moved down the stone path towards the unknown man, but the moment his intentions were noticed the man left the safety of the archway. He ran down one of the paths and disappeared from Mira's sight. Byron ran after him, and Mira followed behind.

She had to move slower to avoid tripping on her skirts. The cemetery was a maze with crisscrossing paths and plenty of hiding places, It was much too similar to the one that held the secret entrance to Circe's tunnels. Mira had to focus on the differences to keep the memories at bay. It was the middle of the day, and while the tombs were covered in frost, it was melting away in the sun. She was there with her family, for an entirely different purpose. By all accounts she was safe. But the shadows still loomed as she dodged crypts and mausoleums to catch up with Byron and the unknown man.

In the end it was a fruitless chase. Whoever he was, he had vanished, like a ghost. Although Mira didn't particularly want to imagine such things, especially given the scenery.

She and Byron found each other behind a marble mausoleum towards the northern edge of the cemetery, both of them out of breath.

After gulping some air Byron said, "He's gone."

She nodded. "Who do you think he was?"

"I don't know. But it doesn't bode well." He took her arm again. "Come on. Let's get back to your family."

January 13, 1889

*T*HE PURSUIT OF THE UNKNOWN MAN IN the cemetery had been so startling, that Mira quite forgot about her interaction with Madame de Bonnemains until the next morning, at church. She was mulling over the particulars of the funeral and wondering if the shadow she saw in the narthex was the same man from the cemetery, when she saw a woman wearing a veil in the pew across the aisle. This one was short, blue, and attached to a hat. It rather suited the woman wearing it. And of course, the veil reminded her of Marguerite.

She hadn't really learned anything by speaking with the madame, but the more she thought about their conversation, the more it felt . . . off. They had only spoken for a few moments though. Marguerite had been in quite the hurry.

Nonetheless, she thought about their interaction for the rest of the service and the majority of the afternoon. Her thoughts were still swirling with possibilities when Walker led Byron and Fred into the sitting room after lunch.

She smiled and set her quilt aside. "I had wondered when you were coming over."

Byron moved over. "I would have been here earlier, but Fred insisted on coming along."

Fred scoffed. "I needed a proper outing, a way to stretch my legs!"

"So the doctor has let off the lead?" Walker said, as the men took up positions on the sofas and armchairs. "Your stab wound has healed well enough?"

"I've been given a clean bill of health. Or, at least, I think I have." He wavered his hand back and forth. "There was a bit of a translation difficulty."

Mira gasped. "That was it!"

They all turned to her. Byron furrowed his brow. "What?"

"The thing that was bothering me about Marguerite yesterday. She didn't understand when I spoke to her in English!"

"Well, she is French," Byron said.

Walker frowned. "She spoke English well enough when I was there with Uncle and Loretta."

Mira set a hand on Byron's arm. "Don't you remember meeting with her a few days ago?"

He flushed. "I remember what was discussed. Did she speak English then?"

"Yes. She did." A pit formed in her stomach and she glanced over at Fred. This was hardly a minor detail to forget. Was his memory that much worse?

"Now that you mention it," Byron said, hesitation in his voice. "I do remember her speaking with me directly," He laughed a little. "I suppose it didn't really occur to me about the language."

She picked up the quilt again. Now wasn't the time to bring up the status of his memory loss, although his excuses were getting thin.

Walker leaned forward. "That is odd if she didn't speak it yesterday."

"I think she was taller too," she said. "Did you notice?"

Byron frowned. "I couldn't say. Was she wearing different shoes?"

"I don't know," Mira stopped in her sewing again. "Maybe I'm imagining it, but I think her voice was different too. And she was wearing a jade scarab brooch."

"What's wrong with that?" Fred asked.

"If Emilie was right, Marguerite *hates* the color green." She turned to Byron. "I don't think that was Madame de Bonnemains at all."

"Who was it then?" Byron asked.

Mira had recognized the voice, even if it wasn't Marguerite's. And the woman's hair was the right shade of blonde. She just didn't have the same build. Or the language skills. "I think it was Angeline."

"One of the maids?" Walker asked.

"I think so."

Walker let out a long breath. "What a rotten thing to do. Just because she doesn't want to come to the funeral, she sends someone to pretend to be her? Might as well just send a postcard with condolences."

Mira sucked on the inside of her cheek. She had completely forgotten that Walker didn't know they were investigating Emilie's death. As far as he was concerned, the death was natural and the case closed. If they kept him in the dark, they wouldn't be able to speak candidly. If they told him, he could help them with the investigation. Her thoughts parsed each option within a few seconds. With a sharp breath, she set her sewing aside and closed the sitting room door. Heaven knows how upsetting it would be if Loretta or her uncle were to overhear and find out that they thought Emilie was murdered, especially before they had more proof.

"Walker, I'm afraid we haven't been entirely forthwith with you about what we've been up to."

He looked up at her, his brow furrowed. "You haven't?"

"Well . . . we've been investigating Emilie's death. We think she might have been murdered."

His eyes blew wide. "What? Why on earth would you think that?"

Mira came to sit next to Byron again. "There are quite a few reasons, but the main one is that she was blackmailing Madame de Bonnemains."

Walker sat back in his chair. "And how do you know that?"

She pointed up. "I found the evidence in one of the drawers in her room. I can get some of it for you."

He shook his head. "I believe you. But that doesn't mean she was murdered."

"There are other factors at play," Byron said. "In any case, if the woman yesterday was not Marguerite de Bonnemains, I think it would be remiss of us to ignore it."

"Marguerite must be part of Circe," Mira said. "It all adds up. The secrecy, her motive. She would have to have some supplier of poison, and since we suspect Emilie was killed with the same poison used on Durant, it would—"

"Durant is dead?" Fred interrupted.

Mira looked at Byron. "You didn't tell him?"

"It didn't occur to me."

She let out a sigh and picked up her sewing again. "We found him when we visited the morgue. Cause of death: seizure. The timing can't be a coincidence. Two seizures within less than a week? And both deaths were unexpected. That suggests that there is some correlation between them."

"And that isn't accounting for their connection to you," Byron said.

Walker swallowed, his complexion turning rather peaky. "Yes, I would say that is all rather suspicious."

Byron hummed. "I think we need more proof before we can definitively say that Marguerite is working with Circe."

"What sort of proof?" Mira said.

"Well, we can't exactly go searching her flat." Byron stood and began to pace, shifting into full detective mode.

"We need more evidence of her using Angeline as a double. Was that only for the funeral or could it have been Angeline that went to the opera with the general last Thursday?"

Fred grinned. "I can watch her flat. After all, a woman can only leave an apartment so many times before she has to come back again."

Byron nodded. "Good. Although I hate for you to go alone, in case there is something dangerous about it."

"I can go with him," Walker said. "After all, I have experience with twins." He winked at Mira and she rolled her eyes.

"And what about us?" Mira said.

"We need the Circe theory to have more teeth. And I think there's one person who might be able to help us."

"Who?" Mira asked.

Byron moved over to the window, lifted the curtain and dropped it again. "Selene's man. Theodore Jaubert."

"Theo?" Fred asked. "How could he help?"

"While he's cut his ties with Circe, if Marguerite is part of the organization I'm certain it isn't a recent thing. Surely, he would have heard rumors of her or the general being members."

"But would the police trust the testimony of a thief?" Walker asked.

"Oh, certainly not. But I would. And right now it's more important for us to get the facts in line." Byron resumed his pacing. "At the moment, there are only three things we know for certain: Emilie is dead, she was blackmailing Marguerite and the general, and Alexander Durant died in the exact same way." He listed the items on his fingers. "One could surmise that those three things are connected, but until we know, beyond a shadow of a doubt, that Marguerite or Boulanger are part of Circe, I'm afraid we can't assume anything."

Mira stabbed the needle in the fabric with too much force and hissed as it hit her finger. "We aren't assuming anything. It's obvious that they are connected."

"Circumstantially, at the moment." Byron stopped by the fireplace. "I admit there is something suspicious about it all, but the police don't arrest people based on gut feelings and emotions. At least, they shouldn't."

"Well, it seems we have a suitable plan," Fred said. "When do we start?"

"I don't see why we can't do it today," Mira said, setting her needlework aside. She sucked at the blood, trying not to let the iron taste recall intrusive memories again. Especially now that they were truly on the case.

‿◦❘◦⸮

THE MIDAFTERNOON SUN WAS HIDDEN BY STORM clouds when Byron and Mira reached the Gallerie de Mestra. Instead of going to the front door, which was certain to be locked, Byron led the way around the back to a secret door.

"I didn't even know this was here," Mira said, pulling her coat tighter around her neck.

"Theo showed it to us when Fred and I came to ask about Selene and where she might have taken you." He rapped on the door.

Images of Selene in her last few minutes crowded Mira's thoughts. Her breath hitched and she could almost feel the blood on her hands.

"Are you all right?" Byron asked.

She nodded, trying to pull her focus away from the past.

The door opened, a crack of light in the darkness, and Theo's face appeared.

"Constantine?" he said.

"The one and only." Byron removed his hat. "Could we come in for a quick chat?"

Theo nodded and led them up the rickety wooden staircase to the main sitting room that Mira was familiar with. It seemed cold, in spite of the crackling fire, and empty. Selene's chair was particularly foreboding.

"I am glad to see you are well," Theo said, nodding to Mira as he took a seat in the armchair closest to the window.

Mira moved to the sofa. "I am only well because you were willing to help Byron to find me. Thank you."

Theo sighed. "I presume you are here to ask more of me?"

Byron shook his head, sitting next to Mira and pulling out his notebook. "Only if you are willing to offer it. We have some questions about Circe."

The thief gave an involuntary shudder. "They have not bothered me since, if that is what you are asking."

"I'm glad to hear it," Byron said. "However, we were wondering about some potential members. Marguerite de Bonnemains and General Boulanger, to be precise."

Theo's eyes widened. "You think General Boulanger is working with Circe?"

"I take it that you hadn't heard anything of the sort?"

Theo shook his head. "I wasn't particularly high up in the ranks. Certainly not enough to interact with anyone of note."

"Were there any rumors you can remember?" Mira asked.

"We were all known to . . . what is the word . . . gossip? But I would have remembered if someone had mentioned that General Revenge was part of the organization. Circe's aim is for a war in Europe, and if he were a member I would think we would already be fighting it."

"And Madame de Bonnemains?" Byron asked.

"I'm not certain I know who that is. The name seems familiar, but I couldn't say." He leaned forward. "Why do you think that they are part of Circe?"

While Byron explained the situation, Mira examined the paintings on the walls. She found herself drawn to the painting Selene had shown her only a month before. It depicted a shoreline with a dark ocean and a few ghostly ships lit by the full moon. The ocean was choppy and dangerous, the brackish waters hiding who knows what. So many secrets.

Movement outside drew her gaze to the window. There was a figure standing in an alcove across the street, a lit cigarette creating an eerie glow near his face, though she couldn't discern who he was. It started to rain, some of the drops hitting the window, but the figure didn't move.

She looked back over to the men. Byron had just finished his explanation.

"Yes, I could see them working with Circe to that end," Theo said. "But I cannot confirm anything."

"Do you have people stand watch over the gallery?" Mira asked, interrupting the conversation.

"Er, no?" Theo said, moving to look.

Byron was close behind. "Do you know how long he's been there?"

Mira shook her head. "I only just noticed him."

"If he were a member of Circe, we would not have seen him," Theo said.

"That is some comfort," Byron said. "I wonder if it is our friend from the cemetery."

"I'm not sure," Mira said. "I didn't get a good look at him then, either."

"Well, I think I'll try to have that little talk again," Byron said. "Theo, do you mind ensuring Miss Blayse's safety?"

"Not at all. There's a knife in the first drawer of the desk as you go out, if you want it."

Lightning flashed across the sky, followed by a crack of thunder.

Mira stared at the man across the street. "What if he wanted to be seen?" She turned towards Byron. "I don't think it's a good idea to confront him."

"This is the second time in as many days that we've noticed someone following us," Byron said. "I think it is more dangerous to not know who we are up against." He moved over and kissed her cheek. "I'll be careful."

The lightning flashed again and for a moment Mira saw blood staining Byron's suit. She blinked the image away and Byron was gone.

The rain continued to pelt the window. The figure continued to smoke his cigarette. Theo continued to stand beside her, watching the scene. Mira's stomach churned. The moment Byron came onto the pavement, she stepped away. She couldn't witness him be murdered. She couldn't stand to have that memory burned into her mind.

"The coward," Theo said under his breath. Louder he said, "He's run away, whoever he is."

Mira let out a breath and sank into one of the armchairs. A few minutes later, the downstairs door opened.

"Do you want this back in the drawer?" Byron called from the side room.

"If you would, yes," Theo said.

There was the soft thud of a drawer being closed. Byron came into the room, clothes soaked and hair dripping. "He ran off down one of the side streets. I still don't know who he is."

Theo closed the blinds. "It would seem someone does not want you to be investigating this matter."

Byron locked eyes with Mira. "All the more reason to investigate."

They met up with Fred and Walker back at the boarding house. The rain had gotten worse, so the whole group was gathered around the fire in the sitting room, trying to dry off and get warm.

"I don't like the idea of you being followed," Walker said, after she had explained their side of the story.

"I assure you, we don't like it either," Byron said. "Theo is fairly certain that, whoever it was, they weren't part of Circe."

"But who else would have an interest in our investigation?" Fred asked.

"It's difficult to say. How did your watch go?" Byron said.

"Strangest thing," Fred said, a slight lilt in his voice. "We saw the woman leave the apartment twice in the time we were watching. And she hadn't returned in between."

"I watched from the back of the house too," Walker said. "I only saw the cook come out into the yard. And the cat. So the madame couldn't have come back through there."

"Was she wearing a veil?" Mira asked.

"Both times," Fred said. "The first time she left with a gentleman, taking his carriage."

"General Boulanger, I would guess," Byron said.

Fred nodded. "The second time, she took her own carriage."

"And did she return?" Byron asked.

"We stayed long enough that the second one returned, but not the first," Walker said. "By that point it was raining too hard and we decided to leave."

Mira moved over to the sofa, feeling overheated from the fire but still damp from the rain. "I wonder what she's up to. There can't be—"

The door to the sitting room opened and Loretta came in with her sewing basket. She paused on the threshold. "Oh, I'm sorry. I didn't mean to interrupt."

"It's perfectly all right," Byron said. "We were just warming up after getting caught in that downpour."

"Yes, it is coming down quite heavily." She moved to an armchair. "I hope it will clear up before Tuesday."

"Tuesday?" Fred asked.

Loretta ducked her head. "It's our wedding at the church. Although I don't think anyone feels much up to it. Part of me wonders if we ought to cancel outright. Cyrus and I have been married in a church before, after all."

"No," Mira said. "Emilie wouldn't want that."

Loretta sighed. "No, she wouldn't. We still have so much to do for it though. I don't even know if I'll have time to pick up the dress."

Byron hummed. "Mira, you'll have time tomorrow, won't you?"

Mira frowned. Was he still trying to stop her from working on the case? She couldn't very well tell her aunt no.

"Of course," she said. "I'll stop by the House of Worth first thing."

January 14, 1889: Morning

THE HOUSE OF WORTH WAS ALL HUSTLE and bustle when she arrived. A tailor moved through the foyer, arms laden with cloth. Several elegant ladies were talking with one another while waiting for their appointments and if Mira weren't in such a hurry, she would stop to listen in on the news of Paris. Instead, she approached the front desk, explained her need to retrieve a dress, and received directions of where to go.

The sewing room was easy to find by the sound of feet pumping on sewing machine pedals. There were two rows of sewing machines, most of them occupied by women working with the most incredible fabrics. Sandrine, one of the attendants Mira had met with Loretta, approached her as she came in.

"*How can I help you?*" she asked, in French.

"*I'm here to pick up a dress. It is either under the name Lavigne or de Bonnemains.*"

"*Very good, Miss. If you will take a seat, I will retrieve it shortly.*"

Sandrine went to a back room and Mira took a seat against the wall facing the sewing machines. Mira had never really seen one at work before. It was fascinating, but quite loud, to see them all working on their projects. No wonder Worth could complete so many gowns in such a short time.

Although, short would not describe the time she spent waiting. Five minutes turned into fifteen, and then thirty, before Sandrine finally returned.

"*I am so sorry, Miss. I'm afraid we only have one of the dresses completed.*"

Mira blinked. "*One?*" She was only there for Loretta's. Were there more?

"*Yes, I know it must be disappointing. But we have only had since Wednesday evening to complete the alterations for the second dress. I hope Madame de Bonnemains won't be upset.*"

"*Oh, I'm afraid I don't know all of the particulars,*" Mira said, trying to play along. Wednesday evening was the night Marguerite had gone to the opera. The night that Emilie died. "*May I see the dress, in any case?*"

Sandrine flushed. "*Of course, but it really isn't ready.*"

She led Mira along the edge of the sewing room to the back room where they kept the dresses. Two women were speaking in hushed tones near the rack, one had brown hair in a braided bun and the other wore a cap.

"*Do you think turpentine would work?*" the one with brown hair said.

"*I don't think it would damage the fabric, but I'm not sure . . .*" The two of them stopped their conversation as they approached.

"*She wishes to see the dress,*" Sandrine said to the others.

The woman wearing a cap pursed her lips. "*It isn't ready.*"

"*She knows that.*"

The woman with brown hair brought over a dress that had been draped on the table. It was deep blue with a hem and the train covered in elegant embroidered florals. The bodice had full length sleeves, so it must have been a day dress, but more elegant than any that Mira had ever seen.

"*Oh my,*" she said. "*It is beautiful. What still needs to be done?*"

The women exchanged a glance. "*We will need another fitting with the madame,*" Sandrine said. "*Due to some . . . circumstances, we've had to let go the assistant that took the measurements and the notes on what needed to be altered were misplaced.*"

"*And then there's the issue of the blood . . .*" the woman with brown hair said, draping the skirt over her arm and holding the bodice up.

"*Blood?*" Mira stepped closer.

"*Cyrille!*" the woman in the cap hissed.

"*I thought we were telling her the problems with the dress,*" Cyrille said without remorse.

Sandrine ushered Mira closer. "*It is not so big of an issue.*" She picked up one of the sleeves and turned it inside out. The lining was cream colored and there were a few splotchy blood stains around the wrist.

"*I just don't see where it could have come from,*" Cyrille said.

Mira picked up the sleeve, running her thumb over the unmarred fabric closest to the cuff. "*The fitting was last Wednesday?*"

Sandrine nodded. "*In the evening, I believe. You will apologize to Madame de Bonnemains for us, won't you? We can send someone over this week, once we figure out how to address the stains.*"

"I'll be sure to let her know," Mira said. *"Might I take the dress that is ready?"*

"Of course. I have it wrapped up for you. Do you have the receipt?"

MIRA DROPPED OFF LORETTA'S WEDDING DRESS BEFORE heading to Rue Geoffroy. This was proof that Marguerite couldn't have been at the opera! Although Byron had proved her alibi, hadn't he? She and General Boulanger had been seen together. But, was the woman seen wearing a veil at the time? If she had been, it could have been Angeline that went to the opera, not Marguerite.

She paid the carriage driver and rushed up the stairs, pausing to compose herself before knocking. Byron opened the door a few moments later, but before he could say a thing, she was rambling on.

"There was a fitting on Wednesday evening! Marguerite couldn't have gone to the opera because she was needed at home. Angeline went to the opera with the general, giving Marguerite an alibi and the opportunity to poison Emilie for blackmailing her! It all makes sense."

He blinked at her. "Might I have some context for this news?"

"Oh. Sorry."

They came into the sitting room, but she couldn't stand to sit still. For once, she was the one pacing while he sat and watched.

"The seamstresses at the House of Worth assumed that I was working for Madame de Bonnemains when I came to pick up the dress for Loretta, because I wasn't sure which name it would be under. There was another dress there for Marguerite, but it wasn't ready. During the conversation it came up that the fitting had been held Wednesday evening!"

"Hence the alibi and the opportunity," Byron said, drumming his fingers on the armrest. "Yes, that does match up nicely."

"The only thing I don't understand is why all the maids are hiding the truth. I can understand Angeline not wanting to be involved, but why didn't Heloise or Sorcha tell us that Marguerite stayed behind?"

"Perhaps they are being paid not to say anything."

Mira moved to sit across from him. "That would explain why Heloise was so nervous."

Byron tipped his head to one side. "We still have the problem of proving it."

"Yes," Mira sighed. "I'm certain that the women at the House of Worth would testify that there was a fitting. Although the actual tailor's assistant who did the fitting has been let go."

"Did they say why?"

Mira frowned. "No, they didn't."

They sat in silence for a few minutes, each of them mulling over the details.

"Marguerite wouldn't have had time to poison her," Byron said at last. "If she truly was being fitted, she wouldn't be able to move, and there would be more witnesses."

Mira slumped in her seat. "Then why send Angeline to the opera?" The moment the words left her mouth, a memory came to mind. "Wait." She stood again, nervous energy flowing through her. "Emilie would stand in for fittings for Marguerite."

Byron frowned. "She would?"

Mira nodded. "Just before Christmas, when I was looking for the man Klasha had been in love with as a girl, I needed to talk to Charles Worth because Emilie and I thought he might have known him."

His brow furrowed. "I think I remember you telling me about it."

"We were able to meet with him because of Madame de Bonnemains. She agreed to send her card as long as Emilie to stood in for a fitting for her. Emilie mentioned that she'd done it before because she was so close to Marguerite's coloring and build and the madame hated fittings."

"So, it is possible that Marguerite went to the opera that night and Emilie stood in for the fitting."

Mira paced over to the fireplace. "But if Marguerite really did have an alibi that night, then who killed Emilie?"

Byron cocked his head to the side. "I think it's high time we gave Madame de Bonnemains the chance to tell the truth."

HELOISE WAS THE ONE WHO ANSWERED THE door when they called.

"*Good afternoon,*" she said, shifting from one foot to the other. "*I'm afraid that the madame is not taking visitors at this time.*"

"*It is urgent,*" Mira said. "*We have information about Emilie.*"

Heloise drew in a sharp breath. "*I will ask. Would you wait in the foyer?*"

She closed the door and went up the stairs, tripping on the first step before righting herself.

"She's still nervous," Byron said once she had left their sight.

Mira frowned. "I still don't understand why they wouldn't tell us that Emilie was being fitted. If they all believed her death was natural, then why hide it?"

"I'm sure the madame can shed some light on that subject." Byron picked up a book from one of the side tables and turned it over in his hands.

Heloise returned a few minutes later. "*She will see you, if you will follow me.*"

They followed the maid up the stairs and to the sitting room. Heloise gave a short knock on the door and allowed them entry.

Marguerite was by the window, wearing a deep crimson dress with a fur wrap around her shoulders. The veil seemed to be a permanent fixture. General Boulanger sat in one of the armchairs, adjusting his cravat.

"I apologize for the intrusion," Mira said.

"It is no matter," Marguerite said, turning towards them. "Heloise mentioned you had news about Emilie. The poor thing."

Mira's jaw tightened. Byron stepped forward. "May we sit down?"

"Of course." Marguerite positioned herself on the chaise lounge.

Byron settled next to Mira on the sofa, but before he could say anything, she said, "First of all, I wanted to thank you for lending my aunt a dress for the wedding."

"Oh, yes!" Marguerite said, sitting up. "How does she like it?"

"It suits her perfectly." She arranged her skirts as she spoke, being careful and deliberate with her word choice. It wouldn't do to spook either of them. "But when I went to pick it up from the House of Worth this morning, the attendants mentioned there was another dress that you had ordered. Unfortunately, the measurements they took last Wednesday evening were lost, so they'll have to come to take them again. I thought you might want to know."

"That is unfortunate," Marguerite said, as if she didn't realize the significance. "Is that why you came?"

"Not exactly," Byron said. "We did also want to ask you a few questions for clarification."

"About Emilie?" Boulanger said.

"Yes, if that's all right." Byron pulled out his notebook and pen.

"Well, yes," Marguerite said, shifting uncomfortably. "What exactly do you want to know?"

Byron asked, "How often did Emilie stand in for fittings for you?"

Marguerite stiffened. "What?"

"That fitting Miss Blayse mentioned occurred on the night that Emilie died."

The madame fell silent. Boulanger sat next to her on the chaise lounge. Byron continued on. "Now, you were at the opera that night, which means that Emilie stood in for that fitting for you, did she not?"

"Y-es. She did."

"Might I ask why you didn't inform us or the police about that detail?"

Marguerite let out a shaky laugh. "It didn't seem important."

"It didn't seem important to let anyone know what Emilie was doing when she was taken ill?" Mira asked.

"Well, it was a natural death." She fidgeted with her veil. "What does it matter what she was doing?"

"Madame, it is my opinion, based on several pieces of evidence, that Emilie was murdered," Byron said. "That is why it matters."

Marguerite stilled. "Murdered?" she whispered. "But why would anyone want to murder Emilie?"

Boulanger took her hand. "*Ma chérie,* I think we should tell them."

Mira held her breath. Were they going to confess?

But both of them remained silent while Marguerite removed her veil with shaking hands. For a moment, Mira wondered if she would see Angeline or someone else entirely, but sure enough, it was the same woman she met with Emilie before Christmas.

"I'm not exactly sure how to explain it. Yes. Emilie did

stand in for me that night. We left for the opera around five and the fitting was at seven."

"Why keep that a secret?" Mira asked. "It is a strange arrangement, certainly, but why not tell the police? And why have your staff been sworn to secrecy as well?"

"She wasn't only standing in for me. She was . . . well she was meant to *be* me."

"Like Angeline at the funeral?" Mira asked.

Marguerite's eyes widened. "You noticed?"

"She was wearing a green brooch." Mira gestured to the lapel of her dress.

Marguerite swore under her breath in French. "Silly girl. I knew I never should have tried with her."

"Regardless, what we want to know is why you have been using your maids as stand ins at all," Byron said.

"It is all my fault, really," Boulanger said. "It started, well, because of our love."

"Must we tell them that?" Marguerite said.

Byron cleared his throat. "If it helps at all, we are aware of your relationship. And the fact that it started before the divorce."

Marguerite flushed. "How?"

"We found the documents in Emilie's room," Mira said. "Letters and receipts, mostly."

"What letters?" Marguerite said. "I wasn't aware of this."

"You mean, she didn't blackmail you?" Mira asked.

"No." Marguerite's breath hitched. "Although, perhaps I can see why she would."

"Why don't you tell us what happened, from the beginning," Byron said.

Marguerite wrung the veil in her hands. "My husband, the viscount, was a horrible man. He cared more for my inheritance than for me and he would often spend more time with other woman than at home. When I met Georges . . ." she looked over at the general. "It was an entirely different kind of love. It was warm and passionate and caring. But if we were to spend any time together, my husband could not know. If I were to report him for infidelity, it would be a small fine. But for him to do the same, I would be imprisoned for years."

"So you see why we needed the secrecy," Boulanger said.

Marguerite took Boulanger's hand. "One time, when Georges came to talk with my husband about matters of the military, he commented on how much Emilie and I looked alike. That was when the idea took hold. Emilie agreed to help me trick my husband. On nights that I wished to be with Georges, I would have Emilie sleep in my bed, pretending to be me, so that if my husband came in, he would think I was asleep. As he was out most nights himself, it worked perfectly. That is how it started."

Byron finished his note and looked up. "You are divorced now, yes?"

Marguerite nodded. "He determined I was an unfit wife, as I hadn't borne him any children."

"Then you had no reason to continue the charade."

Marguerite sighed. "You are right. Absolutely right. Except, she and I were having too much fun. And it is terribly convenient to have more than one of yourself. In fact, I had the idea to have more of my staff look like me, in case I needed it. You may have noticed that my new cook, Dufresne has quite the resemblance to me. And she can even mimic my voice. Although she won't be able to fill in until after the baby comes."

She brushed a stray hair out of her face. "That is why I used Angeline on the day of the funeral. I had the most terrible headache but so wanted your family to feel supported. Of course, as I had never intended for her to be a stand in, we hadn't spoken about the proper way to portray myself in public. And she is much too tall. But I thought the veil would do enough that no one would notice. Obviously, I was wrong."

Mira frowned. "I have a question about the veil. When I came to visit you with Emilie before Christmas, you weren't wearing one, and yet every time since you have."

Marguerite held the veil up between them. "I usually try to wear it around strangers, but when you came with Emilie, I didn't see the reason. Both Emilie and I were in the room. And, truth be told, it is rather stuffy."

"But when you sent Emilie for the fitting with Worth in person, you didn't have her impersonate you. Why is that?" Mira said.

"Oh, there wasn't a reason to. You see, Worth is aware of the fact that I hate fittings and that I send Emilie in my place. A few of his head tailors know too." She tossed the veil to the side. "They know Emilie well enough by now, and let us play our little game with the younger tailors. Worth actually thinks it might help to weed out the less observant ones. When you are in such close proximity to a person you should be able to tell if it is a completely different person than the client you were expecting. Since you intended to see Worth himself, I didn't see the need to go to all the trouble."

Byron tapped his pen on the page. "Did Emilie know of your plans to have Dufresne act as a stand in?"

"Oh yes. I spoke to Emilie about the prospect before hiring her. I thought it would be nice to let Emilie have a little more freedom. I've relied on her so much over the last few years. Although, she may have thought that I was replacing her. She had grown a little distant this past year. And if she was gathering letters to use against me . . ." She closed her eyes. "Oh, I hate that she thought it would have to come to that."

Mira's stomach churned at the thought. The greatest relief was that Emilie hadn't gone through with it, and she wouldn't have needed to with Cyrus coming into the family. But how terrible to know that she had considered it, acted on it even.

Boulanger frowned, standing. "You say it was murder . . . and perhaps it was. But there truly was no reason for Emilie to be murdered."

Byron closed his notebook. "I would agree. The only motive we have found so far is the blackmail, and you were both unaware of it and have an alibi for that night."

"What, you thought we would murder Emilie?" Marguerite said, her eyes going wide.

"It was a theory," Mira said.

"And now that we've disproved it, we're left with the unfortunate truth: Emilie wasn't the target," Byron said.

Mira fell silent, her mind swirling. Emilie was never meant to be dead. They had been investigating in all the wrong places. If Emilie had been pretending to be Marguerite then—

"It was you." Mira looked up at the madame. "Someone wanted to kill you."

Marguerite's breath hitched. "Me? But why would anyone . . ."

Boulanger swore. "It is because of this election." He took her hand again. "They know what you mean to me, and hope to stop my campaign."

Byron stood and paced away. "The murderer couldn't have been one of your maids, as they know about the switch. Whoever it was thought that Emilie was Marguerite. And there was only one other person with the opportunity."

"It was the tailor," Mira said, clenching her fists. "Emilie had called for tea, the way you usually would, and the tailor must have slipped poison into it."

"We still can't prove it," Byron said. "This is all suppos—"

Marguerite interrupted, "It couldn't have been the tea."

"What?" Mira said, turning to her.

"I usually have tea in the evening. When I saw it there I— well, I suppose it was out of habit— I took a sip of it. Ice cold, of course, but if it were poisoned . . ."

"You would be dead," Boulanger said, his voice shaking. "This is all too much." He held his head in his hands.

"Still. It must have been the tailor," Mira said. "He would have been the only person in the house who wouldn't know that Emilie wasn't you."

"Then you must fetch the police and go to the House of Worth at once to arrest him," Boulanger said.

Mira shook her head, that familiar coldness settling in her stomach again. "He won't be there."

"What?" Marguerite said.

"He was fired or quit or something. I don't know." She turned to Byron. "There's no way we'll be able to track him down on our own."

"I think the first thing we need to do is determine who completed the fitting," Byron said. "The House of Worth should have a ledger that can tell us that much. At that point we can bring what we know to Lozé. And if he doesn't believe us, we can take it higher. Who does he report to?"

Boulanger swore again, pacing across the room. "The ministry of the interior. But I'm afraid that won't work. The interior minister and I had a . . . disagreement last year."

"A duel, chéri. It's called a duel," Marguerite said. "And I still haven't forgiven him for wounding you."

"It was more my pride, than my arm," Boulanger said rolling his shoulder back, as if remembering the injury made it hurt again. "But in any case, he has wished ill of me from the moment I entered government. I doubt he would help."

"Then it seems we must convince Lozé." Byron ran a hand through his hair, letting out a long sigh. He drew his gaze across the room, stopping on General Boulanger. "Until we do, and until we can catch this murderer, I would advise you to stay with Marguerite. If the police do not believe us, they will not offer any protection."

"I intended to. They will not have the chance to try again."

"Good." Byron stood, and held out a hand to pull Mira up. "I believe we have some more investigating to do. We'll keep you apprised of any new information."

"Thank you for your help." Boulanger extended his hand for Byron to shake, which he did.

"My pleasure."

A myriad of conflicting emotions were churning within Mira as they left the madame's flat and turned towards the boarding house. Grief, anger, relief, determination, confusion, discouragement—she decided to focus on the determination for the time being. Although it was late enough in the day, they couldn't exactly investigate the tailor immediately.

"We'll go to the House of Worth first thing tomorrow," she said, as they settled into the carriage. "Once we have the ledger it should be simple enough to get the name of the murderer and then—"

"I think you're forgetting something," Byron said.

"I am?"

"Your uncle's wedding is tomorrow, love."

"Oh." She leaned against him, suddenly feeling quite tired. "I hadn't thought of that."

He kissed her head. "That's why I'm here. The House of Worth will still be there, day after tomorrow."

January 15, 1889: Morning

*L*IGHT SPILLED IN FROM THE WINDOWS, STAINING the floors and wall of the church with dancing reds, blues, and oranges. The warm tones of the organ flowed over the small congregation as Loretta stepped down the aisle. The gothic arches stretched heavenward, candles flickering on their stands, and Mira stood with Byron at the front of the pews on the right side, chest bursting with joy and heartache.

Walker stood beside their uncle at the front, acting as best man. Fred and the men from Scotland Yard had come to support. Little Clarisse and Jean-Marie had already made their way down the aisle, the flower girl and ring bearer respectively, and were now standing near the celebrant. Mira caught the gaze of Klasha and Georges on the opposite side of the nave as Loretta passed by them and came to her place beside Cyrus.

The rose colored silk of the gown caught the dappled light, and she looked as if she were glowing. And yet, there was sadness there too. Or perhaps that was Mira's own sorrow coloring the scene. That dress had been Marguerite's and somehow that was all she could focus on.

The celebrant began the ceremony with the preface, but Mira didn't hear the words. She was too caught up in thoughts of Emilie, murder, and Circe. Knowing that Marguerite had been the target only made the tragedy worse. The loss was palpable, felt more acutely on what should have been a joyful occasion.

When no one brought any objections against the marriage, the organ swelled again, leading the congregation into the hymn. Byron held the hymnal between the two of them as they sang loud and clear. But she couldn't ignore the voice that was missing.

After the hymn, everyone moved to sit in the pews as Mira stepped to the front to do a reading from the Bible. She spoke out, her words echoing in the space. "When Jesus saw the crowds, he went up the mountain . . ." Her uncle had chosen the passage from Matthew. She continued on, but paused as she came to the second beatitude. Voice wavering, she said, "Blessed are those who mourn, for they will be comforted."

She looked up, catching her uncle's gaze. He gave her a sad smile, his eyes crinkling at the corners. She glanced at Loretta. Her aunt wasn't wearing a veil, as widows who remarried weren't permitted to. Its absence allowed Mira to see the tears streaming down Loretta's face, open and honest.

"Blessed are the meek . . ." she continued, her gut churning with guilt. Perhaps Mira wasn't wearing a veil, but she was hiding things nonetheless. They knew that Emilie's death hadn't been natural, and yet she hadn't told Cyrus or Loretta or any of

Emilie's siblings. Walker knew, but had been sworn to secrecy. And that wasn't the only secret she was keeping, not the only loss that her family was feeling.

If Cyrus had his way, Professor Burke would be his best man, not Walker. Which would be worse? Believing your best friend dead, or knowing he was a villain and a traitor? A murderer? And in this case, Walker didn't even know the truth. He still believed his godfather to be an honorable man, taken from the world too soon. Here she was, standing at the front of a church, in the sight of God, with all these lies within her. "Blessed are the pure in heart . . ." All she wanted to do was protect them from the truth. "Blessed are the peacemakers . . ." Their peace would shatter if they knew.

She moved back to her seat, her heart racing. Soon enough they would need to tell the truth about what had really happened to Emilie. The matter of the professor could be kept hidden forever, but what was the right thing to do? It wasn't clear. The celebrant began his address to the couple and she took a few deep breaths to calm herself, a tear trailing down her cheek.

"Is something the matter?" Byron whispered.

She shook her head. "I always cry at weddings."

Here she was, lying once again, hiding things from Byron, a man she loved more than anything in the world. And she knew he was keeping secrets from her, at least about his memory. Yet the thought of bringing any of them out into the open, Emilie, the professor, her nightmares, or Byron's memory, brought so much anxiety. Her breath came faster, her pulse racing. It felt as if she would die if she said anything.

Byron wrapped an arm around her waist, pulling her closer and she leaned into him. For a moment, couldn't she pretend that everything was alright? For a moment, couldn't she forget?

Except even as she thought that, the mystery was before her mind again. The tailor. They had to figure out who it was. And then they had to track him down, and could only do so with the help of the police. But the police wouldn't help them without evidence. It was a continuous circle of ruin, spiraling down. One was only possible with the other. What if they were wrong and Emilie really had died naturally, by a seizure, and it was just a coincidence that Durant had died too? After all, the tea hadn't been poisoned and Emilie hadn't eaten anything else that they knew of.

The celebrant said, "Marriage is a gift, and it may come with many riches. But these are not the riches of the world, but rather the riches of the heart and the treasures of heaven. And these are more precious than any of the treasures of the earth. For Jesus said, 'It is easier for a camel to go through the eye of a needle, than for a rich man to enter into the kingdom of God.' And together you may . . ."

A needle.

Mira didn't hear the rest of his speech. There was blood on the inside of the dress Emilie had worn during the fitting. Just a few drops near the cuff on the inside. She hadn't thought much of it, after all Emilie had scratches there from the cat. But what if it hadn't been the cat? What if it had been a needle?

Byron pulled her to stand for the next hymn, but she couldn't focus on the notes. What sort of poison could be administered with a needle? And how easy would it be to get it? If she was right about Durant having the same cause of death, Circe would have access to something like that. And if the tailor was part of the organization the whole murder would be simple. He would only have needed to work at the House of Worth for a short time, find a way to be assigned to Madame de Bonnemains, and administer the poison during a fitting. Then disappear, like a ghost. A phantom. A shadow.

She looked back towards the narthex, almost expecting to see the shadowy figure that had lurked there only a few days previous. But no one was there. When the hymn was finished and they were seated again, Byron leaned over.

"Are you sure that everything is all right?"

She shook her head. "I'll tell you afterwards."

The ceremony ended with a prayer over the bride and groom and all the congregation. Cyrus and Loretta kissed and they all cheered. And with that, they were married in the eyes of God and man. The party left the church in high jubilation, and yet Mira's thoughts were elsewhere. She smiled and preened with everyone as congratulations were given in front of the church, but she was entirely preoccupied.

She caught Byron's arm and pulled him away from the others.

"I know how the tailor did it," she said.

"Is that why you went still during the ceremony?" Byron asked.

She nodded. "It was a needle. Or pins. Something of that sort. Those punctures on her body weren't from the cat but from the tailor. There was blood on the inside of the dress that she wore around the cuffs. But what sort of poison can be administered in that way?"

He tilted his head to the side. "It's difficult to say." He spoke slowly as he ordered his words. "Many poisons can be administered intravenously. But to only prick the skin?" He furrowed his brow for a moment. "It must be an incredibly potent substance, whatever it is."

"One that Circe would have access to?"

"It's probable. And if it is that toxic, it likely could be administered in multiple ways. Hence, Alexander Durant having a seizure but no puncture wounds."

She shuddered, the image of his corpse coming into her mind. Byron wrapped his arm around her back and pulled her closer.

"These are dreadful things to be speaking of when your uncle has just been married. You should be celebrating with everyone else."

"Everyone else doesn't know that Emilie was murdered," she whispered. "And by accident, no less. And the longer we wait to investigate, the more likely it is that her murderer will get away."

A few moments of silence passed between them. Eventually, Byron said, "Let us at least have a little cake and congratulate them."

"And then we can go to the House of Worth?"

Before he could answer, Clarisse ran over to them. "Maman is going to toss the bouquet! You must come!"

She grabbed hold of Mira's hand and tugged. Mira let herself be pulled along to stand with the other women gathered for the toss. Klasha, Clarisse, a few former boarders that Mira vaguely recognized, and a few friends that she didn't, all stood together. Loretta held her bouquet of winter jasmine, heath, and snowdrops in front of her, breath clouding around her face. Once everyone was assembled, she turned her back to the crowd and tossed the bouquet.

There was a scuffle of hands and petticoats, and Klasha was the victor, plucking it from the air. But before anyone had seen, the old woman pushed the bouquet into Mira's hands.

"Oh look!" Klasha said. "We have the lucky one to marry next!"

Mira blushed, her gaze flicking to Byron. He gave her a quiet sort of smile. Meanwhile, Fred was grinning from ear to ear and moved over to slap Byron on the back. Walker came up to her.

"Is there something we should know?" He waggled an eyebrow at her.

She pushed him back. "You are incorrigible. Especially considering you and Liza."

Walker laughed. "You were the one who always dreamed of having a double wedding."

Mira looked down at the bouquet in her hands with a smile,

rearranging the greenery so that the flowers weren't crowded. How wonderful that would be! Although in truth, she hadn't been the one to catch the bouquet. Klasha was a little way away, completely pleased with her scheming. No one needed to know the truth.

Despite her moment of revelry, Mira couldn't help but wonder if the toss might have gone differently had there been another in the running. Emilie would have loved the bouquet. All of Mira's good feelings left in a rush, leaving a cold, empty void. Tears pricked in her eyes.

She looked up at Byron again. It seemed he understood the change in her emotions, his own good humor fleeing. He brushed off Fred's teasing and came over to her, turning her away from the others. He pulled out a handkerchief and wiped away a stray tear.

"I'm sorry," he said. "I'm so very sorry."

"So am I," she said. "So am I."

January 15, 1889: Afternoon

*T*HEY SLIPPED AWAY FROM THE FESTIVITIES AT the boarding house and called for a carriage to take them to the House of Worth. Mira steadied her breath as they rode along, trying to order all of the questions she wanted to ask the tailors. There must be something they could find there, some real, concrete evidence that could be brought to the police.

Byron passed his hat from one hand to the other. "You mentioned before that the last time you visited the House of Worth, they assumed you worked for Madame de Bonnemains, is that correct?"

Mira nodded. "It was because I wasn't certain if Loretta's dress had been filed under Lavigne or de Bonnemains."

He hummed. "It might be best if we let them continue to

operate with that assumption. After all, it is one thing to answer questions for a client, and an entirely different one to answer questions for a detective."

"You think they would conceal things?"

"Not necessarily. But I believe they would be more forthcoming if they didn't know they were under investigation."

The carriage went over a rather nasty bump.

"And how do we explain you?" she asked. "When I was there yesterday I was alone."

Byron paused a long moment, before untying his cravat.

"I am the valet of General George Boulanger, come to compare one of his ties with the dress of Marguerite de Bonnemains to ensure that it will match for an event they are expected to attend." He tucked the cravat into his pocket.

"You don't speak French."

"That isn't an issue if it is believed that I don't speak at all." He raised an eyebrow at her.

She laughed. "I won't be able to tell you what is being said."

"Then I will have to trust that you know what questions to ask. And, as I won't have to pay attention to the topic of conversation, I will be free to observe what is going on behind the words."

"You can't go in there with your collar undone like that," Mira said.

"I need some kind of fabric to corroborate my story."

She pulled out the matching handkerchief he had given her earlier and tucked it into his suit pocket. "Then use this. If you don't look the part, they will never believe the story."

The carriage slowed to a stop in front of the House of Worth as Byron retied his cravat. He exited first, paid the driver, and held out a hand to help her step down. Once both of her feet were planted firmly on the ground, he let go and took a step away from her, already beginning the charade.

She led the way into the building and approached the receptionist, the same one as the day before, with Byron at her heels.

"*Excuse me,*" she said in French. "*I am here on behalf of Madame de Bonnemains. I was here yesterday.*"

"*I remember,*" he said. "*Did the dress not meet expectations?*"

"*Quite the contrary. It was received incredibly well. What was not received well, was the news that another fitting would be needed. She has sent me to find out more about the tailor that completed the original fitting.*"

The man froze for a moment, clearly nervous about the prospect of a complaint.

"*I see. I'm sure that we can help you with that. May I ask who is with you?*"

She turned to glance at Byron. He stood as straight as a railroad tie, every inch of him oozing with decorum—the very picture of a perfect valet.

"*This is the valet of General Boulanger. The dress that Madame de Bonnemains has requested is to be worn at an event with the general. Monsieur . . .*" She hesitated a moment, as they hadn't determined a code name to be used. "*Monsieur Ambrose is here to compare the color of the dress to a handkerchief in the General's wardrobe.*"

"*Ah. We are honored to have you here, Monsieur Ambrose.*"

"*I'm sorry,*" Mira said. "*He doesn't speak.*"

A flicker of surprise crossed the receptionist's face. "*Mm. I will inform Monsieur Worth that you are here.*"

Mira swallowed. Charles Frederick Worth would surely recognize he. He would know that she didn't work for Madame de Bonnemains.

"*There is no need. Might we first examine the dress?*"

"*Of course. I will call for an attendant to take you to the sewing room, if you will wait here a moment.*"

Mira led Byron over to the benches to wait. He pulled out his notebook, scribbling down something quickly. He passed it over to her.

"Must you have used my real name?" it read.

She laughed a little and stole his pen.

"A little bit of truth in every lie," she wrote in small, swirling letters. She leaned over and whispered. "Besides, it was the only name I could come up with on short notice. Did you understand anything else that was said?"

He shook his head and took the pen back. "He seemed rather nervous," he wrote.

"I agree," she said.

He closed up the notebook and tucked it away as an attendant came to lead them up. Sandrine met them at the top of the stairs.

"*I did not expect you back so soon,*" she said to Mira. "*The dress is still not ready.*"

"*I am aware of that,*" she gestured to Byron. "*This is General Boulanger's valet. He is here to compare colors.*"

"*Oh, I see. By all means, come with me.*"

She led them past the army of sewing machines in motion and into the back room where the dress was waiting.

"*We still haven't been able to remove the blood,*" Sandrine said.

"*Don't,*" Mira said, and immediately regretted the harshness of her tone. She laughed a little, trying to recover. "*I didn't mention it yesterday, but we have our own way of dealing with stains.*" In this case, the stain needed to stay in place as evidence. "*The madame is very sensitive to certain chemicals.*"

Byron moved to compare the handkerchief to the dress. The stark difference in color was laughable, as the dress was blue and the handkerchief was a royal purple.

Sandrine frowned, glancing between the handkerchief and Byron's tie. Mira stepped in, snatching the handkerchief from his grasp. "*I thought I told you that the dress was blue. Did you bring any other samples?*" She gave a very small shake of her head, which thankfully he caught onto, shaking his head as well.

Mira gave a deep nasally sigh and turned back to Sandrine. *"I suppose it is just as well that the dress isn't ready. But Madame would still like to know everything possible about that tailor. After all, it is highly unprofessional to require another fitting without any alterations to the dress."*

"Yes, and we cannot apologize enough for the inconvenience. Although it was not a tailor that attended to that fitting."

"It was not?"

"No, the tailor was unable to attend at last minute. We sent his assistant. And considering the circumstances, I can assure you that she has been let go without recommendation."

"And who was it?" Mira asked. *"I must know the name."*

Sandrine squirmed. *"It was Liliane Aguillard."*

Mira's eyes widened. That had been the attendant that had helped Loretta when they came for the wedding dress fitting. At the time, Mira had felt sorry for her because of how the tailor had treated her. It had all been an act. Of course she made for a terrible tailor's assistant. She was "highly recommended" and yet had none of the skills because she was there for an entirely different purpose. Liliane was a member a Circe.

And hadn't she poked Loretta during the fitting? Had she been practicing to see what she could get away with?

"I see. How long has she worked with the House of Worth?"

"I'm afraid I do not know, miss."

"Surely you have employment records. I demand to see them."

Sandrine nodded hurriedly. *"Right away. Come with me."*

Mira couldn't help the small smile that graced her lips. Pretending to work for Madame de Bonnemains was a little fun. She could throw all the fuss she wanted without any repercussions.

Byron followed behind them as Sandrine brought them to the records room. She rifled through several stacks of files before she found the one on Liliane.

"*Here you are. It would appear that she started work for us in late October. She had many references, yet her skills did not match. We've had numerous complaints about issues with pins.*"

"*I can imagine,*" Mira said, looking over the record. She pointed to a gap in the paperwork. "*It would seem she never listed an address with you.*"

Sandrine frowned, but scanned the line. "*It must have been an oversight. I apologize.*"

"*I'm sure it wasn't your fault,*" Mira said, putting a little more warmth into her tone. "*Are her references here as well?*"

"*Everything is there.*"

Mira closed the folder. "*If you don't mind, I would like to borrow this.*"

"*I'm afraid I can't let you do that,*" Sandrine said, taking the folder from her. "*We need to keep it for our records.*"

"*I assure you that it will be returned. We only need to—*"

"*And what, might I ask, is happening here?*" A loud male voice sounded from behind them. Mira turned and found herself face to face with Charles Frederick Worth. His beret was askew on his head, his grey mustache twitching. But his demeanor changed as he saw her, a little less strict and harsh. He switched to speaking English.

"Miss . . . Blayse, wasn't it? You were here with," his gaze flicked to Sandrine and he adjusted his posture. "Madame de Bonnemains a few weeks ago."

A small wave of relief washed over her. He was keeping with the charade, even if he didn't realize it. "Monsieur Worth," she said. "I'm here on behalf of the madame."

He raised an eyebrow. "And this is?" He gestured to Byron.

Mira swallowed. "This is Monsieur Ambrose. He is General Boulanger's valet."

Worth narrowed his gaze for a moment. "I see. Why don't we go to my office, hm? It will be a little more private, you can tell me what the issue is and we'll sort it all out."

They left an incredibly confused Sandrine in the records room and followed the father of fashion down the hall and into a large office and workspace. Sketches were pinned on the walls and his desk was a mess of organized chaos. There were two seats in front and one behind, but Worth chose to perch on the edge of his desk. He picked up a pipe from its stand and lit it.

"Now, I believe you must have some story for me, because unless something has changed in the past week, General Boulanger does not have a personal valet."

Mira slowly sank into one of the seats, trying to think of another lie, but Byron was the one who answered.

"You certainly know your business, sir. The deception was necessary for us to do ours." He extended a hand. "Detective Byron Constantine."

"Ah!" Worth shook his hand. "It's always a pleasure to speak with another Englishman. And I do believe I've read something about you in the newspapers. Incredible that you can solve so many cases with a shoddy memory, if you pardon my saying."

Byron gave a bit of a nervous chuckle. "It has improved in recent months, but yes."

Mira fidgeted with the handkerchief in her hands. She hated not knowing whether that statement was a lie.

Worth shifted his weight, puffing on his pipe. "I take it that you are investigating something, then? May I ask what?"

"The death of Emilie Lavigne."

Worth nearly dropped the pipe, tobacco spilling onto his lap. He brushed it off of his dark suit. "Marguerite's girl? What do you mean?"

"She had a seizure on the night of the ninth, just after standing in for a fitting with one of your attendants," Byron said.

"Unfortunate, but I'm afraid I don't see the connection. Unless you are accusing the attendant of murder." He laughed a little, but it petered out as soon as he realized the two of them weren't even smiling. "You're in earnest, aren't you?"

"I'm afraid so," Mira said. "We think the poison may have been on one of the needles or pins."

Worth coughed. "On the pins? Why I've never heard of such a thing!"

"Regardless, we believe it to be the cause of death," Byron said. "Which is why we are here."

Worth let out a puff of smoke and paced away from the desk. "This is a serious accusation."

"And we are taking the matter seriously, sir," Mira said. "Based on our investigation, it was one of your newer women. Liliane Aguillard."

"We also believe that she was planted by a criminal organization with the intention of killing Madame de Bonnemains," Byron added.

Worth sighed. "But they had the wrong woman. I see."

"So it's true, then? You were aware that Emilie acted as a stand-in?" Mira asked.

"I knew from the first time that she attempted the swap," Worth said.

"And you didn't question it?" Byron asked.

"Madame de Bonnemains is not the only eccentric member of the nobility that I work with." He tapped the side of his pipe. "I would have complained about it, but their size was almost identical and the madame did not care if there were minor issues in the fit as long as she didn't have to be there for it. It was rather hilarious to see which of my staff would catch on. Most of them know at this point, although the newer attendants wouldn't."

"How do you hire on new attendants?" Mira asked.

"Oh, it is quite the process. Although, I've been in the business long enough that I don't have to do it myself. I have Bernier handle the hiring and dismissals. He's my personal assistant and the one in charge of records."

"May we speak with him?" Byron asked.

"By all means." He stood and ducked his head through a side door, calling for his assistant in French. A few moments later and a short, dark haired gentleman with spectacles stepped in.

"*These people have some questions for you,*" Worth said, continuing in French.

The assistant inclined his head towards them.

Mira sat forward. "*Do you remember when you hired Liliane Aguillard as an attendant?*"

The man nodded. "*It was only a few months ago. She had references from Dentelle & Brocart and had a personal recommendation from Emile Pingat.*"

Worth gave a short whistle. "*I didn't know we had anyone recommended from him.*"

"*Yes, sir. That is why we brought her on. Although her recommendations seemed to have been wrong about her ability. I let her go last week due to complaints about fittings. She seemed to always misjudge where the fabric ended and where her client's skin began.*"

"*Thank you,*" Mira said. "*Would you happen to have a means of contacting her?*"

"*It would be in her employment record. I can fetch it.*"

Mira shook her head. "*We've already seen it and those lines were blank. Although, if we could borrow it, it would be much appreciated.*"

He gave a short nod and left the room. Mira relayed the information to Byron.

"There's one other thing I think we would like to borrow," he said, "If it is amenable."

"I'm sure most anything could be arranged," Worth said.

"The dress that Emilie wore when Liliane was fitting her. It has blood on the inner cuff. I believe that might be enough proof to reopen the case with the police."

"By all means. I'm sure we can come up with an explanation for Madame de Bonnemains."

Mira stood. "Oh, I'm sure she'll be all right with it. Thank you, monsieur."

Worth stepped forward and took her hand, kissing the back. "The pleasure, as always, was mine."

January 16, 1889: Morning

"YOU'VE BEEN AWFULLY BUSY AS OF LATE, Mira," Cyrus said at the breakfast table. Due to Emilie's death, he and Loretta had decided to postpone their honeymoon. Loretta particularly didn't want to leave Clarisse to grieve alone.

Mira poked at her porridge, not wanting to give anything away. "We've had quite a bit of new evidence come up in relation to the Durant case. In fact, we'll be going to the police prefecture today to discuss it with Prefect Lozé." If asked, she would insist that her response was entirely truthful. Technically, Emilie's death was related to the Durant case, and they were going to the police prefecture. The only untruth that one could derive from her response was the matter of Lozé. Mira wasn't sure they would be allowed to meet with him.

"They really draw these things out, don't they?" Cyrus sighed. "Better to have the nasty business over and done with, I say."

"It's more complicated than that," Mira muttered.

"Walker, what do you have today?" Cyrus asked.

The man in question paused, a spoon halfway to his mouth. "I have that meeting with Monsieur Augustin this afternoon."

"Oh yes. I nearly forgot," Cyrus said. "How long do you think you'll be at the police prefecture this morning, Mira?"

"A few hours. Why?"

Cyrus said, "I think Walker ought to go along with you."

Mira drew in a sharp breath. "Uncle, this is business. We don't need a chaperone."

"You've been unaccompanied far too much. And that may be more acceptable here in Paris, but we'll be returning to London soon enough." He pointed at her with his spoon. "I don't want you getting used to it."

Mira glanced at her aunt. If memory served, Loretta hadn't seemed too keen on leaving Paris. "Do we have a date set to return?"

Loretta was the one who answered. "Not yet. Before we do anything, we have to get the boarding house ready to sell."

Clarisse's eyes widened. "Sell?"

Loretta turned to her youngest, her expression softening as she switched to French. "*There are too many memories here, love.*"

Tears pricked in the corners of the little girl's eyes and she rushed from the table. Loretta hurried after her.

Klasha glared at Cyrus. "You had not told the child?"

Cyrus had the decency to look sheepish. "We hadn't finalized any plans."

The old woman scoffed, but remained silent.

Georges cleared his throat. "I have always wanted to visit London."

"I'm sure we'll be able to find you a good apprenticeship too," Cyrus said, but there was a sadness behind his words.

Mira swallowed. She remembered having to leave her house in the country when her parents died. At the time, she was much younger than any of the Lavigne children, but to lose your home of many years at any time is a terrible thing. Yet another thing to grieve. Mira wondered if it was Emilie's death that prompted Loretta's change of heart, or if her uncle was pressing his advantage.

A knock sounded from the entryway and she pushed her chair back. "I'll answer it."

She left the room before anyone could argue and opened the door. Byron stood on the step, a dusting of snow on his hat and shoulders.

"Good morning, Byron," she said, stepping aside so he could warm himself a moment.

"Good morning, Mira." He gave her a small smile and took off his hat. "Are you ready?"

"I just need to fetch my coat and hat. Won't be a minute." She left him there and rushed up the stairs, hoping to leave before her uncle could finish arranging for a chaperone. She stopped on the second landing, hearing sniffles around the corner.

"*I know it is a difficult prospect,*" Loretta said. "*But life is full of changes like this.*"

"*Everything is changing!*" Clarisse said. "*All at once! It is one thing for you to be married again. But Emilie is dead and now we're leaving?*" There was a strain on Clarisse's voice making her sound much older than she ever had before, even with her sobs. "*I've never left Paris. I can't even speak English properly.*"

"*You're getting better all the time.*"

"*Do you want to leave or is he making you?*"

Mira's stomach dropped. Loretta sighed.

"We had agreed, before even the civil ceremony, that we would decide together where to live. Cyrus is a gentleman. He wouldn't force me to leave simply because we are married. When we first spoke of it, I thought we would spend some time here and some time in London. But now with Emilie . . ." Her voice hitched and there was a long pause. *"I think it would be good to have a fresh start."*

"And leave Papa and Emilie behind?"

"Oh, dear one. We could never leave them behind."

Mira continued up to the third landing. She had violated their privacy long enough. She retrieved her hat and coat—her heart aching for Clarisse—her new almost-sister.

When she came down the stairs, Loretta was speaking with Byron in the foyer. Her eyes were red, but she was hiding her emotions well.

"Is Clarisse going to be all right?" Mira asked.

"Eventually. She's with Klasha now." Loretta sighed. "I should have spoken to her about it before now, but I didn't know how."

Mira slipped into her coat. "It's understandable. You've had a lot happen this past week."

Loretta pressed her lips into a thin smile. "Unfortunately. Now, you ought to get going."

"Oh yes," Mira took Byron's arm. "Cyrus intends to send a chaperone after us."

"Speak of the chaperone and the chaperone arrives!" Walker said, midway through donning his coat.

"You really don't have to come," Mira said.

"Nonsense. It is my brotherly duty to make sure you two maintain proper decency." He looked far too pleased with himself. Mira groaned and turned to her aunt.

"I promise we will only be speaking of business."

"I'm not the one you should ask. And I doubt your uncle will relent." She laughed a little. "Although he is one to talk, after all we were the ones who eloped all those years ago."

MIRA AND BYRON, WITH THEIR CHAPERONE CLOSE behind, reached the police prefecture just after ten. Byron held a small parcel under his arm that contained the dress and a written statement from the House of Worth about the fitting that had occurred the night of Emilie's death. Mira silently prayed that they would be able to meet with Lozé instead of Grandpierre.

She led the way to Lozé's office and the constable there looked up at their approach.

"*How may I help you?*"

"*We need to meet with Prefect Lozé.*"

"*In regards to what?*"

Mira hesitated. If she told the exact truth about the matter, they would likely be referred to Grandpierre again. But most of the prefecture was aware of the burning of the catacombs and how serious it was.

"*We have more evidence for the Durant case.*" Yet another half-truth.

The constable consulted his notes. "*There is an opening in thirty minutes, if you care to wait.*"

"*Yes, thank you.*" She took Byron's arm and they moved together to one of the nearby benches. Walker made a point to sit between them.

Byron leaned forward so he could see Mira better. "Good news, I presume?" he asked.

"We have a chance of seeing him, if that's what you mean."

"Is this about Emilie?" Walker asked.

Mira inclined her head. "We can explain more afterwards."

Walker gave a nod and they lapsed into silence. Byron settled the parcel on his knee. Policemen walked to and fro in front of them, each busy with something. It made her homesick for Scotland Yard, in a strange sort of way. They had such an easy relationship with the police in London, especially with Chief Inspector Thatcher. He would have believed them. The police prefecture was a similar building, but unlike Scotland Yard, she hardly recognized anyone, and no one recognized her or Byron.

Perhaps she had thought too soon. She caught sight of Constable . . . oh what was his name? He had been in the interrogation room when she gave her statement to Lozé and the judge. Chauvin? Chauvet? Whatever his name was, he was standing down the hall, consulting a file, but his gaze kept flicking up to them. She shifted in her seat.

When he left his place on the wall, heading for the stairs, Mira let out a small breath of relief. That is, until he changed course and moved in their direction.

"*Good morning, Mademoiselle Blayse,*" he said, a sharpness to his voice.

"*Good morning, Constable.*" She wished more than ever that she had remembered his name.

"*Back again so soon?*"

"*We have additional evidence.*"

He glanced towards the package on Byron's lap, his eyes narrowing. But he said nothing about it, gesturing to Walker instead. "*And who is this?*"

She straightened. The question was not asked out of politeness. His tone was cold, and his stance was too rigid, as if he was suspicious of something. It was exactly how he acted during the interrogation. Was that his usual approach or did it speak to something else? Something specific to her? What had she ever done to him?

Walker was the one who answered, standing and holding out a hand for him to shake. "*Walker Blayse. Brother and chaperone.*"

The constable shook his hand. "*Leonard Chabot.*"

"*Good to meet you. Have you worked for the police for long?*" Walker asked.

"A few years. Excuse me, I must file this."

He moved back to the stairs and she fisted her hands in her skirt.

"Everything all right, Mouse?" Walker whispered as he took a seat again.

"Fine," she said. Although it didn't feel fine. His questions were innocuous enough, but she couldn't shake the sense that he was digging for something deeper. Could he be a member of Circe? It would certainly explain how antagonistic he was. And if he had only worked for the police prefecture for a short time, he could have been planted.

Byron leaned forward again. "Are you certain?"

Of course he would see through her. He always did. She huffed. Why could he not forget these things when it was convenient?

Before she could come up with yet another lie, the door to Lozé's office opened. A man came out, tall and thin, with dark black hair and an unruly beard. He was kempt in every other regard, his grey suit without a single wrinkle.

Lozé came out behind him, still deep in conversation.

"Thank you for your opinion on the matter," Lozé said.

"It is always a pleasure to work with you," the man said.

When Lozé saw them, he brightened and came over, switching to English. "Good morning, Detective Constantine." He inclined his head towards her. "Mademoiselle Blayse. And who is this with you?"

There. That was how a gentleman was supposed to behave. His tone was much warmer than Constable Chabot's.

Her brother extended his hand. "Walker Blayse. I'm here to watch over them."

Lozé frowned a moment before breaking into a wide laugh.

"Ah, I see. The chaperone. I am pleased to meet you." He turned to Byron. "What is it that brings you in?"

"We have new evidence related to the case," Byron said.

"Oh really? We were just discussing the matter." He gestured back to the man, who was standing near the desk with the secretarial constable. "Have you met Dr. Moreau yet? He's the police physician."

The doctor stepped forward. "I'm afraid we haven't had the pleasure. Detective Constantine, was it?"

Byron shook his hand. "Yes, sir."

Mira frowned. There was something familiar about the doctor, although she knew she'd never seen him before.

"I was actually planning on sending for you," Lozé said. "So this is rather fortunate. Why don't we go into my office?"

"I'll wait out here," Walker said. "As long as you promise to keep an eye on them for me, monsieur."

Lozé laughed again. "I promise. And I won't keep them long."

Mira followed Byron, Lozé, and Moreau in, keeping a keen eye on the doctor. Why was he so familiar?

Once the door was closed, and everyone situated, Lozé said, "I'm afraid I have some news, which could be seen as good or bad. Durant is dead."

A shiver ran through Mira, the image of Durant's corpse coming to mind again. She looked at Byron. Were they going to pretend not to know?

"I see," Byron said. "What happened?"

"A seizure," Dr. Moreau said. "In the prison. It took him almost instantly."

"Are we certain it wasn't brought on by an outside influence?" Byron asked. "After all, Circe wouldn't want Durant to reveal anything during the trial."

"What, you think it was poison?" Moreau said, his nose wrinkling. "I have done a full autopsy on the body, and found no traces of poison."

His voice. The more he spoke, the more familiar he became. Mira's stomach churned. She'd overheard his voice in the catacombs, when she was hiding with Durant. She looked over at the man. He'd been the one to speak with her godfather about toxins and poisons. They had been planning a murder. In fact, it could have been Marguerite's murder they had been discussing.

"That does mean you no longer need to be here for the trial, Miss Blayse," Lozé said. "Your written testimony on the matter should be sufficient when we try the other men found in the catacombs."

Moreau pulled a silver-engraved snuff box from his pocket and tipped a dash of brown powder onto his hand, inhaling it. He said, "You mentioned that you had new evidence about the case?"

Panic gripped her. They could not reveal what they knew in front of a man implicit in the murder. He was likely the one who had sourced whatever poison had killed her cousin and Durant. As the police physician, he would be the one to identify the cause of death. And he could have had direct access to Durant at La Santa prison.

She reached over and placed a hand on Byron's wrist. "We actually came to tell you the same. You see, we saw Durant in the morgue when we went to retrieve a cousin of mine for burial. We weren't sure if you knew. Although, thinking back, of course you would know."

She gave Byron's wrist a gentle squeeze, hoping that he would understand.

"Yes, but I see why you wanted to inform us," Lozé said. "From what you've told me about how Circe operates in London, it would make sense for you to be on guard here. Although, I can only hope that this Circe business has been flushed out of Paris with the arrests you helped us make."

"We can hope," Byron said.

"Thank you for your time," Mira said, standing. The men stood as well.

Moreau cocked his head to the side, gaze set on the package under Byron's arm. "If I may ask, what is that parcel you're carrying?"

Mira laughed a little, answering for him. "Oh, he's being a dear and carrying a dress for me. We picked it up this morning."

Her heart pounded as they all said their farewells. As soon as possible, she pulled Byron from the room, trying not to make a spectacle.

Walker followed them. "That was quick."

Mira took his arm as well, so she was standing between them, and tugged them towards the stairs. Byron said, "Mira, what about—"

"Not now," she whispered.

She kept silent until they were safely in a park a few blocks away from the prefecture, just in case. Even then, she felt as though someone were watching them, and not just Walker.

"Are you going to explain?" Byron asked.

"Dr. Moreau is a member of Circe," Mira said.

Silence passed between them. She could almost see the new knowledge slotting into place in Byron's brain. After a moment, he said, "Tell me more."

"When I was escaping from my cell in the catacombs, I needed a map from the Charger's office. Durant was with me, and when we approached, we heard voices. Bur . . ." She stopped and glanced at Walker. His eyes were wide with concern and nothing else. She redirected her statement. "O-one of them was the Charger's and I am certain the other was Moreau's. In fact, if I remember correctly, the Charger even referred to him by name. They were discussing poisons and toxins to be used to murder someone. I never saw him, but I know it was his voice."

"Hence your changing the subject in the police prefecture. Good show, love. If he had known what we know . . ."

"I'm a bit lost," Walker said. "Does this mean that the doctor was involved with Emilie's murder?"

"I think so," Mira said. "If only to acquire the poison. I just hope he doesn't suspect anything from what we said."

"I think our conversation was benign enough," Byron said. "Thinking back, you were incredibly careful."

Another couple was walking towards them, so Mira remained quiet for a moment. Once their group rounded a dry fountain and moved out of earshot, she said, "When I overheard him in the catacombs, he mentioned something about needing to isolate a toxin and that he would need to test it. You don't think he tested it on Durant before giving it to the tailor to use on Madame de Bonnemains, do you?"

"I believe it is as likely a possibility as any at the moment, but once again we have no proof. If we are to convince Lozé of Moreau's involvement in Circe, we'll need more concrete evidence. With his connection to the police force, this will not be an easy feat."

Walker whistled. "Can you imagine? Having a police doctor be so corrupt?"

Mira shuddered. "He could give any cause of death and be believed."

"Exactly," Byron said. "Which is why we must find a way of exposing the truth, whether he is involved with Emilie's death or not."

She frowned. "Do you think the list of individuals that are contracted with the police would have his information in it?"

"Which list?" He furrowed his brow.

Her stomach twisted. He really was forgetting. Why would he not tell her?

"When I went in for my statement last week, you searched Lozé's office and borrowed a file."

He hummed. "Oh, that list. I think it's back at Rue Geoffroy. Shall we take a look?"

January 16, 1889: Afternoon

MIRA SAT WITH WALKER IN THE SITTING room at Rue Geoffroy while Byron searched for the file. Part of her wondered if Byron was bluffing about remembering the file. And even if he had a vague reminiscence of taking it, would he know what it looked like?

She swallowed. She really should ask him about his memory, but the thought made her throat tighten. What if he had been forgetting more? Would it regress to the point that he would no longer remember her?

Had that happened already?

After all, his journal would tell him everything he needed to know. He could simply read about her and pretend to remember. If she asked him, would he tell the truth?

Oh, how she hated these feelings. Why did Fred have to mention it at all? For him it was a passing comment. For her it turned her world upside down. Again.

Walker cleared his throat. "This whole business with Emilie is terrible."

She nodded, grateful for the distraction. "It is."

"Once it all comes out . . ." He shook his head. "Uncle is going to be devastated. And poor Loretta, of course. Have you thought at all about how you are going to tell them?"

In truth, Mira hadn't put much thought into it. There was a small hope that she wouldn't have to, erroneous as that hope was. Before she could answer, Walker continued, saying, "It's a similar situation to when you told them of the professor's death, I shouldn't wonder."

Her guilt came back in full force, her nerves plunging into ice-cold water.

"It must have been terrible," Walker said. "To witness that."

She blinked, unsure of whether he meant that night on the bridge when she watched their godfather "die" or when she told her aunt and uncle about it. She looked down at her hands, feeling nauseated regardless of his meaning. "It was."

"And then, after all of that, for you to be held by Circe. I can't begin to imagine how frightening that was for you." He paused, turning to face her. "Perhaps I'm putting too much credence in our twin sense, but you've seemed more guarded as of late. You know you don't have to put on a brave face for me, don't you?"

"Of course I know."

He hesitated, placing a hand on top of hers. "Mira, be honest with me. Are you sure that you're all right?"

She swallowed and averted her gaze. "And if I'm not?"

"Then I'm here to listen." He leaned closer to her and lowered his voice. "And to keep secrets from Uncle, if needs be."

Her shoulders tightened. She wanted more than anything to be able to tell him the truth about their godfather, Circe, and Alexander Durant. It wasn't a matter of trust. She knew that he would keep it to himself, as he had done with dozens of secrets over the years.

She was saved from making a decision by the sounds of footsteps on the stairs.

"Here it is," Byron said. "Sorry to keep you waiting."

"That's all right," Mira said. "Is Moreau listed?"

"I haven't checked." He sat beside her and flipped the file open. She read over his shoulder as he skimmed the list of names.

Across from them, Walker tapped his foot. After a moment, he stood. "Time has gotten away from me, it would seem. I'm afraid I need to be off to my meeting."

Mira looked up from the list. His tone was cold, distant, and his brow was furrowed. Was he angry with her? "Oh. I had forgotten about that."

"So had I. Good luck with all of this." He made a vague gesture at the paper and shot Byron a glare before turning back to her. "You can fill me in later." The full meaning behind his words shone through the intensity of his gaze and the way his voice wavered at the end. His following smile was a little too wide. "And for our uncle's sake, keep things proper, won't you?" The teasing was only half-hearted and that was even more worrisome.

"We'll do our best, I assure you," Mira said, her mouth going dry.

Walker gave a short nod, took his coat and hat, and left the room.

Byron frowned. "He seemed upset."

"I think it must be something to do with the business," she lied. Twin sense went in both directions after all. Walker was upset because he knew she was keeping secrets. She sighed.

Maybe she should tell him everything. Then he would be able to help her determine the best way to tell her uncle.

"Here he is," Byron said, turning the file towards her and pointing to a name. "Dr. Pierre Moreau. There are two addresses. One for his flat, and another for a laboratory."

Mira leaned back. "If he's been testing toxins and poisons, would it be more likely for him to keep his notes at home or at his lab?"

Byron frowned. "Difficult to say."

Mira brushed off her skirt and stood. "Well, I suppose we'll need to take a look at both."

"And what rash decision are you considering now?" Byron asked, his eyes laughing.

"We need evidence of his involvement in Circe, do we not?"

He flicked the folder closed. "And so you want to steal it?"

"Do you have a better idea?"

He considered the question a moment. "No, but I do have an amendment."

"Oh?"

He stood. "We'll consult an expert first."

THEO JAUBERT, THIEF EXTRAORDINAIRE, RAN A HAND over his face as he paced in the upper room of the Gallerie de Mestra. Mira and Byron sat on the sofa opposite.

"I've heard whisperings of a doctor working with Circe on the poison front, but never knew his name. Are you certain this is the man?"

"Positive," Mira said.

"I'll help you then. By all means. I can't imagine that it will be an easy job though. He's bound to have extra security."

"That's why we came to you," Byron said. "We have little experience in the field of breaking and entering."

"And you say that there are two possible addresses?"

"According to the file, yes," Byron said, handing the relevant page over.

Theo parsed the information. "Hm. Seems they are both in the fourteenth arrondissement. We ought to see what we are working with."

"I agree," Byron said. "I think a walk around the neighborhood would suffice."

"There's a restaurant in the area," Theo said. "Best to add as much as possible to the narrative to avoid suspicion."

THEY DECIDED THE BEST COURSE OF ACTION was to have Theo pretend to be Walker still acting as chaperone. It would explain why she was with two gentlemen and gave them a framework to create their cover. He had a surprisingly good English accent and Mira doubted that anyone would question their relation. Their first stop was Moreau's residence, which they quickly decided against searching, as it was a boarding house. Not only would it be more difficult to break into, but it was highly unlikely for the man to leave secret papers in a more public building.

The second address brought them to a street with buildings crowded together, staring down like old sentinels. The laboratory was an old stone building standing at the end of the street. The facade was stained with frost and a brass plate on one of the columns read "*Laboratoire de Moreau*" in cursive script.

They circled the block twice before going to sit at the restaurant across the street. They requested a table near the window and settled in to watch.

"It doesn't seem too difficult at first glance," Theo said, voice hushed. "There are a few windows that are promising."

"There is quite a bit of bustle on this street though," Byron said.

Theo nodded. "We'll have to wait until dark."

Mira kept her gaze on the opposite side of the street. The sun was already going down, and some light could be seen from one of the lower windows. A shadow moved across it.

"And if he's still there?" she asked.

"There will be other days," Theo said.

They were halfway through the consommé when the door to the laboratory opened and Dr. Moreau stepped out onto the street.

"Fortunate," Theo said, once the doctor had disappeared from view. "I'll be back in a moment."

He left his napkin on the table and slipped out, crossing the street. He disappeared down the alley to the side of the laboratory.

Mira pushed her salad around with her fork, anxiety coursing through her. It was one thing to discuss breaking and entering. It was an entirely different prospect to do it. And, yes, she had a little experience from when she and Byron had investigated the airships, but that seemed different too, in a way.

"You're deep in thought," Byron said.

Mira sighed. "I'd just rather get this all over with." She glanced back through the window. A figure was at the mouth of the alleyway, but it wasn't Theo. It was the man in the blue coat!

"Byron, look," she said in a rush.

His eyes narrowed as he caught sight of the unknown man. He scanned the other people in the restaurant and stood, saying, "Stay here." He left before she could argue with him.

The figure, whoever he was, wasn't expecting anyone to come from behind. Byron came close to him and planted a hand on his back, startling the fellow.

A few moments later, Theo joined them, and it was a much different picture. The unknown man, imposing as he was in every other instance she had seen him in, shrunk back for a moment, before standing straight and waving a finger at the two of them. Byron kept his hand on the man's shoulder and turned him towards the restaurant. Soon enough, they were in the light of the streetlamp again and Mira could see that the man wore a police uniform beneath his coat. It was the constable from her statement. Constable . . . Charoux? Oh, what was his name and why could she never remember it?

The restaurant was busy enough that no one looked her way as she pulled another chair to their table. She'd just settled in again when the three men came in, the constable looking incredibly sheepish.

"May I introduce our shadow," Theo said. "Constable Leonard Chabot."

Chabot, that was it. Mira cocked her head to the side. "Now why have you been following us, Constable?"

He clenched his fists and released them, a sure sign of tension, even if his shoulders hadn't been starched back, but said nothing.

Byron answered for him. "You'll never believe it, but he thought we were members of Circe."

Theo pulled out the chair for the constable and gave him a look that had Chabot sitting.

"Us? You've been following us around all these weeks because you thought we were members of Circe?" Mira laughed. "Why, we thought you were!"

"Do not play act with me," Chabot said. "I know that you are not who you say you are."

"And what do you mean by that?" Byron asked.

"You say that you are a detective from Scotland Yard. I say there is no such 'Detective Constantine' on their records. Grandpierre told me himself."

Mira let out a long breath. Inspector Grandpierre was really starting to grate on her. "That is because he works with them under contract."

"Well then, why are you sneaking around with a thief, eh? Colluding." He gestured to Theo. "I know of his history."

"I'm semi-retired," Theo said.

"And in answer to your question," Byron said, "Because of his prior occupation, he is useful for information. Aside from the fact that I like the chap. Is that a crime?"

"Impersonation is," Chabot said. He pointed at Mira. "You have been calling him by your brother's name. There is no reason for that unless you were up to something."

Byron leaned across the table. "If you truly think we are part of Circe, you are incredibly brave to go after us alone. I'm afraid you don't know enough about the organization to realize the danger you've unwittingly put yourself in."

Chabot paled and pulled back.

"Luckily, we aren't with Circe," Byron said. "In fact, we are trying to stop the very corruption you accuse us of. You see, that laboratory across the street belongs to Dr. Moreau, a man who actually is part of Circe and is the reason for several recent deaths."

"Dr. Moreau? You mean to say, one of the police physicians?" Chabot asked, brow furrowing. "Do you have proof of this?"

Byron let out a breath. "In a word, no. Not yet." He paused, considering. A flicker of humor crossed his expression, just a little crinkle at the corners of his eyes.

"But, if you'll bear with us for a little while, we can get you some proof. And if we don't, you'll have reason to arrest us."

"Byron . . ." Mira said, a warning in her tone.

"And how is that?" Chabot narrowed his eyes.

"Well, Constable," Byron said, "We intend to break into that laboratory across the street."

Theo swore under his breath.

"Byron!" Mira hissed. What was he thinking?

"I believe it is best to be honest with law enforcement whenever possible," Byron said. "I don't see the issue."

"You admit that you are planning a crime?" Chabot asked.

"Whole-heartedly. All I ask, is that if we do find the evidence we believe we'll find, you'll listen to us."

Chabot frowned. "I could arrest you now."

"Ah, but there isn't any evidence. Just your word against ours. Although with the corruption in your police force, I suppose that just might work . . ." Byron trailed off.

"No!" Chabot said. "The prefecture is above such things."

"Well, in that case, you'll need to wait until we've actually broken into the laboratory so you'll have more concrete evidence. And at that point, you might as well see what proof we come up with about Moreau, hm?"

Mira held her breath.

Chabot considered the situation a moment. He studied each of them in turn, looked over at the laboratory, then nodded at the group.

Theo's mustache twitched. "You'll allow us to break into the laboratory?"

"Under two conditions," Chabot said. "One: I shall supervise."

"Fair enough," Byron said.

"Two: This one," he pointed at Theo, "Shall stay with me."

"What?" Theo said.

"We had no evidence to convict you before, I have heard of your reputation, Monsieur Jaubert. This will be enough evidence, that even if these two try the funny business and run, I will have you."

Theo swallowed and turned to Byron. "We had better pray that your evidence is in that lab."

January 16, 1889:
Evening

THE MOON SHONE BRIGHTLY ABOVE AS THEY approached Dr. Moreau's laboratory. It certainly wasn't the best conditions for their objective. If Mira could arrange it perfectly, a cloud would have blocked out the moonlight, and she could have gone home to change into something darker, perhaps something with less fabric to deal with. And, of course, there wouldn't be a constable waiting to arrest them. What if they were wrong and there was no evidence whatsoever?

The group stopped in the shadows of the alleyway and pressed against the wall. Chabot had his own pistol which he kept a firm hand on. His other hand was attached to one of Theo's with handcuffs.

"I'm not going to run, you know," Theo said.

Chabot's nose wrinkled, but he remained a silent judge.

With a sigh, Theo pointed with his free hand. "There's two entrances there in the back. A door off the kitchen, I believe, and a cellar." He pulled lock picks from his pocket and handed them over. "You might want these."

"Now, see here—" Chabot said.

"You already agreed to let us break in," Byron said, taking the lock picks. "This is included in that agreement."

"I-I," Chabot stammered, but the rest of the sentence got lost on the way to his mouth.

Mira moved to the corner and peered around it. There was a rather squarish back courtyard with trees and shrubs. The area was likely shared by the adjoining buildings. It seemed no one was particularly attentive to it, as it was overgrown and crumbling. There was another alley between the buildings on the opposite side.

"Are we clear?" Byron asked.

"For the moment."

He hesitated. "Are you certain that you don't want to go home? I'm sure your uncle is—"

"Need I remind you of the last time you left me behind to do some serious investigating?" She narrowed her eyes at him.

"Last time?" He frowned.

Her heart sank. How could he not remember? "The catacombs?"

He let out a breath. "Right. Come on."

They left the constable and the thief watching at the corner and made their way around. The kitchen door was up some stairs on the left side of the house, but Byron moved past it, coming around the opposite corner to where the cellar doors lay. There wasn't a visible lock or chain or anything, so he gave a tug on the handle. The door opened an inch or so, and then was stopped by a chain on the inside.

Byron straightened. "If I were to hide something, it would certainly be down there."

"If it's locked from the inside, there must be another way in," Mira said.

Byron nodded. "Let's go back to the tried and true." He took her hand and they went back around to the kitchen stairs. The door was in an alcove away from prying eyes.

Mira stood by one of the columns and kept watch while Byron worked the devil's magic with the lockpicks. She gave a short wave to Chabot and Theo where they stood at the corner.

"This reminds me of our first case," she whispered, just loud enough for Byron to hear. She knew she was testing him, trying to see if he would admit to forgetting on his own.

He remained silent, likely listening for the clicks of the tumblers. A few moments later and the door was open.

"When I taught you how to pick locks?" He asked as he led her inside.

Did he remember that or did he read about it in his journal? Oh, dash it all, they were back to the very same problem that had plagued her when she first started working with him. Why couldn't she just trust him?

The door opened onto a small kitchen. A sliver of moonlight came in from two small windows at the back. A large table stood at the center, caked with dust. The counters stood empty. It seemed that Moreau did not use the room at all. The far corner jutted out awkwardly, as if one of the adjoining rooms had been extended into the space. The building had likely been a house once before the doctor—or some other tenant—converted it.

The floor creaked beneath them as they moved to the only other door in the room. It opened inwards, revealing a dark hallway. Mira could tell the length by a dim bit of moonlight on the floor at the far end. She placed a hand on Byron's shoulder as they walked into the darkness, her heart beating rapidly.

"What if I'm wrong?" she whispered. "What if Moreau isn't the man I heard?"

The hallway led to the front entry where a kerosene lamp sat on a side table. Byron opened the drawer and felt around, pulling out some matches and lighting it. He kept the flame low and held the lamp away from the window. A golden bell attached to the front door reflected the glow.

As the hall became illuminated, Byron said, "There was more evidence against him than your memory. If you consider the facts, we know that Moreau was the one to identify the cause of death in both Durant and Emilie." He turned in a slow circle, lifting the lamp as he considered the various paths in the house. "He is either incompetent and doesn't know it, or competent and knows exactly what he is doing. Your memory of him only serves as further proof to investigate." He came to a stop facing her and the lamplight caught his eyes. "Your feminine intuition is useful, but not the only thing that brings us here," he teased.

"How can you joke at a time like this? If I'm wrong, we're all going to be arrested. And if I'm right, we're still in here illegally. He could come back at any moment."

"Fair point," he sobered, heading for the stairs. "I think we should start from the top and work our way down."

They spent more time than they ought in the small attic at the top of the house due to the amount of clutter, but found nothing that could be considered evidence. Together they checked each room on the second landing. A little parlor, a water closet, and an unused bedroom covered in dust were all quickly crossed off the list of hiding places.

Coming back to the main landing, they double checked the kitchen, found an unused dining room, another bedroom, and something much more interesting: an office attached to a surgery. Byron set the lamp on a table at the center, turning the knob all the way up. Slowly, the room came into view in the dim light and the two of them separated to search.

The main point of interest was the desk which stood on the far wall. A telephone was built into the wall next to it and every other available adjoining wall was lined with shelves. An empty worktable sat near the center of the room. The surgery was accessed through pocket doors on the righthand side. They were currently open, revealing white tiled floors and reclining tables that reminded Mira more of the morgue than anything. Byron started at the desk. Mira swallowed and, not wanting to breach the surgery by herself, decided to study the shelves instead.

They were filled with books and various oddities. Two toads, set in taxidermy as if they were dueling. Some sort of electrical apparatus. Bottles of labeled remedies. Laudanum. Quinine. Iodine. A case containing syringes and other instruments. A mortar and pestle. An empty snuff box, black instead of silver. Preserved specimens in formaldehyde that had Mira gagging at the sight of them.

All in all, nothing seemed particularly unusual.

Most of the books he had were French medical textbooks and treatises. There were two exceptions. The first was a set of medical books in English. The second was a set of three tomes that had Asiatic symbols instead of letters. Chinese, or something.

A clink sounded behind her and she turned to find Byron by the desk fiddling with the lock picks again. He was crouched beside an open cabinet on the side of the desk.

"What have you found?" she whispered.

"Nothing, as of yet. But this does show promise." He gestured to the lock he was working on. "Have you found anything?" he asked, whilst twisting his tools in one direction and then the other.

"No." The longer they searched the more anxious she became. So far, there was no indication whatsoever that he was involved in anything untoward. He seemed to be the usual sort of doctor with the usual sort of supplies.

"Ah, here we are," Byron said, swinging the door open to reveal a compartment towards the back. A hidden cache had three shelves. The top two were a fairly short—Mira could probably measure out the height of each with her hand—while the bottom one was tall enough to hold the medical bag sitting within it. The shelves certainly went farther back than the depth of the desk. It was likely built into the wall, which cemented her theory that the house had been renovated for Moreau's purposes.

Byron retrieved the contents of the compartment and set them on the central table: a journal, a folder, a little black box, and the medical bag.

"Where shall we start?" Byron asked, moving the light closer.

Mira picked up the box and opened it. The walls of the box were lined with velvet and had about a dozen little slots vertically holding glass slides. She took one of them out and found that it was stained red. Blood? Or some other chemical? Upon closer inspection, the slide itself was made of two thin sheets of glass, protecting whatever substance was pressed between them. A small numeric value was written beneath it.

$$4211811420$$

She passed it to Byron. "What do you make of it?"

He held it over the lamp. "It appears to be blood. Dried and preserved to be examined under a microscope." He tucked it into his pocket before continuing to pull out each of the slides in turn. Half of them had the same label, whilst the rest were unique. And one of them wasn't of blood at all. It looked more like fish skin.

After carefully packing away all of the slides save the one, Byron snapped open the medical bag and peered inside.

"What have we here?" He pulled out several vials of

unknown content and set them on the table. Mira picked up the one closest to her and examined the label.

Atropine

She picked up the next.

Aconite

And the next.

Digitalis

"Are these medicines?" Mira asked.

"In the right dose, they could be," Byron said. "But they are more commonly used as poisons." He pointed to each of the vials she had looked at. "These are the scientific names for nightshade, wolfsbane, and foxglove." He held up the one he had been studying. "I don't recognize this one, though."

She took the vial from him and read the label.

Japon P-G

"The Charger was looking for a new poison," Mira muttered. "That was what their meeting in the catacombs was about."

Byron took the vial back, tucked it into a separate pocket from the slide, and reached for the journal.

"This, I believe, will be the most useful. Though it will require closer study." He pressed the book under his arm and set about replacing everything into the hidden cache.

"Shouldn't we take it all?" Mira asked.

"We don't know when Moreau will return or if he will access this compartment before we can examine the evidence and present it to the police. If only one or two objects are missing, we can hope he will assume he was the one to misplace them."

With the hidden door locked again, he stood and scanned the room.

"Let's look over the surgery before we leave." He picked up the kerosene lamp and brought it to the adjoining room.

Even with the yellowish light from the lamp, everything seemed tinged with a sickly sort of green. There were cabinets with glass fronts on most of the walls crammed with more of the same instruments and apparatuses as the office. On the far wall stood a large steel door. It looked new.

Byron set the lamp down so he could lift the heavy latch keeping the door closed. As he opened, it a low hum sounded from within and a cool fog descended on their feet.

"It seems Moreau has borrowed some of the technology of the morgue," Byron said.

Mira stepped closer and the chill of the air pricked at her skin. Moreau couldn't be holding bodies in there, could he? Surely not.

Byron opened the door a bit more, then, finding it too dark to see, picked up the lamp again and held it inside.

All three walls were lined with metal shelves, each containing different samples and specimens. The floor was covered with a thick rug, likely to help with insulation. There were bottles of medicines, a few vials filled to the brim with crimson, and a half dozen trays with some rather unsettling fleshy things. Upon closer inspection, she found one of the trays held an ugly, bloated fish mid-dissection, and the rest held organs and tissue samples.

The blood rushed to Mira's head. "You don't think . . ."

"It's difficult to say whether any of this is illicit," Byron said. "I'm certain Moreau would have an entirely reasonable explanation. After all, this room was not hidden away or locked like this journal was," he said, gesturing to the tome beneath his arm. He stepped farther into the room and Mira held the door open, unwilling to get any closer than necessary.

"Look here," Byron said. "I do believe this lung has the same numerical label as those slides we found."

"Human?" Mira's stomach turned.

"Undoubtedly," he said, fascination in his tone.

She half-turned away. "I think I'll stay here while you look at everything."

"Oh." He paused, frowning. "Are you all right?"

"It's just a bit—" she gagged. "It's a bit much."

A bell sounded at the front of the house and she jolted.

"What was that?" she whispered.

"Someone came in the front door. We—" he cut himself off as hurried footsteps echoed down the hall.

"It's Moreau," he hissed. "Get in here."

"He might not come this way," she said, eyeing the lung on the slab.

"We don't have time to gamble." Byron grabbed her by the arm and pulled her inside. She drew close to him as he doused the light and closed the refrigerator door as much as he dared.

Mira took a bracing breath. "I don't like this."

Byron found her hand and gave it a squeeze. "Shhh."

The door to the office opened and an eerie glow started up as the gas lamps were lit. Mira tried to measure her breaths. They seemed too loud. Surely he would hear them. Byron kept a firm hold on her hand, the only warmth in the space.

Shuffling footsteps, rustling papers. And two voices speaking in French.

"*And what did you think, eh? That you would be able to disappear and throw the whole mistake on me?*" Moreau said, his voice filling the space.

"*There wasn't a mistake, I tell you. The woman was Marguerite de Bonnemains. I know she was,*" a woman said. Mira couldn't quite place the voice.

"*Well, the corpse would say differently, and so would the Charger.*"

Mira's eyes widened, another wave of nausea passing over her. If they were speaking of Emilie's murder, the second voice had to be that of the tailor's assistant—Liliane Aguillard.

She could make out two human-shaped shadows on the wall opposite the little refrigerated room. With all her heart she prayed that they wouldn't come into the surgery and find them there. Moreau continued. *"When he came to me, asking for recommendations for this job, I could have given him any number of people, and I chose to send you. It was as simple as murder can be, even."*

"How was I to know that she was an imposter? It cannot be my fault if I am given faulty information. There must be something we can do."

Moreau sighed. *"I will handle it for you. But we must get you out of Paris, and I think it is high time we stopped hiding from Circe, hm? That is where the troubles always begin."* His tone was warm—almost familial—towards her.

One of the shadows disappeared and she heard Moreau turn the crank on the telephone.

"Yes, I need to make a call to 47 Rue des Terraces, Troyes," he said. A beat. *"I know I will need to wait."* More papers rustled. Mira's own heart was beating out a symphony. A few tense minutes passed before Moreau spoke again, this time, in English.

"Put the Charger on."

Mira's stomach dropped. He intended to speak to her godfather. Byron squeezed her hand as they both leaned closer straining to hear better.

"Good evening, sir. Yes, I have her here with me." A beat. "Yes, she knows. But sir, how could we have known about the double, hm?" A pause. "No, I am not giving excuses." Another beat. "I understand, and I will tell her that, but in the meantime we need to know where you want her to be sent in case the police do go that way."

A drop of water fell on Mira's forehead and she shuddered.

There were a few moments of silence. "No, I did not mean that. I am certain the police have no reason for suspicion. In fact, that detective you warned me of? He was at the prefecture this morning and didn't suspect a thing. He's more concerned with Durant's dea—" His voice cut off, presumably as the person on the other end interrupted.

"Well yes, sir. He is aware of it. But there is no way that they could trace it to me. And surely, he would expect Circe to retaliate against the traitor. Durant is taken care of, regardless. I've already removed the affected organs for study and I ensured the disposal of the remainder."

Bile crept up Mira's throat.

"Yes, I am certain. Even if the grave was found he would be unidentifiable."

Moreau gave a sharp exhale. "I intend to finish the job before the election. Regardless of the outcome, Boulanger will be ripe for the coup, I guarantee it. Do you not believe my word?"

More silence. "I'll see to it personally. And maybe it will be better than before, hm? We could do the Prussia angle. His heartbreak and anger might lead him to declare war before the week is out."

A beat and some shuffling papers. "Let me check my notes. One moment."

There was a small thud as he set the receiver down and moved over to the desk, muttering. Based on his movements and the sounds, he may have been getting into the hidden cache they had broken into minutes before. And if she was right, he was searching for the book that Byron had tucked under his arm.

"*What does he want?*" Liliane said.

"*Oh, information about that poison we used. The Hound might have need of it soon.*"

Moreau swore, loudly, and moved back to the telephone.

"There's been a complication."

He let out a dry chuckle. "Well, I wrote it down in my research notes and it seems I have misplaced them." A pause. "My notes are not here," he said, louder this time, as if the person on the other side hadn't heard him originally.

"No, no one else knows of the cache."

A few moments of silence. "You think I do not know the danger?" Moreau said, his tone becoming heated. "This is my life's work! I would not just leave it about. I know I had it locked up."

Another pause. "If the police had it, we wouldn't be speaking, now would we?

A pause. "I know, I know. I don't like it either. It was here earlier today, I know it was. And there were no signs of forced entry. It has to be here somewhere."

Byron let go of Mira's hand and her breath stuttered. He reached under his arm and carefully grabbed the journal they had taken. Then, without any warning, he pushed the heavy steel door open wide enough for him to slip through.

Mira's whole body went numb as Byron took step after careful step towards the closest cabinet and set the journal atop it.

"Give me a moment." He switched to French. "*Can you check in the surgery? I may have left it there.*"

Byron moved back into the safety of the refrigerated room just as Liliane rounded the corner. She let out a sigh as she found the journal. Mira's stomach turned as she waited for her to retrace her steps. But instead, Liliane paused and took a step closer to where they were hiding.

She clicked her tongue, muttering, "*And he blames me when he is so careless himself,*" as she pushed the steel door closed and set the heavy latch. Mira's breath hitched.

Liliane's steps were dampened, as was Moreau's voice finishing the conversation on the telephone.

"I have it—and I—yes—where would—I will take—station—myself—locking it—goodbye."

There were a few mutterings between him and Liliane, but it was difficult to make out. The office soon became quiet as both of them left earshot, hopefully leaving the building. Mira squeezed around Byron and reached the heavy door, pushing on it.

Her heart sank. "We're locked in."

January 17, 1889: Early Morning

MIRA SHIVERED AS ANOTHER DROP OF CONDENSA-TION landed on her. The confined space, the walls closing in, felt all too familiar. Even the cold. They were trapped in the darkness. Her breathing became ragged. A hand grasped her arm and she flinched back, her hand brushing the cold, metal shelves. No. The iron bars.

The stench of the catacombs was staunched by the cold, but it was still there. The clinging dust filling her nostrils, the smoke and soot from the kerosene. She couldn't run, not without a map, not without light. She would die down here, trapped with Alexander.

"Mira, love, I need you to breathe."

The hand brushed her shoulder this time, the only warmth

in this small place. Was Byron trapped here too? Her lungs burned, but she managed to take a few breaths, her vision coming back to her, spotty but there. When had he lit the lamp again? And where were—

She jolted, pushing away from the shelves. She was on the floor, though she didn't remember how she got there, and her eyes were wet. Had she fainted?

She traced her fingers along the edge of the rug, catching the rough texture and took in the space with a little more clarity. Cold metal. Steel door. Human organs that she would rather not think about. They were still locked in the refrigerated room in Moreau's laboratory. Byron was crouched beside her, his hair in a state and his eyes wide with concern.

"Mira, are you quite all right?"

She shook her head slightly and forced a smile. "Oh, it's probably the enclosed space." Her brain whirled for the proper response, her words coming out with a disingenuous, cheery tone. "Sorry for fainting on you."

He frowned. "You didn't faint."

"I didn't?" She swallowed, her insides twisting.

"No. Certainly, I don't think you were conscious of what you were doing, but you were quite upright for most of it."

"Oh." She bit her lip. "What did I do?"

He sat back against the shelves. "Well, you grew quite distant, as if you weren't seeing this room. And then you started muttering about the catacombs. You were calling for me, and even when I answered, you didn't respond." He squeezed her hand, though she didn't remember when he had taken it. "You scared me, love."

"I'm sorry," she said. "I-I don't know what came over me."

Byron looked up at the space. "I would imagine this place is frightfully similar to the cell Durant held you in."

"Yes, a little." After a moment she said, "How long was I . . ."

Byron checked his pocket watch. "A good twenty minutes, I would say."

"Twenty minutes?" She blinked at him. It had never been that long before. She stood, using the shelves for support. "We need to get out of here."

Byron's shoulders slumped. "There isn't a way to open the door from this side. I've tried."

"Oh."

"I'm sure Chabot or Theo will wonder what's taking us. It's just a matter of waiting."

Her breath came faster again. They really were trapped in this frozen room. She closed her eyes, forcing herself to breathe slowly, and slid to the floor again.

Byron said, "That . . . episode earlier. You don't seem surprised."

She opened her eyes again and found his scrutinizing, blue gaze locked on her.

When she said nothing, he said, after a moment of hesitation, "Has that happened before?"

A numbness swept over her, a cold beyond the nature of the room. He was never meant to know. She hardly knew what was happening herself. The corners of her eyes burned as tears came to the surface again. When he offered a handkerchief, it only made her cry more.

He shifted so he was sitting next to her, one arm around her shoulders and she turned, sobbing into his chest. He rubbed her back, shushing her gently.

"It's all right, Mira. Whatever it is, it is all right."

She shook her head. "No. No, it isn't."

The chilly air nipped at her tear tracks and she shivered. Almost immediately, Byron had set his coat around her. "Won't you tell me?" he said.

She hiccupped, sitting up again, dabbing at her eyes. "It's ridiculous."

Silence settled between them for a few moments. Byron let out a sigh. "Whatever it is, it is obviously affecting you. *Hurting* you. And I can't help you if I don't know what it is." He shifted so he was facing her again.

"We really ought to focus on finding a way out of here," Mira said, though she made no move to stand.

"So you can pretend as if this never happened?" Byron said, pained. "Why don't you want to tell me?"

She closed her eyes for the space of two breaths, the cold air filling her chest. There were so many reasons to keep it to herself. When she first started working for him, she felt she needed to prove herself. As time went on, that feeling did not alter. In some ways it was made worse. The longer she worked for him the more she ought to have been getting better at the whole detecting business.

Instead, she was faced with nightmares, dissociation, and ill-placed memories coming to the surface. There was a reason she hadn't told anyone. She would be seen as weak, labeled as hysteric. She looked up at Byron. If she told *him* the truth, what would he think?

She was entirely wrung out, exhaustion emanating from her bones. She wasn't sure if that tiredness came from her latest experience with her past or the idea of telling him about it. Or if, perhaps, it came from the thought that, if his memory was failing him, she would have to go through this explanation again, and again. Oh, how could she bear it?

To his credit, he sat patiently, his own worries heavy on his face as he watched her search for an answer. She opened her mouth and closed it again. Then, taking a bracing breath, she decided to trust him and be brave.

"I-I," her voice was hoarse and she cleared her throat. "I've been having these . . . episodes on and off for the past few months. Although, they were mostly nightmares before, well, before the catacombs." She averted her gaze. "I don't really remember much of the episodes, other than something will happen and all these memories surface. It's not in any particular order or anything that makes sense. And really, it's more sensations and emotions than anything else."

It came out easier than she had thought it would. Just a moment before it felt as though she would die to say it out loud. And yet, she was breathing. It hadn't broken her.

"So, when you've gone quiet in the past few weeks . . ." Byron said, his cogs all awhirl to put the pieces together.

"Yes, in all likeliness I was somewhere else entirely."

He fell silent. She shifted her position on the floor, wrapping her dress tighter around her legs. They sat there together for a while, and Mira wondered if the thief and constable would ever come to find them.

At last, Byron said, "You still haven't explained why you didn't tell me."

"I suppose I haven't," she whispered, averting her gaze. "I-I thought maybe it would change your opinion of me. That you wouldn't think me fit to investigate things with you because I couldn't handle it." She sighed. "Maybe I can't. How can you trust me if I fall to pieces at such trivial things?"

"Such as?" he pressed.

"Enclosed spaces, for one," she gestured at the room generally. "Fire is another. I split my lip the other week and the taste of my blood was enough to send me back. And I don't know what sets off the dreams."

"Those may be, as you say, trivial now. But they weren't at the time. And they are more than nightmares, because you lived them."

She scoffed. "Yes, but that was in the past. Why should it come up now?"

"I wish I knew," Byron said. "If I did, I certainly would find a way to stop it happening."

"You can't save me from everything, Byron."

"I wasn't talking about you, love," he said. "It happens to me too."

She finally brought her gaze up to his. "It does?"

"I believe you've witnessed it once or twice. Surely, you must have in the time we've known each other. Moments where it takes just a little too long for me to respond? Or where I detach entirely?"

Mira frowned. "There were a few times in October. I thought you were just remembering things?"

"Is that not what is happening to you? Something mundane happens and suddenly you're back at the very beastliest moment. And then there are the nightmares."

"So . . . it is normal?"

"I'm not sure either of us could be considered as such. If we were, I doubt we'd be in this situation. But I think it is quite natural." He shifted so he was leaning in a different way against the shelves. "Especially considering what happened to you just recently. I suppose it's the brain's way of figuring it out. Dashed inconvenient though."

She laughed a little, and he smiled. "I am sorry you've had to carry this alone for so long," he said, and the little mirth she had petered off.

"I'm not the only one keeping secrets," she whispered, trying to stop any bitterness from entering her tone. Maybe she should tell him that she knew he was forgetting her again. That his memory wasn't improving, it was getting worse. The hypocrisy was astounding, as he likely was keeping it from her for the same reasons she was hiding her own memory troubles. Granted, hers came from an inability to forget while his were the exact opposite.

And both of them didn't want to hurt the other.

He drew back. "What?"

She shook her head, and the teardrops fell heavy into her lap, her courage going with them. "It doesn't matter."

That silence was back again, punctuated by the consistent drip from the ceiling. Mira was quick to focus on something else, squeezing one hand with another as hard as she could to stay present. It wouldn't do to dive back into the icy past so soon after her last visit. They really should have been focusing on getting out of their refrigerated prison. Chabot or Theo surely would have come already. And as they hadn't, they needed to find another way. She was about to suggest it when Byron said, "You know."

There was such weight behind those two words that it gave Mira pause. She hadn't meant to say anything to hint at his secret. Why had she said anything at all? Her breath stuttered. "I do."

He sat back against the shelves and ran a hand through his hair. "How long?"

"A week or so."

"I ought to have expected it. You are too clever by half. Of course you would figure it out." His tone was surprisingly warm, considering the topic.

"Fred was the one who put me onto it."

Byron frowned. "What did he say?"

She pulled his coat tighter around her shoulders. "He said you were spending more time reading your journal. And that you had—well—had some troubles back in November. And after he mentioned it, I couldn't help but see it all."

Byron's brow furrowed. "But what would my journal . . ." he trailed off. "Oh. Oh, I see." He let out a long sigh. "We were speaking of two different secrets."

Her stomach twisted. "There was more than one?"

A depreciating chuckle crossed his lips. "I believe you landed on the more grievous one. My memory, yes?"

She nodded.

He swallowed, heavily. "I suppose I didn't hide it well enough."

"No. You didn't."

"You aren't going to ask me why I was keeping it from you?"

She tucked a stray hair behind her ear. "I think I already know. You wanted to spare me the heartache."

"And yet, your heart is aching." He sighed again. "I should have told you."

"You can tell me now. We have all the time in the world, unless someone finds us."

He gave her a sad sort of smile. "Tell me what you know."

"The facts of the case?"

"As you like."

She sat up, trying to ignore the chill seeping into her bones. "Well, to start, there was an accident that happened almost five years ago, come February. The detective was investigating an organization known as Circe and went incognito into their ranks. He involved himself in a dynamite plot in order to further understand the organization and find evidence."

"You can skip ahead a bit. I haven't forgotten that."

She shook her head. "It's relevant because while there he met Grace Trimble. And had a terrible accident from an explosion that caused him to lose his memory. In fact, every day he would wake up and forget everything of the day before. His last memory was always of preparing the night before the accident occurred. Until, that is, he met Miss Trimble again and his memories started to come back."

"You missed the most important part," he said. "How after years of forgetting, his world was upended by a beautiful and clever artist-turned-secretary."

"You are letting emotion cloud your judgement," she said. "Because the detective never remembered his secretary until after Miss Trimble jogged his memory."

"Oh, but the emotions are quite relevant. Because memory or not, the feelings were still there."

Heat flooded Mira's face, even with the chill of the air. "All of that aside, little by little his memory became better." She decided to leave out the bit about her own envy for Grace Trimble, and the fact that he took so long to remember Mira. "Eventually, he could remember things one day to the next without the use of his journal."

"For the most part, yes. Any other facts?"

"A few. One being that he left his journal in London when traveling for a case in November and happened to forget something important, something he didn't even tell his best friend about and certainly didn't mention to the secretary. Another being that he began using his journal as reference again. And the last being that he started to show outward signs of forgetting, such as not remembering that certain people are bilingual and that sort of thing."

"You are incredibly thorough, Miss Blayse."

"Thank you. Now, I shall call my first witness. Byron Ambrose Sherard Constantine to the ice box, please."

He let out a surprised laugh. "You're making rather light of all of this, considering."

"If I don't, I might cry again, and it's much too cold for that."

"Fair enough." He rubbed at his arms. "First, I would like to make a correction. Since my memories 'filled in,' so to speak, at the end of October, I still could never remember everything from one day to the next. Did I remember more? Yes. Important things, definitely. But minor details always slipped through the cracks. I used my journal to track what I remembered—and what I didn't—day to day. It did seem that my memory was improving. I decided to leave my journal behind for the case Fred and I investigated in November. In part due to my pride. The interim commissioner was questioning my abilities, and in turn made me question them myself."

He paused. "I didn't even realize I was forgetting things.

Fred kept me apprised of the details during that silly sheep case. But towards the end, I realized there was something quite important I was missing." He looked up at her. "You."

Her heart sank, all of her fears coming to the surface. "I had wondered."

"It is inexcusable. But you must know that I knew I was missing something. I knew it was crucial, whatever it was. When I finally returned to London, it came to me. I realized that it was you. And I felt positively sick about it. But when I came to Swan Walk . . . you were so happy and content. How could I shatter that peace?"

"You brought me flowers," she said, remembering the day.

"Camellias. They were actually what made me remember. Your favorite flower."

"You could have told me later," she said, knowing full well why he hadn't.

"Yes. And I should have. Especially after . . . well." He rubbed the back of his neck and repositioned himself, nervous. "I-I . . ." He gave another false start before finally saying, "When I came to find you in the catacombs, there was a bit of a struggle. One of those Circe thugs hit me with a crowbar or pipe or something."

"I remember that you were bleeding." She scooted closer to him.

He rubbed the spot on his forehead, as if it still hurt. "My faculties have been worse since then, I grant you that. But I thought maybe I just needed time." He looked up at her again. "I never forgot you again, I promise you that. You are what I think of as I go to sleep, and the first thought I have when I wake."

Tears pricked at the corners of her eyes again. "I believe you."

He placed his hand over hers, and the warmth made her skin tingle. "I thought I was protecting you but it only hurt you."

She laughed a little. "I think one cannot help hurting those that one loves." She lay her head back against the shelf. "I'm so tired of secrets. I have too many."

He moved closer, so he could put his free arm around her. "I can help carry them."

She shifted so her head was on his shoulder. "Oh, you know most all of them now." She sighed and her breath clouded the air. "It's everything I'm keeping from my family. The truth about the whole Circe business. The fact that Professor Burke is still alive. Emilie's death. It's all so much. So many things left untold."

He squeezed her hand. "I understand why you haven't told them."

"Yes, but where do secrets land us? It was a secret that got Emilie killed. And a secret that led Professor Burke down his path to Circe. Did you know, it all started with cheating on his exams at Cambridge? One indiscretion that has led to so much pain."

"He had a choice at every point. Even now, he could change."

"Yes. There is always a choice." She shivered and pulled closer to him. "What if they don't come?"

"Who?"

"Chabot and Theo. It's been at least an hour, maybe more, since we left them. Shouldn't they have found us by now?"

"Perhaps Theo is doing too good of a job keeping Chabot from barging in." His teeth chattered towards the end.

She sat up, shrugging off his coat. "Here I am, taking all the warmth. You must be freezing in just a suit jacket."

He shook his head. "It's not so bad."

She draped the coat around his shoulders just the same. "Take it for a little while at least."

The ceiling was still dripping, soaking a spot into the rug near the door. They nestled together in a way that was almost comfortable, if it weren't for the cold, and the organs, and the fact that they were trapped. A thin tendril of anxiety took hold. If Theo and Chabot never came there were only two possible outcomes. Moreau would certainly return to his laboratory. It was just a matter of whether he would find them alive or not. And even if they survived the cold, starvation, and dehydration of the little room, they likely wouldn't survive whatever he would plan for them upon their discovery.

Perhaps the cold was getting to her, because that little spark of panic ebbed away almost immediately. Her limbs were too heavy and she was too tired to think about it. The kerosene lamp burnt low and Mira fell into a doze without realizing it.

"It's strange that we never found another staircase," he said after who knows how long.

"Hm?" was all she could manage, half awake and half asleep.

"One going down, I mean," Byron said. "We know there is a cellar, and we know it has to have another entrance since it was locked from the inside."

Mira blinked, trying to make sense of his words as she came back to full consciousness. "I think Swan Walk has a cellar," she said. "But it has a trapdoor from the kitchen. Not a staircase. Landon never let me down there. Walker said it had a lot of spiders."

A pang of grief hit her heart. She'd never see Swan Walk again, would she? Or her uncle, or Landon, or Walker. She sat up, fighting the urge to fall back into unconsciousness.

"What's wrong?" Byron said, his words slurring just a little.

"There has to be another way out," she said. "You're right, we didn't find another staircase. And I didn't see a trapdoor in the kitchen, did you?"

He yawned and pulled his arm out from behind her. "I don't remember seeing one."

"But there was that strange set of new walls jutting out.

You don't think that they took space from the kitchen in order to build this room do you?"

Byron's eyes brightened considerably. "And what better insulation for a refrigerated room, than a cold storage cellar?"

Hope was swelling within her chest now. Could they be so lucky? They both stood. Mira noticed a little numbness in her feet.

"If Moreau were to access the cellar regularly, surely he wouldn't move the shelves each time he needed to roll away the rug," Byron said, crouching again.

Mira hadn't paid much attention to the rug before. In the dim light, she could just make out the oriental pattern. When Byron ran one of the lock picks around the edge of the decorative border, he was able to pry it up. He pulled the center away from the outside revealing a perfect, rectangular cut out that could be rolled back at any time to reveal the flush trapdoor beneath.

"'Hope springs eternal,'" Byron said. There was a little notch in the wood, which he took with two fingers and pulled the trapdoor up.

Chilled air rushed over them at the change of pressure within the room, nearly the same temperature the refrigeration had provided. A ladder descended into the darkness.

"This really is too much like our first excursion in breaking and entering," Mira said, teeth still chattering. "Do you think we'll find a hidden smuggling hold here too?"

"There is an easy way of finding out." Byron took hold of the kerosene lamp. "Would you like to go first, or shall I?"

"You go, and I'll follow."

He nodded and handed the lamp to her. "I'll go down a way, and then you can hand it to me."

Mira held the lamp over the trapdoor while he descended, then handed it down. Soon enough, he was helping her off the ladder and they found themselves in the cellar, safe and sound.

Byron held the lamp out, determining the layout of the place. There were crates and old furniture, and much of the same detritus they had found in the attic.

"We can search here more thoroughly with the police, I think," Byron said, taking hold of her hand and guiding her towards the stairs that led to the inclined double doors at the far end. "I say we get out, breathe some of the fresh January, air and then break into that office again to take the journal."

"But he took it, didn't he?"

"You really were in another place, weren't you?" He stopped at the door and handed her the lamp. "He told your godfather that it was locked up again. Certainly, he could have lied, but I would bet it is back in that cache." He took up the lock picks again, setting to work on the last obstacle to their freedom. "Once we have it again we can put things to rights and toddle off to read the journal in peace."

"And show Chabot the evidence."

"That too. Heavens, it will be nice to have the police on our side again. I must send Chief Inspector Thatcher a fruit basket or something once we get back to London."

She let out a laugh, out of relief more than anything. The lock came free from the chain and he pushed one of the cellar doors open with an inelegant thud. The moon was still shining, although it had traversed quite a distance over the sky, and Mira had never been happier to see it. Byron helped her up the stairs and then set a finger to his lips, whispering, "Best get the evidence before going to find our absent constable."

She nodded and they snuck around to the kitchen door again. It was a simple matter to pick that lock and to make their way to the office, although this venture was a little more tense. Logically, she knew that Moreau wasn't likely to come back within such a short time, but what if he did? She fidgeted as Byron worked his magic with the hidden cabinet in the desk. Within a few minutes, he passed the journal over to her.

But instead of going for the door, he moved back towards the surgery.

"Stay here, won't you, and make sure I won't get locked in again?"

"What are you going to do?" Mira asked, following him back to that beastly refrigerated room.

"If we are to find more evidence later, we must make it appear as though we were never here at all. Do you mind if I take the light? I'll need it to fiddle with the lock."

She nodded and, quick as anything, was left in darkness as Byron shimmied down the ladder again. She held onto the heavy door, the cold air leeching out around her. Her mind began playing those silly tricks on her, making her think someone was behind her, or reminding her that the organs they had been locked in with were most likely Durant's. The thought made her nauseated. But soon enough, light was coming up the ladder, and then Byron was too.

She pulled him into a hug, and the chill of the room, in contrast to his warmth, made her shiver again. He ran a hand over her back.

"Not much longer now."

He pulled away, closed the trapdoor, and set the rug over it as if nothing had happened. "Come on. I'm sure Theo is chewing his nails to bits waiting for us."

"I just don't understand why they didn't come for us." Mira kept a firm hold of the journal as she followed Byron to the entry. He extinguished the kerosene lamp and set it back on its table. She took his arm as the house fell into darkness again.

They left through the kitchen door, taking a moment to lock it behind them. Byron did a quick scan of the courtyard before gesturing for Mira to follow him around the corner to where Theo and Chabot were waiting.

Or, at least, where they should have been waiting.

Bile crept up Mira's throat. The two of them really had left.

If that trapdoor hadn't been there, they would have fallen into a cold-induced sleep and then . . . Her breathing was coming faster, her vision blurring.

Byron placed his hands on her arms. "Take a deep breath. We're safe. The cold you feel is the wind. The light is from the moon. You're standing on cobblestone. And I'm here."

She swallowed, pushing back the panic. "Sorry."

"Don't apologize. What were you thinking?"

"They aren't here. And if they aren't here then . . ."

He caught her gaze. "We could have died."

She nodded.

He pulled her closer to him and used his hand to guide her head to his chest. The steady thump of his heart sounded in her ear, soft and calming.

"Do you hear that? We're alive, Mira. We're safe now."

"We're safe now," she repeated.

"Although I agree, it is rather unsettling to know that our reinforcements have left us."

Mira pulled back. "You don't think . . . Chabot didn't arrest Theo, did he?"

"It is a possibility," Byron said, brushing some hair from her face. "But I didn't take Chabot for the impatient sort. After all, he followed us across Paris for who knows how long without evidence. Surely he wouldn't fizzle out just as he was about to achieve victory."

A new coldness came over her. "You don't think Moreau did anything to them, do you?"

Byron shook his head. "No. He was more focused on getting that tailor's assistant to—" He stopped mid-sentence and then burst out laughing. "Maybe Chabot is more of an idiot than I took him for."

Mira frowned. "What do you mean?"

"Well, imagine this: a man and a woman break into a laboratory. A little while later, a man and a woman leave. But instead of coming to talk with the nice constable who let them break into that laboratory in the first place, they leave through another alley and start heading for the train station."

Her eyes widened. "No. He didn't think that Moreau and Liliane were us, did he?"

"I can't say for certain, but I do believe if Moreau had found him and Theo lurking, he would have brought them inside."

Mira laughed. "No wonder they didn't come looking for us. Poor Theo."

"He can handle himself. At least for tonight." He patted her arm, yawning. "Let's get you home."

He led her through the little alley, back to the street and called for a carriage. Once they were settled inside and on their way to the boarding house, she said, "What was your other secret?"

"Hm?"

"The one you thought I knew, but that I didn't. What was it?"

He laced his right hand with her left, running his thumb along her fourth finger. He pressed a kiss into her hair. "Oh, I think you know."

January 17, 1889: Morning

*I*T WAS LATE INTO THE NIGHT WHEN they reached the boarding house. So late, in fact, that the sun was already coming up. Mira braced herself, preparing for the onslaught of lectures her uncle would certainly have prepared. If she were more alert, she might have attempted to sneak in and up to her room, so as not to arouse his puritanical sensibilities. Then again, she really had nothing to hide. Except the fact that they had broken the law. On second thought, maybe that would be more favorable to him than being out all night without a chaperone.

She and Byron were both dead on their feet as they headed up the path together. An unspoken agreement hung between them that they would endure the abuse of her uncle together.

All was quiet as they came inside. There were moving crates and steamer trunks in the foyer, which meant they had already begun the process of packing. She sighed, remembering the pained look on little Clarisse's face at the news. Hopefully, she was feeling better about the prospect of moving to London.

She peered into the sitting room and found her uncle there, fast asleep in one of the armchairs closest to the fire. Walker was sprawled out on the sofa. A fond smile came to her lips. Of course, they had waited up for her.

She set her coat and hat on the hook in the hall and gestured for Byron to stay there before moving into the room. She stoked up the fire a little, which roused her brother. He shifted drowsily and turned towards her. With a glance at their still sleeping uncle, he whispered, "And where have you been?"

"Investigating Moreau."

"Am I going to get the whole story, or is this a secret too?" he whispered, bitterness outweighing his humor.

She set the poker aside. "I never wanted to keep secrets from you."

"So there is something." He ran a hand through his hair and stood. "You are keeping something from me."

She sighed, a bone weary exhaustion taking over her. "Walker, I'm too tired for this conversation."

"That's your own fault for staying out all night. Do you know Uncle was almost sick with worry? He thought you'd been kidnapped again."

"Well, I wasn't. There were just some unexpected difficulties."

"Like what?"

For a moment, she considered lying, if only to get him to stop asking questions. She had always intended to make herself known to her uncle, ask for Byron to stay the night in one of the spare rooms, and to finally get some rest. But even her sleep addled brain knew that ignoring Walker would only make things worse. And she was tired of the secrets. Tired of caging her words and thoughts in certain company.

"I had my reasons for not telling you," she held a hand up when he tried to interrupt. "It doesn't make it right, I know that. And I'm prepared to tell you now, if you'll let me."

He blinked. "You aren't going to argue?"

"Do you want me to? I thought you wanted the truth."

"Of course I want the truth."

Cyrus stirred. After a few mutterings and a stretch, he looked over at them. He reached out and took Mira's hand, giving it a squeeze. "You're safe," he said, voice gravelly from sleep. He frowned. "Are you two fighting?"

"No," they both said at the same time.

"I just have something I need to tell you," Mira said. "Loretta too."

Cyrus nodded. "I'll fetch her, if you want to start some tea."

BYRON DRUMMED HIS FINGERS ON THE KITCHEN table while Mira filled a kettle and set it on the hob.

"Are you sure you're ready to tell them?" he asked.

"No." She came to stand next to him. "Part of me wants to delay it forever."

"Nerves?"

She rubbed her arms. "A whole barrel of them. After all, it is rather a difficult prospect to tell one's relations that you've been lying to them, even by omission. That one's cousin was murdered and that one's godfather is alive and a murderer. It's the same problem as before. I don't want to—"

A loud thump sounded near the door. In a swift motion, Byron opened it and stepped out.

"I say, Walker. Did you trip?"

Her brother appeared in the doorway, pale as a sheet. "I-I just came to see if the tea was ready."

"Almost," she said. "Are you all right?"

He hesitated, rubbing the back of his neck. "I . . . er. Well. I heard you."

Mira froze. "Oh."

"Is it true?" Walker's voice was thick, his eyes misty. "About Professor Burke?"

She swallowed, and gave a short nod. "That's part of the secret."

He swallowed. "Right. Well. I suppose there are quite a few gaps to fill in. The most I heard was 'alive' and 'murderer.' My imagination is probably making it out worse than it really is."

"Therein lies the danger of eavesdropping," Byron said.

Walker gave him a glare. "I expect you know everything, then?" He turned to Mira. "Why didn't you tell me?" he said, voice pained. "I know that we're grown, but I never thought we would grow apart. We used to tell each other everything."

Her chest constricted. "I'll explain it all, I promise you I will."

"That doesn't change the fact that you've left me in the dark all this time. Sure, you told me about Emilie, but I barely knew her." He clenched his fists. "I saw Professor Burke as another father and I've been mourning him all this time and you said nothing. I've made myself an idiot."

Mira's heart constricted. This was exactly why she didn't want anyone to know.

Byron stepped forward. "If I may—"

Walker shook his head. "She doesn't need her white knight to defend her. You're the reason we're in this mess."

"That isn't true and you know it," Mira said. "If you'll just let me ex—"

Her words were drowned out by whistling of the kettle. She poured the water into the teapot and when she turned back,

Walker was gone. She set teacups next to the teapot, tears coming to the surface. Her fists clenched around the handles of the tray.

Byron reached over and placed a hand over hers.

"He's shocked and angry. But I don't think it will last."

"He's right though. We used to keep secrets for each other. Not from each other." She shivered.

He took the tray from her. "Then let's right that wrong." He started down the hall back to the sitting room and with each step she took behind him, the dread increased.

Walker stood by the hearth, avoiding her gaze. Cyrus and Loretta sat on one of the sofas, a little tired but unsuspecting. Byron set the tray on the table, and Loretta immediately jumped in to serve with Mira helping to hand the cups around. When she handed one to Walker, he set it on the mantle and turned away. Once everyone was settled with a cup, Cyrus said, "What was it that you wanted to tell us?"

His hand was entwined with Loretta's and there was a shine in his eyes, some good humor as he looked between her and Byron. Oh heavens, did he think they were engaged? How was she to break the news?

"Do you—" Mira's voice had given a false start and she cleared her throat a little. "Do you remember when I told you the truth about our parents' accident? This is rather a similar situation."

Cyrus' posture tightened. "I see."

"I haven't told you up to now because, well, because I didn't want to hurt you. But I see now that secrets can only cause more heartache." She said, glancing at Walker, who remained aloof and cold. She took a deep breath. "Professor Burke is alive."

Her uncle's eyes blew wide and he glanced at Loretta, mouth falling open.

Loretta said, "Is that not good news? Why wouldn't you tell us? And why wouldn't he come to us?"

Byron reached over, taking one of Mira's hands and stopping her from fidgeting. He gave it a squeeze and she pressed on.

"Professor Burke is a member of Circe. He faked his death on the bridge so he could continue to act without interference from any of us. In fact, he is one of the leaders. He—" she paused, trying to find the right words. "He became the Charger after your father, Loretta."

Loretta paled, her expression distant as the words sank in. "How do you know?"

"I found him when I tried to escape from Durant in the catacombs. He pretended he'd had been captured as well, but his true identity became clear soon enough. At least he had the decency to give me an explanation."

She continued, the words tumbling out. "Loretta, your father actually wanted you to marry Burke, as a means of helping him rise in the ranks of Circe. Burke refused because he knew of your elopement, but he was the one who told your father about it."

"Oh," Loretta said, hollow.

Mira continued, "He was also the one who changed the plans of the airship my father was building." She turned to Walker. "When Father found out, Burke arranged for him to be abducted, but Mother was accidentally taken as well. He thought he could coerce Father to work with him, but he refused."

"Imprisoned. Not killed," Cyrus said. "Does that mean—"

Mira's heart twisted. She'd had a similar thought when the Charger revealed the truth to her. "Mother died of an illness. When Father still wouldn't work for Circe, well . . ."

"Burke . . . he didn't. They were friends. He wouldn't have . . ." Walker said, voice stuttery.

"Was Burke responsible?" Cyrus asked.

She gave a short nod, taking a shaky breath. She couldn't even say the words.

"I knew that Circe killed them," Walker said, bitterly. "I didn't realize it was our own godfather who ordered it."

She found her voice again, though it was hoarse. "It would be difficult for me to believe if I hadn't witnessed the change in him." She paused, her throat tight. "He was prepared to kill me to keep his secret."

Cyrus ran a hand over his face. "I never suspected a thing."

"None of us did," Loretta said.

A heavy silence fell over the room. Finally, Cyrus said, "At least we won't have to worry about a funeral."

Walker let out a startled laugh. "Is that all you can say, old man? We find out that your oldest and dearest friend is a lying, murderous beast, and you are thinking of the finances?"

"More logistics than anything. I intended to split our residence between London and Paris until the body was found."

"Why, we never would have found the body!" Loretta said.

Mira laughed a little in spite of herself. She had expected their reactions to be similar to her brother's. "You aren't angry?"

"I'm sure I will be once the shock has worn off," Cyrus said, before amending, "Not at you dear. Never at you. I can't imagine the burden this has been for you to keep."

She sank into her chair, the tension in her shoulders dissipating. "I just didn't know how to tell you. I thought maybe it was better to believe he was dead, rather than to know the truth."

"You presumed quite a bit," Walker said, his voice still tense.

"Yes, but I understand why you did it," Loretta said. "And we know the truth now. There were so many things that never made sense and now we know why."

"Poor Rose," Cyrus said, choking up. "My dear, sweet sister."

"Are you going to tell them the rest?" Walker said, pointedly.

"There's more?" Cyrus asked, brow furrowing.

Mira's stomach churned. "I know that you've noticed my absence as of late."

"You've had business at the police prefecture, haven't you?" Loretta asked.

She nodded. "Yes, but not about Durant. Or at least, not directly related to him. You see, well . . ." She looked to Byron. How was she meant to tell her aunt and uncle that their daughter had been murdered?

Byron cleared his throat. "We have been investigating Emilie's death."

Cyrus took Loretta's hand again. "It wasn't natural, was it?"

Mira closed her eyes as Byron said. "No. It wasn't."

Loretta's eyes misted over. "But who would want her dead?"

"That is the worst part," Mira said. "She wasn't the target."

When her uncle asked for more specifics, Mira let Byron take the lead, explaining their investigation, and all that had led them to this point. He glossed over a few details, particularly when it came to their breaking into Moreau's laboratory, but soon all present were filled in on everything related to Emilie's death and the catacombs and Durant and the Charger.

"I see," Cyrus said once it was all out. Walker had taken a seat, simmering down from his earlier ire.

"It is difficult to grasp but . . ." Loretta bit back a fresh round of tears. "You'll find them, won't you? Emilie might have some justice?"

"That is the intention," Byron said.

"What's to be done?" Cyrus asked.

"I have a few ideas," Byron said. "But I'm afraid all of them hinge on being well rested."

"Oh, of course," Loretta said, wiping her eyes. "You must be exhausted from being up all night." She stood. "There should be a spare room for you, Mr. Constantine. On the second landing. I'm sorry, but it might be a bit crowded. We've been storing the trunks there as we've been packing."

"Thank you, Mrs. Griffon," Byron said. "I'm much obliged."

WHEN MIRA WOKE, HER ROOM WAS FULL of light and the clock indicated it was well past midday. There had been no nightmares, no anxiety to keep her up. Just simple, calm, quiet sleep. She lay there for a moment, reveling in the warmth of the bed. Then she forced herself to brave the chill and get dressed.

The boarding house was certainly awake with footsteps on the stairs and echoing voices. She left her room and headed down to the second landing where Byron had been put up. He opened the door only a few moments after she knocked, journal in hand. It was such a familiar sight that it took a little longer than it ought for her to realize whose journal it was.

"Is that Moreau's?"

He nodded and ushered her inside. "It contains a wealth of information. Lists of poisons and their toxicities, a key that matches individual names and specimens with numerical values, and this," he held the book open for her.

There were sketches of what looked to be a pin cushion with a vial in the center. The notes on the side indicated the difficulties of keeping liquid in such a contraption and how one could administer poison with a needle.

"Oh dear. I hadn't thought of how it was done." She sat down on one of the packing crates, feeling a little dizzy.

Byron closed the journal and set it on the side table. "There is quite a bit I wasn't able to decipher from context. After all, the whole thing is in French. "From what I have been able to understand, Moreau is an expert in poisonings and it's clear enough he was involved in this particular one."

Mira picked up the journal and flicked through it, skimming a few of the pages. A little over halfway through, she came to a sketch of that strange fish they had seen in the refrigerated room. The note next to it said, "*Japon Poisson-Globe.*"

"That vial of poison we borrowed . . . do you still have it?" she asked.

He nodded, removed it from the bedside table, then brought it and the slide they had found back over to her. She ran her hand over the label.

"Japon P-G. This is pufferfish toxin from Japan."

"Is it really?" He whistled. "Does the journal list what it is used for?"

She summarized the text for him. "The toxin is well known in Japan and poisoning usually occurs through ingestion. There are some notes about how it might be introduced via needle. Symptoms include paralysis and difficulty breathing. He has a note here about what diagnoses could be given that would mirror the symptoms. One of them being Grand Mal Seizure."

Her hands shook as she closed the journal. It seemed such an awful way to die.

"Poor Emilie," she said.

"Yes. But we finally have the proof we need. Although, we still have a minor difficulty."

"And what is that?" she said, setting the journal aside.

"Proving that the journal belongs to Dr. Moreau. I've checked it over and haven't found any means of identification outside of handwriting."

"Won't that be enough?"

He sat on the edge of the bed, curling his fingers under the wooden frame. "From my experience, those who entrench themselves in the evils of Circe are slippery as eels in this sort of thing. He'll probably find some way to prove the journal is a forgery and a slander on his name. Or it's possible he uses a different hand when writing in it. And since Chabot did not witness us coming out of the laboratory with journal in hand, there is some doubt thrown on the subject."

"But surely the police will believe this evidence in conjunction with the testimony of the tailors at the House of Worth."

"Perhaps. But I think we'll need to be incredibly clever in how we go about this."

A knock sounded on the doorframe and Walker poked his head in.

"I thought I heard two voices," he said. "What would Uncle say, to know you two were alone together, hm?"

That teasing lilt was back in his voice. Mira rolled her eyes and stood. "We've been discussing the case."

"A likely story." Walker rocked back on his heels.

"Might I ask why you're listening at doors again?" she said, testing the waters.

"Oh, I don't think I'll ever break the habit," he said. "Besides, you left the door open."

Mira felt a little relief when his tone remained the same. Maybe he wasn't irreparably angry with her.

He continued. "I came to let you know that there are some gentlemen downstairs wishing to speak with the two of you."

"Did they give their names?" Byron asked, opening the door wider.

"Chabot, or something like that, and a man named Jaubert? I left them bickering in the sitting room."

Byron crossed back to the bed, retrieving Moreau's journal. "Seems our wayward constable has turned up again."

"It is promising that he didn't immediately arrest Theo," Mira said, following him and Walker into the hall. Byron started for the stairs, but Mira lingered on the landing a moment, detaining her brother with a hand on his elbow.

"If you were wondering, we really were discussing the case." She tucked some hair behind her ear.

"Oh, I don't doubt it." He pulled the strand loose again, his mouth ticking up at the side.

She smiled and blew it out of her face. "You must be feeling better about things to tease."

He sighed. "I see the logic in why you kept things secret. But it still doesn't make it right."

"I know that. How might I make it up to you?"

"I just need time, Mouse. It is difficult to reconcile the man I thought I knew, with who he really is."

"I still have difficulty. In some ways, I think I've been pretending he's two different people. That the man I knew as my godfather died on that bridge."

He placed his hands in his pockets, looking down. "Which explains why you've actually been mourning all this time."

"Do you forgive me?"

"Not yet," he said, looking up at her. "But I think I will once I find a secret to keep from you."

She laughed, recognizing the spark in her brother's eyes. "Please do. You've more than earned a secret."

January 17, 1889: Afternoon

*T*HERE WAS A RATHER COMICAL SIGHT WAITING for them when she and Byron entered the sitting room. Constable Chabot and Theo were seated on the sofa looking all out of sorts. Clothes wrinkled, hair mussed, and deep under eye bags revealed a certain exhaustion. There was a stain on the shoulder of Theo's suit and they were still handcuffed together. Her Uncle Cyrus was keeping a wary eye on them from a seat across the room. When Theo saw Byron come in, he stood, dragging Chabot along as he extended the cuffs.

"Please tell me you still have them."

Byron fished into his pocket and threw the lock picks over. Theo caught them with his unbound hand and immediately began working on his freedom.

"What happened to the key?" Byron asked.

Chabot flushed. "I . . . er . . . lost it."

Cyrus furrowed his brow. "Are those lock picks?"

"Perfectly legal ones, eh, Constable Chabot?" Byron raised an eyebrow. "I assume since you are here, and not trying to stop Jaubert from escaping, that you believe us?"

Chabot swallowed, nodding.

"He had better, after what we've been through," Theo said as he pulled his hand out of the cuffs with a sigh of relief.

Cyrus stood, "Perhaps I should leave you all to your business, hm?"

Mira smiled and kissed him on the cheek as he passed her. "Thank you, Uncle."

"Perhaps you should start from when you left the laboratory in pursuit of Moreau," Byron said, moving to the fireplace and leaning against the mantle.

"You know of that?" Chabot said, eyes widening. He shook his head and carried on. "Yes. I thought the couple that left was you. In the dark—"

"I told you it wasn't them," Theo said. "And yet you dragged me along."

"It was for the best, eh? Seeing what we found out," Chabot said, gesturing vaguely. The movement brought his attention to his hand, which was still attached to the handcuffs. He said, "Will you finish the job?"

Theo sighed and set to work again.

"What did you find out?" Mira asked, sitting down.

"We followed them to the train station," Chabot said. "It was then that I realized it was Moreau. I was going to turn back when I heard the word Circe. The girl had said it. I had never seen her before and she doesn't work with the police, so why would she say it? The more we listened, the more it became clear that they were discussing a failed murder! The girl was apologizing for ruining the job and Moreau was trying to quiet her down."

"But we didn't hear anything else," Theo said, pulling the handcuffs free and dropping them on the sofa with triumph. "Moreau left after purchasing her a ticket to Le Mans and I suggested we follow the girl."

"I would have followed her without your input," Chabot said, offended. "If she was the murderer, my superiors would not have wanted her to disappear."

Theo rolled his eyes. "We bought two tickets under the guise of a prisoner transfer, seeing as we were attached to the alibi."

"So, you went all the way to Le Mans and back this morning?" Mira asked. "You must be exhausted."

"We took turns sleeping on the train," Theo said. "Or we tried."

Chabot folded his arms. "I do not care what you say. I did not snore."

"Yes, and I'm sure you didn't drool either." Theo rubbed at the stain on his suit. "But we did end up in the same compartment as the girl. It took a minute to warm her up, but with a little charm we found out that she is Moreau's niece."

"She asked if I was a part of the police." Chabot shrugged. "It was a natural progression."

"His niece?" Byron said, drumming his fingers on the mantle. "That would explain the familial attention he was giving her."

"And why he is so willing to set everything to rights for her," Mira said.

"Set it all to rights?" Chabot said. "What do you mean?"

"The election is in ten days," Byron said. "Emilie's accidental murder was an attempt to remove Marguerite as a distraction or obstacle to Boulanger's victory."

Chabot's mouth dropped open. "There has been rumor of a coup. If he wins, they wish for him to take power immediately."

"Exactly, and it is my theory that Circe thinks Marguerite will somehow prevent that from happening," Byron said.

"They failed the first time because Emilie was in her place, but based on what we heard in the laboratory last night, Moreau will try again. And this time, his aim will be to manipulate Boulanger into not only taking power, but declaring war on Prussia."

"Not if we arrest him first," Mira said. "We have the journal as proof, as well as the testimonials from the tailors, and a police officer as a witness now. Surely that is enough to convince Lozé."

"Journal?" Chabot said.

Byron handed it over. "We borrowed it from his laboratory."

Chabot skimmed over the contents, nodding in one moment and shaking his head in the next. After a few pages he closed it and ran a hand over his face. "I'm not certain that this will be enough. There has been much talk in the police station against you and your British interference. And much of the force is poisoned against Boulanger as well. Lozé may listen to you, but this is a serious accusation against a respected member of the prefecture. It would call into question hundreds of cases he ruled on." He handed the journal back. "There is nothing in the journal to indicate that he wrote it, and even if he admits to it, he studied under Gaultier."

"Gaultier?" Mira asked.

"He was one of the premier toxicologists of this century," Byron said. "And if anyone had reason to study poisons, it would be a police physician."

"*Exactement*," Chabot said. "Lozé will need more evidence than that. Especially with the case being considered closed and your cousin's death natural."

Byron paced away towards the window. "If we can't arrest Moreau with the current evidence, then he shall have to make more for us."

"What exactly are you thinking of?" Mira asked.

He turned towards her. "Moreau intends to kill Marguerite de Bonnemains. I say, we let him try."

"Let him kill her?" Chabot said, brow furrowed.

"Heavens no." Byron straightened his suit sleeves. "We'll stop him before he gets that far. We know from his conversation with the Charger that Moreau will make another attempt sometime this week. It would be simple enough for us to arrange a watch on her apartment, and ensure she doesn't leave during that time. Moreau would have to come to her. And if we also keep a watch on him, we will be one step ahead of him."

"I can watch him," Chabot said.

Byron pursed his lips, but before he could say anything, Theo laughed.

"You? He will see you following him from the very moment you start."

"No, I shall remain hidden in the shadows."

Theo shook his head. "I have been cuffed to you, remember? There is not a sneaky bone in your body. I could sneak better handcuffed to an elephant, than you could on your own."

Byron cleared his throat. "And we'll need you at Marguerite's. Theo will watch at Moreau's home. I think we'll have Fred watch at the laboratory. You see, the moment that either of them catches sight of Moreau moving in the direction of Marguerite's, he will make two calls. One to us to give us warning at Marguerite's, and another to the police prefecture to ask for men to be sent there.

"Meanwhile, Chabot and I will hide in a room adjacent to Marguerite's sitting room. With finesse, and a little luck, when Moreau comes we will have some additional members of the police force with us in that room to overhear the conversation. We can burst out, catch him in the act, and arrest him for attempted murder."

"And what am I to do?" Mira said.

"Oh, you have the most important part," Byron said.

She interrupted. "If you say that I am to stay home and wait, I shall slap you."

He shook his head. "No. You are to pretend to be one of the maids. You will stall Moreau a little in the entryway and then inform Marguerite, and subsequently us, of his arrival. When the police come, you will escort them up a back way to where Chabot and I will be waiting."

"He's seen me before, Byron. Won't he recognize me?"

"Not if we are careful about your disguise. In any case, I doubt he remembers much from his interaction with you at the police prefecture. You'll remember he only mentioned me on the telephone to your godfather?"

"Right." She took in a shaky breath. "We have ten days until the election. How will we know what day he is coming?"

"That is the tricky part. We won't. Which means we will have to be in position for the duration." He turned to Chabot. "Will you be able to get the time off?"

"I believe I can do better than that. Lozé has been struggling to know what to do about the death threats towards Boulanger. The interior minister has given orders to ignore them, but it hasn't sat well with the Prefect. If I suggest that I stand as guard over him, it might give Lozé a little peace and allow me to be in position."

"Perfect. I believe that settles it."

"Not quite," Mira said. "We still need Marguerite to agree to it."

"ABSOLUTELY NOT!" BOULANGER SAID, HIS FACE RED. He followed it with some ungentlemanly words in French.

"But beloved, don't you see?" Marguerite said. "We must catch him in the act."

"Using you as bait? I hardly think so." Boulanger clenched his fists and turned away from the group, calming his anger.

Mira sat on the sofa across from the chaise lounge. Marguerite sat there with the cat on her lap and no veil concealing her features. Byron stood behind Mira, while Theo and Chabot sat in chairs closer to the door.

"No harm would come to her," Byron said. "Someone will be close by at all times."

"It is too much of a risk," Boulanger said. "All we have to do is keep her safe until after the election, and then they will stop this nonsense."

"There is no guarantee of that," Byron said. "And aside from that, we would be letting Emilie's murderers go free if we cannot provide the proper evidence."

"Then we use a duplicate," Boulanger said.

Mira glanced at Byron. What an interesting thought.

Boulanger turned to Marguerite. "We ask Angeline."

"I cannot ask her to take such a risk for me," Marguerite said.

He sat on the edge of her chaise. "Then we take you away to Royat. Marie can hide us there."

Marguerite reached over and set her hand over his. "You cannot leave Paris until after the election, love."

Boulanger swore again.

Theo said, "Sir, there are ladies present."

"*Pardon,*" Boulanger said. "This entire situation is most intolerable."

"I could do it," Mira said.

The whole group turned towards her. Before anyone could argue against the idea, she stood and moved closer to the madame. "I believe there is enough of a resemblance in form between the two of us."

"No," Byron said, taking a step towards her and then aborting the motion. "He's seen you before."

Mira turned to him. "You said yourself that a simple disguise would be enough to fool him. What disguise is better than a veil?"

"It is still dangerous," Marguerite said, though she seemed to be considering the prospect. "I would hate for you to be hurt, when it is me he is after."

"We'll have warning and can be prepared for when he comes," Mira said. "It will be perfectly safe. And you did not ask me. I offered."

Marguerite hesitated for a moment before moving next to her, studying her features. "Your hair is quite a bit darker than mine, but the veil should cover that." She moved to a side table and opened a drawer, removing a black veil from inside. She placed it over Mira's face and cocked her head to the side. "Yes, I think it will work." She handed the veil to Mira before walking around her in a circle. "We have quite a similar figure and height, which is more important. And you speak the proper languages. If you are certain you wish to do this."

"I am."

Byron opened his mouth to argue again, but nothing came out.

Boulanger's shoulders relaxed. "If she stands in for you, I see no faults with the plan."

"I see one," Marguerite said. "If she is to become me until the election, there is quite a bit that we will need to go over. And yet, there is no time. So, if she shall take on my part, I shall take on hers."

"What do you mean?" Mira asked.

Marguerite grinned, her eyes sparkling. "I shall be your maid. And so, if anyone comes to visit, anyone outside of Moreau that is, I can tell you all there is to know."

Boulanger grimaced. "I would much prefer for you to go to Royat."

"She is risking her life for me, *mon chéri*. It is only right that

I shoulder some of the risk. Besides, do you really think I would miss all the fun?" She took Mira's hand, tugging her towards the dressing room. "Come, we shall find something for you to wear." She laughed. "And something for me to wear too."

Byron stepped forward. "Just a moment."

The two ladies turned back and he closed the distance, catching Mira's gaze and holding it.

Once he was close enough, he whispered, "Are you certain you are up to this?"

Mira pulled her shoulders back, lifting her chin. "If I don't do this, Moreau will continue working with Circe. We won't be able to bring him or Liliane to justice. I have the chance, the power, to set things right. Emilie's death doesn't have to be in vain. So, whether or not I am 'up' for this is irrelevant."

He let out a slow breath. She could tell that he didn't like the prospect of her being in such a vulnerable position. And yet, to say anything—especially in front of Boulanger—would make him a hypocrite. She stepped closer.

"I'll be all right." She reached up on her tiptoes and kissed his cheek. "After all, I have you looking after me."

He nodded. "You'd better get ready. We don't know when Moreau will enact his plan."

January 24, 1889: Morning

THE VEIL WAS A MONSTROUS THING. EVERY breath was trapped by the fabric, making the interior incredibly stuffy. An unbearable itch broke out at every point where the fabric met her skin. And though it achieved its intended purpose of blocking the view of her face, seeing out of it was almost as difficult. Was this what it had been like for Emilie?

Mira had worn veils before, of course. They were usually much lighter, in both material and color. And usually she only wore them for short periods of time. She had been wearing this one on and off for nigh on a week.

At first, the thought had been for Mira, Byron, and Chabot to stay at Marguerite's until the call came from Theo and Fred. Then Mira could assume the role of Marguerite, wait for

Moreau, and the men could make the arrest. However, there was no guarantee that Moreau himself would come. And with each passing day, it became more possible that he would make another arrangement.

Which would mean that the threat could come from an unknown and unexpected source.

After the first three days, with the increasing tension and uncertainty, Boulanger insisted she assume the role of Marguerite until their trap was sprung. Mira thought it would be a simple task, and yet, the longer she sat upon Marguerite's chaise, wearing her clothes, petting her cat, entertaining visitors, the more she felt ill at ease. They had to keep up appearances, lest it rouse Circe's suspicions. But the waiting was driving her mad. Byron had been concerned about the danger of the situation. He should have been worried for her sanity.

There were a few comforts that kept her from completely losing her head. The first being that Byron had been close to her the entire time. The second was that she had become good friends with Marguerite and her cat, Aveline. The third was that the election was in three days, which meant she wouldn't be in this position forever. And the last was that she needn't always wear the veil. It was only when visitors arrived that the deception was crucial.

Unfortunately, during the week that Mira had played the part of Madame de Bonnemains, she had received visitors nearly every day. Most of them were admirers who had heard of her beauty and wished to see it for themselves, only to be disappointed. There were also a few women who wanted to form an acquaintance in hopes of ingratiating themselves with the nobility. Those visits were much harder to navigate. Marguerite would always answer the door and tell the relevant party to wait before coming up to tell Mira how to handle them. Mira wasn't sure what she would do without her help.

The only other issue was the matter of the telephone. Thankfully, there hadn't been many calls, but the few that had come through had her on edge. Every time she imagined it was Theo or Fred calling to confirm Moreau's movements. And every time it was some benign situation. The uncertainty of it all was ridiculous. When would Moreau come and why was it taking him so long?

Mira blew some hair out of her face, waiting for Marguerite to take her turn. They'd played all manner of games together at this point, but piquet was her least favorite. Unfortunately, it was Marguerite's preferred way of passing the time so Mira played and lost, and was glad for the company while they waited for Moreau to make his move.

Marguerite sat across from her. She wore the stiff maid's uniform and had her hair in a simple style—no trace of her usual elegance and finery remained. The effect was a remarkable disguise. Yet, she remained a lady of nobility in her grace and poise. She tucked her legs beneath her chair, with an air of regality as she considered her cards.

They sat together like actresses waiting in the wings for their scene to arrive. No matter what they were doing beforehand, the doorbell would ring and each would slip into her role. Mira's was the harder of the two, as she not only had to be another person, but was expected to maintain an aura of *noblesse oblige*. Marguerite could fade into the background, as people rarely paid attention to serving staff. And those closest to the madame knew that at least one of her maids bore a striking resemblance to her mistress.

The true Madame discarded several cards and drew the same number. "That would be nine, eight, and seven of diamonds."

Mira sighed and considered her hand. Now, was Marguerite bluffing with her sequence or telling the truth? She gave a short nod. "Yours."

Marguerite smirked and set down a nine of diamonds.

The door that led to the dressing room opened and Byron and Chabot popped out.

"It's getting rather stuffy in there again. Thought we'd air it out," Byron said. Out of everyone involved, he somehow had the same spark for the plan that he'd had on day one. Everyone else was just about ready to chuck it all in. Perhaps there was a benefit to resetting some of one's memory each day.

"Who's winning?" Mira asked, setting down her seven of diamonds. The men had played multiple games of chess during their confinement.

"Oh, we aren't keeping track," Byron said. "We've moved onto discussing ways of drawing Moreau out."

Mira looked up. "Really? What have you come up with?"

"Nothing of consequence," Byron said. "Unfortunately."

"I think we could have success with the false murder," Chabot said.

"False murder?" Marguerite asked.

Byron pinched the bridge of his nose. "We have Boulanger call the police, saying there's been a murder. Moreau will want to come along, of course, and when they get here we tell them it was a false alarm. The assumption is Moreau will convince everyone to let him see Marguerite alone and we might get a confession out of him."

"A perfect plan!" Chabot said. "With any luck, an inspector will even be nearby to overhear the confession."

"I still say that it depends on too many unknown variables. What if Moreau doesn't have poison on him? What if he decides it is too much of a risk to try with more police in the vicinity? What if a different police physician comes?"

"And your plan does not depend on the unknown? We have been stuck in that closet for seven days, with no sign of Moreau coming."

"It is rather inconvenient," Marguerite said.

Byron sighed. "I think I'll check on Dufresne and see how

lunch is coming along." He moved to the door and disappeared. Perhaps the monotony was getting to him after all.

Marguerite placed her final sequence. "I do believe that is the game."

Mira set her cards down with half a laugh. "One of these times I will win. I just need to understand the strategy."

"Shall I deal again?" Marguerite said, eyes sparkling.

The doorbell rang and her countenance fell.

"Don't people know that it is rude to visit just before luncheon? Why, we will need to inform Dufresne to add another plate."

"Perhaps it will be a short conversation," Mira said.

"We can only hope," Chabot said, moving to hide in the dressing room again.

Marguerite checked her hair in the mirror and slumped her shoulders a bit, slipping into the role of Noemi, the maid. They'd enjoyed determining her personality, her history, her family, simply as a way to pass the time, but Mira hoped it made her disguise all the more convincing.

Mira stood as Marguerite left the room, anxious energy flowing through her. Aveline meowed as the movement disturbed her, but Mira paid the little cat no mind, pacing over to the window and back again. She wasn't nearly as good at pretending to be someone else. Perhaps it didn't help that she was impersonating a real person. She picked up the veil. Did Emilie ever feel as though she were a stranger in her own skin?

After a minute or so, Marguerite returned.

"Who is it?" Mira asked.

"It is strange," Marguerite said, her brow furrowed. "I don't remember receiving a letter from this one."

"Another admirer?" Mira sighed as she set the veil in place over her face, yet again.

"From Prussia. I haven't had one come from so far before."

"Shall I act disinterested or with concealed annoyance?"

Mira sat on the chaise again and Aveline settled next to her, curling into a ball.

"Perhaps both." Marguerite frowned. "It might be a little more difficult to dissuade him."

"Well, should I need the cavalry, I'll be certain to call."

Marguerite disappeared down the stairs, reappearing with a man in tow. He was large and broad shouldered, with dark whiskers that covered most of his face. For a moment, she thought it was Moreau in disguise. But his build was wrong, as was his eye color. Her heart raced regardless, and she braced herself, unsure of what sort of interaction this might be. The last man had nearly groveled at her feet, asking her to remove her veil.

"*Monsieur Richter for you, Madame,*" Marguerite said.

The man brushed past her without a second glance, his eyes sharp as he took Mira in.

"*Thank you, Noemi,*" Mira said.

Marguerite gave a slight bow and stepped off to the side.

"*I hear you have traveled a great distance,*" Mira said.

"*No distance would be too great for my purpose,*" Richter said, surprising Mira with how fluently he spoke French. There was a trace of a Prussian accent, but it was faint.

"*Will you sit?*" she asked, gesturing to one of the chairs.

He followed the direction of her hand with his gaze before casting it about the room and finally resting it on her again. "*There is no need. I will not stay long.*"

"*How may I help you, Monsieur Richter?*"

"*I simply wished to see the woman who so captivates the General of Revenge. Your beauty is much spoken of, even in my country.*"

"*You are too kind,*" she said, though his statement made her frown. How did he know that Marguerite was Boulanger's mistress? And why would he come if he knew that relation?

"*I would not say that,*" he said, his tone cold.

Something was unsettling about his manner. It was possible she was imagining it, but there was an intensity to his presence—a precision to his words—that set her on edge. He wasn't like the other admirers and that made him dangerous.

Moreau had mentioned a "Prussian angle" on the telephone with the Charger. What if the doctor had sent Richter? She glanced at Marguerite. They had meant to protect her, but she was still in the room. If he realized that Mira wasn't Madame de Bonnemains, surely he would turn to the maid.

Byron was still in the kitchen, and she couldn't risk calling for Chabot. She shifted, making Aveline mew again, and a plan formed.

"Oh, excuse me, sir. I forget my manners. Would you like anything to eat or drink?"

"No, thank you."

Mira nodded, turning to Marguerite. *"Will you inform Dufresne that we shall need to move luncheon back?"*

Marguerite frowned, but nodded. *"Yes, Madame."*

She turned to leave but Mira said, *"Oh, and . . ."* Mira plucked the little cat from the chaise and held her out. *"Would you ask for a saucer of milk for my little Ambrose?"*

Marguerite's frown deepened, but she took the cat from her arms. *"Of course, Madame."*

She left the room and a small part of Mira's anxiety went with her. Not only would Marguerite be safer outside the room, but there was a chance Byron would receive her message and understand it. She had to hope for that. She moved to the fireplace to put a little more distance between her and her foreign visitor.

"I'm so sorry for that, Monsieur Richter. Where were we?"

He straightened. *"Will you remove the veil for me?"*

The abrupt shift in subject startled her. Yet another bit of evidence to suggest he was here for another purpose. Although, there was still a chance he was only another admirer.

"I prefer to keep the air of mystery, sir."

"*Unfortunate.*" He shifted his stance, reaching into his coat. "*I have a gift, you see. And I want to ensure it is given to the right person.*"

"*And you doubt who I am?*" Mira swallowed, her mouth becoming dry. No one had ever questioned it before. The heat of the fire emanated through the skirts of her dress.

"*It would be a shame if I am mistaken.*"

Mira's breath hitched in her chest as the light caught a glint of silver, the kind that brought death. And blood. And dust. The lace of the veil brushed her skin— hot and sticky. No. Not lace. It was smoke, clouding her vision. The flames leapt higher behind her. She blinked. The Prussian blurred. Her godfather stood in his place. Then Durant. No—no. She forced herself to take a breath. Durant was dead. She'd seen his body, cold and lifeless. And yet her mind made him breathe again. That was all this was. It was her mind.

"*Whether you remove the veil or not is no concern to me,*" the man was saying, but the voice—Durant's voice—was all wrong. "*If you are not Marguerite de Bonnemains, I would suggest that you prove it.*" There was a click as he pulled back the hammer of the revolver.

She drew in a ragged breath, trying to push the memories away. She had a precious few moments to act, and she needed to stay present. Chabot was in the dressing room. Marguerite had gone to the kitchen. Had Byron understood her signal? If she could stall Richter long enough, perhaps she could find some way of alerting one of them.

"*I don't understand. I have never met you before. How can I possibly prove it?*"

"*I have my methods. Now, remove the veil, so I can be certain.*"

"*D-don't hurt me. I'll prove it,*" she said, feigning the beginning of hysterics.

Slowly, she brought one hand up towards the veil, while

the other reached for the poker in the stand behind her. She fumbled for a moment but masked the movement by removing the veil from her face.

His hold on the gun was unwavering as he narrowed his gaze. His other hand reached into his coat, removing something else. A bit of newspaper. He glanced at it, but before he could look back at her, she pulled the poker free and swung it up against the hand holding the gun. A shot rang off, plaster and dust raining down from the ceiling. The newspaper fluttered to the floor as he grabbed hold of the middle of the poker to wrench it away.

She pulled on the poker with half of her strength, expecting him to pull with all of his. When he did, she released her hold, letting his momentum throw him off balance while she lunged for the gun. Dust filled her nostrils, too much like the catacombs, too much like her nightmares. The darkness and bone and flame. Footsteps pounded through the tunnels and a door slammed open. She curled her hand around the cold metal, kicking her assailant away, but his hands were on her shoulders, he was dragging her away and holding her fast, pinning her arms.

"Mira, you're safe," a voice whispered, a hand running through her hair. "Please breathe."

She half sobbed into him, the gun falling from her grasp onto the floor with a dull clatter. Byron. He had come for her. She gasped for air.

"That's it, my love. Breathe." He shifted. "Marguerite, do you have smelling salts handy?"

Mira didn't hear the response, but soon the sharp, caustic tang of ammonia hit her nose and made her eyes sting. The room came back into focus and she came fully to the present.

The Prussian—Richter—was on his knees. Chabot stood behind him, restraining him with handcuffs. Marguerite sat on the edge of the chaise lounge, eyes wide. Mira sat up, Byron's steady presence behind her, his arms supporting her.

"There you are," Byron said. "How are you feeling?"

"A little shaky." Mira swallowed. Her hand brushed the veil and she picked it up, staring at it.

"Can you tell me what happened?" Byron asked, shifting so that he was by her side while keeping an arm around her.

"He asked me to remove the veil." The stifling fabric caught as she ran her hand over it. "He pulled the gun from his coat and pointed it at me. I . . ." she drew her gaze around the room, finding the poker lying on the floor. "I used that," she pointed, "to disarm him, but the shot went off."

Byron nodded. "Marguerite told me that something was off. I was coming up the stairs when I heard the shot. When I came in, you were in a scuffle with him and Chabot."

The door opened revealing General Boulanger standing on the threshold. A heavy crease formed in the center of his forehead as he took in the scene.

"What has happened here?" he asked.

"An attempted murder," Byron said, helping Mira to her feet and over to sit next to Marguerite.

Boulanger clenched his fists. "This is Moreau?"

"No," Marguerite said. "He said his name was Richter. He is from Prussia."

"Prussia?" The general's face reddened, his voice quiet. He turned on Richter, speaking in a language that Mira didn't understand. German, perhaps? Richter responded with equal ire and Boulanger stalked away, incensed.

"This is what we have been fighting against!" he said. "To think that the Prussians would stoop so low as to attack my love, as a means of stopping my ascent."

Byron stood. "Think, man! What would Prussia have to gain from killing Marguerite? They have everything to lose."

Mira looked over at Richter. He didn't seem to understand what was being said, but he glared at them all.

"It must have been a ploy," Boulanger said, though his words had cooled. "Something that we cannot see."

"No," Byron said. "I believe that whoever sent him intended to incite you to declare war immediately. And I do not believe it was Prussia who did so."

Marguerite stood, moving to the general's side. "Think for a moment. There is sense to what he is saying."

Richter's gaze slipped down to where his bit of newspaper had fallen, flicking between it and Marguerite, understanding crossing his face.

Mira moved to pick up the paper, finding that the clipping contained a woodcut print of Marguerite. A portion of an article relating her divorce was beneath it. The likeness was good, although the ink was a bit smudged.

"He knew about the veil," she said, interrupting whatever geopolitical discussion was happening above her.

"What?" Byron asked.

She stood. "He knew there was a possibility that the woman claiming to be Marguerite was someone else." She turned towards Richter, switching to French. "*Where did you get this clipping?*"

He pointedly remained silent.

Boulanger marched over, pulled Richter up by the hand-cuffs, deposited him in a chair, and stood over him. "*She asked you a question. I suggest that you answer.*"

"*I have nothing to say that I have not already said.*"

Mira considered the clipping. The article was in French. And the only way that he could know about the veil would be if someone had told him. If he really was from Prussia, then someone would have needed to send for him.

"Have we searched him?" she asked.

Chabot frowned. "Erm. No." He checked Richter's pockets, finding an envelope in his right breast pocket and handing it over. A large water splotch spread out over the majority of the envelope, along with a boot print. When she took the letter out, many of the words were smudged, although legible.

"The postman must have dropped it," Byron said, looking over her shoulder.

She skimmed over the contents, hope rising in her chest like never before. "He was hired, given directions of where to find Marguerite, and how to go about murdering her. All from an anonymous source. It even mentions that the anonymous bene-factor would ensure that if he was caught, he would be released. But the handwriting . . ." She lifted it up for Byron to see closer.

"It matches the handwriting in the journal. Now, if we can tie the handwriting to Moreau, we can prove that he has been working to murder Marguerite, and that he was involved in Emilie's death."

Chabot spoke up. "His physician's reports will be in his hand. Could we not cross reference them?"

"There is still the chance that he uses a different hand when working with Circe," Byron said. "But we won't know until we check."

January 24, 1889:
Afternoon

T HE SUN WAS HIGH IN THE SKY as they approached the police prefecture. Byron and Chabot held Richter fast between them to ensure he did not escape. Mira walked on Byron's other side, grateful for the fresh air and sunshine, even if it was cold. After being cooped up in Marguerite's for a week, it was a welcome reprieve. As they drew near the building, a gentleman in a long, tan coat moved to intercept them. It wasn't until he was directly in their path that she recognized Fred.

"Didn't expect to see you here, chap," Fred said. "Our man is in there. It doesn't seem as if he has any inclination to even go near Rue de la whatsit."

"We know. He opted for a different method," Byron said, gesturing to Richter.

"I was going to ask who your friend was. Is everyone all right?"

"As well as anyone can be when shots ring out," Byron said, glancing at Mira.

"I'm perfectly fine," she said. And she meant it. They were so close to the end of it all.

Fred frowned. "Shall I resume my post?"

"For now," Byron said.

Fred nodded and headed for a newspaper boy, pulling out a few francs in exchange for a reason to loiter.

Chabot continued to drag Richter up the steps of the pre-fecture with Byron and Mira following. Once they were inside, Chabot took care of the particulars of finishing Richter's arrest and filing the proper paperwork. After putting their names down for an appointment with Prefect Lozé, Byron and Mira sat in the foyer to people watch and wait.

Byron broke the silence after a few minutes.

"I'm proud of you."

She blinked. "What?"

"What happened back there. We let our guard down after so long a wait. You were left alone, when I promised you—and myself—that you would never be in any danger." He sighed. "He could have killed you."

She set her hand on his arm. "But he didn't."

"No. He didn't." He turned towards her. "But that's only because of how brilliant you are."

She flushed. "I nearly wasn't. The moment he pulled out the gun I-I froze. I was back there again."

"And yet you fought. Against him, against your memories. You managed to send me a message without Richter knowing." He laced his hand with hers. "That is all the more impressive."

Chabot rushed out of the records room with a file in hand.

"Here it is," he said, holding it out to Byron. "The report from Emilie's death."

Byron took the folder and skimmed through it, a small smile forming on his face.

"AS YOU CAN SEE, SIR, THE HANDWRITING is the same," Chabot stood before Lozé's desk as the prefect read over the journal and letter. Mira sat in one of the armchairs while Byron took the other. They'd explained the entirety of the case, omitting Moreau's identity. This was done with the hope that Lozé would take the information seriously before discovering the possibility of interior corruption.

Chabot continued, "We have testimonials from the House of Worth about a fitting that occurred on the night of the ninth of January. Eye witnesses that show Marguerite de Bonnemains at the opera. Proof that Emilie Lavigne would stand in for fittings for her employer."

"You'll notice," Byron said, "there is a passage within the journal outlining a particular poison and its effects. Specifically, that it can cause symptoms similar to seizures. And based on the diagram for a pin cushion with a receptacle for poison, I believe we have enough evidence to show that this is the means by which Emilie Lavigne was killed. And with the letter—"

"Yes, yes," Lozé waved a hand. "I see the whole of it. Circe intended for Madame de Bonnemains to be the victim. Have you identified the individual whose hand this is?"

"That is the difficult part," Byron said, placing the physician's report on the desk.

Lozé frowned. "Why, this is from the prefecture."

"Yes, sir," Chabot said.

Lozé opened the folder, his brow furrowing more and more as he read.

"Moreau," he said at last. "I can't believe it."

"The evidence is before you, sir," Chabot said.

"I recognize that." Lozé rubbed at his temples. "It is simply difficult to grasp. To have a member of Circe in such a position."

"This is part of the reason why we wanted to ensure the validity of the evidence," Byron said. "If we were wrong, it would have needlessly tarnished the reputation of the police."

"And yet it shall be ruined in any case." Lozé sighed. "Chabot, will you ask Cartier to bring Moreau here?"

"Yes, sir." Chabot straightened and left the room.

Lozé looked the two detectives over with a considering eye. "Things were much quieter before you came here."

"Perhaps," Byron said. "But I think the truth is worth the upset."

"I'll have to send some men to La Mans to work with the police there to find that tailor's assistant." He pulled a notepad closer to him and jotted something down.

"I will say, your Constable Chabot has been invaluable in this investigation," Byron said.

Lozé's eyes crinkled at the corners. "He can be a bit, as you say, overzealous, at times. But yes, he is a good man."

As he set down his pen, a knock came to the door and Lozé called in French, *"Come in."*

Moreau stepped in with Chabot right behind.

"You wished to speak with me, sir?" Moreau asked, addressing Lozé.

"Yes. I wanted to ask a question about this report of yours." Lozé switched to English and held up the physician's report.

Moreau took it and opened it. "The Lavigne case, yes." He glanced over at Byron and Mira. "I thought we discussed it already. Has new evidence come to light?"

"We believe so," Lozé said, tone cool. "That is the report you wrote?"

"Yes."

"Do you recognize this?" Lozé picked up the journal.

Moreau stiffened for a moment. "I couldn't say."

"And this?" Lozé held the letter out to him.

The doctor took the letter, a slight tremor in his fingers. "Should I recognize it?"

Byron stood. "It is in your hand. All of them are. And I believe that we have a Mr. Richter in one of the cells who would be willing to verify the letter was sent to him and that it instructed him to murder Marguerite de Bonnemains."

Moreau let out a breath, setting the letter on the desk. In a heartbeat he made a dash towards the door, opening it and careening into the constable standing guard outside. Between the constable, Chabot, and Byron, Moreau was pulled forcibly back into the room and made to sit in one of the chairs. The two constables stood on either side of the doctor. Mira moved next to Byron by the fireplace.

"I will take that action as another piece of evidence against you," Lozé said. "Do you have any explanation for yourself?"

Moreau looked around the room, taking in each person. "I have no explanation. Arrest me if you will."

"We will," Byron said. "But I believe we ought to know exactly what we are arresting you for."

"What do you mean?" Moreau frowned.

Byron clenched his fists. "How many reports have you falsified?" A thread of anger was strung tight within his voice. "How many people have you helped to kill?"

"In truth, I don't know," Moreau said. "I never kept track." His voice was detached and without emotion, as if he were resigned to the fact he had been caught at last.

Lozé stood and moved around the desk. "I can't believe what I am hearing. Do you not have any proper feeling? Any regret?"

Moreau straightened in his chair. "What I do, what *we* do, is something that none of you would ever understand. And my role," he laughed. "My role was magnificent."

"Testing poisons and facilitating murder?" Byron said. "That is what you call magnificent? To take innocent lives?"

"There are no innocents," Moreau said. "All of us do evil to achieve the good." He gestured to the journal. "For you to have that means a crime was committed, and yet you must think it justified." He reached into his pocket and the rest of them tensed, ready to step in should he produce a gun. When Moreau retrieved a black snuff box from his pocket, the room relaxed.

Mira's jaw tightened. "I've heard all the delusions of a new world order, of peace and prosperity that Circe promises to its members. But I also know what Circe intends to do. There is no justification for starting a war, killing millions, to establish a utopia."

He looked up at her, his mouth stretching into something between a grimace and a smile. "You are Miss Mira Blayse, yes?" He didn't wait for an answer. "It seems Burke is right about you after all. You *are* dangerous. I didn't see it when we met before."

He laughed a little. "Ah, but it is so easy to judge the mistakes of our past." He opened the box, and tipped some white powder into his hand. "At least I shall have a choice in my future."

Before anyone could process what he said, he lifted his hand and sniffed the powder up. At first, there was no effect. He coughed a little and pulled back against the chair, his eyes widening. His body began to spasm and convulse—the jerky movements brought him out of the chair and onto the floor. The snuff box fell from his hand, spilling the grayish-white powder on the carpet beside him.

Lozé moved to help him, but Byron caught him by the arm, pulling him back. "Don't touch him," he said, standing between Mira and the body. "We ought to be wary of that powder. It may be cyanide"

The convulsions stopped and Moreau lay motionless on the floor. Dizziness came over Mira and she held onto Byron's arm for support.

Lozé stepped back, clearing his throat. "Chabot, go fetch Dr. Ogier. Tell him to bring gloves. Then call the morgue and inform Brouardel of the death. Cartier, stand guard outside." He moved to the door but paused before opening it, looking back at Byron and Mira. "He spoke of Burke as if he were still alive. I think you ought to come with me and tell me everything you know."

❧◦❡◦☙

IT WAS ALMOST FIVE BY THE TIME they left the prefecture. Between the meeting with Lozé, discussions of whether or not they would be required for Liliane's trial, and filling out paperwork, Mira was more than ready to go home. But before they made it to the corner to call a carriage, they heard a sharp, "Wait!"

They turned and found Constable Chabot fast approaching.

"Whatever is the matter?" Byron said, his hold on Mira's arm tightening. She found herself looking past the constable, expecting some threat to come bursting out of the prefecture doors.

"Nothing," Chabot said, a little out of breath as he reached them. "I wanted to thank you. This case was unlike any I have been allowed to be a part of."

"It would not have been possible without your help," Byron said.

Chabot inclined his head. "I also wish to apologize again. For believing the two of you to be criminals."

Mira laughed. "It was an easy mistake. Especially when we associated with one."

"Monsieur Jaubert is a better man than I thought he was. Even with his past."

Byron smiled. "His past could still prove useful to the prefecture. You might want to ask him if he wants to consult for you."

Chabot tipped his head to the side. "An interesting thought."

"We ought to be going," Byron said. "Although . . ." he reached into his bag and pulled out the folder he had "borrowed" from the station. "Would you mind returning this?"

The constable's eyes widened. "It was you? Why, we have been looking for that file for weeks!" He laughed. "You are thieves after all."

Byron's eyes shone with mirth. "Only sometimes."

WHEN THEY ARRIVED AT THE BOARDING HOUSE there weren't nearly as many crates and trunks in the foyer. For a moment, Mira wondered if, in the week since she'd seen her family, they had up and moved, although she knew them well enough to know better than that.

"Hello?" she called. "Is anyone home?"

A scattering of footsteps down the stairs announced Clarisse into the foyer. Her face lit up as she saw them and she ran to give Mira a hug.

"You're home!"

Mira hugged the little girl back, a little confused. "You seem in good spirits."

Clarisse pulled back. "I missed you."

"Where is everyone?" Byron asked, helping Mira out of her coat.

"Oh, Maman and Papa are in the library with Klasha," she said, oblivious to the way that paternal term of endearment affected Mira. She'd never called her uncle anything but "uncle." And yet to hear "papa" from her cousin made her heart glow. Clarisse continued, "Walker is with Jean-Marie and Georges in the study. But everyone will want to see you."

Mira smiled. "I'll be sure we make the rounds."

Clarisse bounced on her toes, a liveliness in her that Mira hadn't seen since before Emilie died. "Might I come with you? I want to be there when you hear the news."

"News?" Mira frowned, heading towards the library.

Clarisse bit her lip. "You'll see."

The door to the library was open, but Mira knocked on the door regardless. Her aunt, uncle, and Klasha looked up from whatever it was they were working on.

Cyrus stood to give Mira a hug. "When you said you would be gone for a time, I did not expect it to be a week."

"We didn't expect it either," Mira said, hugging him back before sitting across from the rest of the group. Byron shook hands with Cyrus before joining her.

"Is it settled, then?" Cyrus said with hope in his eyes.

"As settled as it can be," Byron said.

"Tell them the news!" Clarisse bounded in behind them.

Loretta smiled. "Do you want to tell them?"

Clarisse grinned. "Klasha is going to take over the boarding house!"

"Why, that's a wonderful idea!" Mira said.

Klasha pursed her lips. "It is only sense. I do not wish to move. The children do not wish to lose their family home. So. I manage the house. The money from the tenants will ensure that all stays in repair. Whatever money is left, we save for the children."

"And I can come visit!" Clarisse said, beaming.

"It's the perfect arrangement," Byron said.

"Yes, we thought so," Loretta said. "I think everything has worked out for the best."

February 1, 1889

*S*MOKE BILLOWED OUT OVER THE PARIS TRAIN station, the steam engine heaving as it came to a slow stop. Mira stood on her tiptoes, trying to spot Landon through the crowd. Byron caught her by the crook of her elbow and pulled her closer to him.

"He'll be on the next train," he said.

"I know," she said, smoothing out the skirt of her traveling dress.

Passengers trailed off of the current train, making their way to whatever destination awaited them. Mira strained to see the times on the board. The next train wasn't meant to arrive for another ten minutes. She and Byron navigated the crowd to where Cyrus was waiting.

Her uncle had planned the day meticulously. When they had written to Landon to inform him that they would be returning, he had written back insisting on coming to meet them. He had ignored all subsequent letters telling him that he didn't need to make the journey and sent a final letter with his travel arrangements. His train would come at half-past ten, whether they liked it or not. Of course, he had phrased it in a much gentler way. It seemed he had missed them as much as they had missed him.

Cyrus had intended to meet him alone, but Mira insisted on coming along, bringing Byron with her. The rest of the family would come by quarter to eleven with the luggage. They would all board the train back to Calais at eleven sharp. This, of course, relied on there being no delays for either locomotive, but so far it seemed to be a successful venture.

The last few weeks had been comparatively calm. The election had been in favor of General Boulanger, but he chose to spend the night of his victory with Marguerite, instead of inciting the coup and taking power immediately, as so many had thought he would. Unless something happened in the government, he would take office in July.

The police prefecture had tracked down Liliane Aguillard and a date had been set for her trial. Chabot had received a commendation and promotion for his work on the case. He would be acting as witness and supplying all the evidence so that Byron, Mira, and her family could finally go home to Swan Walk.

She couldn't wait to see Landon. It seemed as if it had been ages since she had seen the old butler. The whole family would be together again. Or, at least, most of the family.

It was such a strange juxtaposition of emotions. She was sad to leave, but wanted more than anything to go home. And yet, home would be so different. Paris had taken so much from them. How could it ever be the same?

The crowd dispersed and the conductors called for final passengers. The engine huffed and puffed, pulling out of the station. She turned away from the main platform and sat with Byron on one of the nearby benches.

This pain in her heart was familiar. It was an old one, now mingled with a new sorrow. The same grief had led her to Byron in the first place, that urging of her sorrowing soul to find closure in her parents' deaths. But, even after learning the truth, the pain remained. It would always be there, as long as she remembered what she had lost—as long as she loved them.

Her heart ached with all the love she felt. For her parents. For Emilie. For Cyrus, standing nearby. Somehow, she still had love for the man she thought her godfather was. Even with all the pain he had caused to her family, the losses endured by her uncle and Loretta because of his actions over the years. And yet, they had found each other, in the end. Their love would support them through the grief.

She loved Byron, even if his memory would always be incomplete. She loved him so much that it hurt. But the pain was worth it because of what it meant.

Grief had been her constant companion since childhood, and for the first time it felt *comforting*. Tears sprang to her eyes, but there was a joy to them.

"What's the matter?" Byron asked, concerned. He pulled out a handkerchief and handed it to her.

She dabbed at her eyes with a smile. "Nothing at all."

He frowned. "I thought we agreed to have no more secrets?"

"So we did." She folded the handkerchief into a square again. "I was thinking of everyone I've lost. Everyone we've lost." She looked back at Cyrus. "And how much I love them."

"Ah. Happy tears, then?' Byron asked.

"Definitely." She tucked the handkerchief into his suit pocket. "I was also thinking of how much I love you."

He laughed a little. "Is that so?"

She looked up at him. "Is that so hard to believe?"

"No." He took her hand and brushed his lips over her knuckles. "Because I was thinking the same about you. In fact I—"

His sentence was drowned out by the approach of the next train. Mira stood, excitement running through her. Cyrus checked his watch and called to them.

"I do believe this is the one!"

Once again, Mira stood on tiptoe to see over the crowds and steam. This time, she spotted Landon making his way towards them. If she were younger, she might have run to meet him. As it was, she allowed him to approach at his own pace.

"It is good to see you, sir," Landon said when he reached them. "And I look forward to meeting Mrs. Griffon when she arrives."

Cyrus shook his hand. "She is eager to meet you as well."

Landon's eyes sparkled when he saw her. "Good morning, Miss. And Mr. Constantine, you look well."

"Thank you, Landon," Byron said.

"I'm so glad you've come," Mira said. "Although, you really didn't need to come all this way just to travel back again."

"It is no trouble at all. I would hate for you to make the journey without help, especially with everything that has happened." He stepped closer. "And I will have you know that little Nero has been the nuisance he's always been."

Mira laughed. "I'm glad that he is doing well. I've missed him too."

The rest of the family arrived soon thereafter, and it was all a flurry of limbs and luggage as they settled in. Mira sat by the window in one of the compartments with Byron next to her. Walker and Georges would be riding with them, once they had sorted out the bulk of the luggage with the porters. How strange was it to have so many family members that two compartments were needed?

She looked out the window, smoke billowing up around it, ready for the train to depart. There were a few people still on the platform. She recognized one of them and ice formed along her spine.

Professor Burke.

She blinked, thinking perhaps it was her imagination. Those memories coming back to haunt her again. And maybe it was. When the smoke shifted and he was no longer there.

"Are you all right, Mira?" Byron asked. "You've gone rather still."

There was a split second where her inclination was to lie, to hide her fear, to keep it from him. But she pushed that feeling away. No more secrets. Not between them.

"For a moment, I thought I saw Professor Burke on the platform."

Byron moved to look out the window. "Are you certain?"

She shook her head. "Not at all."

As the train started to move, she kept her gaze on the platform, half expecting to see him again. In the misty light, she could almost imagine other figures standing there. Emilie, her parents, even Alexander Durant. But no. It was only smoke, only steam.

The awful truth was she knew Professor Edward Burke was out there. Maybe not in the station, but somewhere out there, in Paris or Spain or Prussia. And Circe was out there, too. She was beginning to think that they always would be there, haunting her. Haunting them.

The door to the compartment opened and Landon entered with a tray.

"I took the liberty of finding some tea for our party, Miss. Would you like a cup?"

"Yes, please." She turned away from the window, away from the ghosts. "And do pour one for yourself, Landon. We have so much to tell you."

Author's Invitation

Welcome to the end of the book! Since you've made it this far, I have a favor to ask. Whether you enjoyed the book or not, please leave an honest review on Amazon or Goodreads. It only takes a few minutes and makes a significant difference for the future of this book. Reviews are essential for its success and longevity, and you'll be helping other readers decide if it's worth their time. If you loved the book, don't hesitate to recommend it to your friends!

To make it even easier, scan the QR code below to go directly this book's page on Goodreads:

AND IF YOU WANT TO KEEP UP with my news and inklings, you can join my newsletter by scanning the QR code below.

Acknowledgements

Well, here we are again. I do believe I'll leave out the piffle and get straight to the gratitude this time.

My dear Becca, thank you once again for your continued support and careful reading of the manuscript. I appreciate that you are always one text away.

To Hannah, Rachel, and Mary—thank you all for being part of such a fantastic writing group. I still can't believe you insisted on reading the rest of this book over the course of three weeks when you realized I had a deadline. Your suggestions (like the bell in the laboratory) were wonderful.

Matt, I might not have figured out the climax of the book were it not for one conversation. I don't even know if you remember it, but thank you for that.

As one of my treasured rubber ducks, I would be remiss to not mention you, Alex. Especially since your advice has changed the course of my life so much. You can forever say "I told you so," about the suggestion to "just write the next book."

Becky, I thought the book was in a pretty good state when I gave it to you. I'm so grateful you didn't use red ink—those pages would've been bleeding. I feel so privileged to have you. I don't know if I've ever had a better editor. The feeling was electric as I made my revisions because I could see just how much better the book was becoming. Thank you.

Mum, as always, you are such a support. I would not be able to do this if it weren't for you. I love you!

About the Author

NATALIE BRIANNE grew up steeped in British mystery—from Poirot to Lord Peter Wimsey, she learned early to love a good twist and a cleverly placed clue. Some of her fondest memories involve curling up with her family, trying to out-solve the detectives on screen. When a friend floated the idea of an amnesiac investigator, she couldn't resist—especially once Byron Constantine walked into her mind, top hat and all.

While writing the first book, Natalie lived in London—walking the same streets her characters do, even staying at 27 Palace Court, the detective's future home. Her time there brought a tactile authenticity to the fog, cobblestones, and candlelight of 1880s London.

When Natalie isn't writing, she's drawing, trying to keep her cat off her keyboard, and forgetting that she has vegetables in her fridge.

Looking For More?

CONSTANTINE CAPERS SERIES:

The Pennington Perplexity
Flashes of Memory
There Comes a Midnight Hour
The Veil of Death
A Song Without Words

SHORT STORIES AND NOVELLAS:

FROM CONSTANTINE'S CASEBOOK

Byron's Oblivion
The Great Sheep Panic
In the Silence of the Catacombs

FROM SAMIRA'S SKETCHBOOK

The Forgotten Letter

GENERAL FICTION

The Glade of Sionn O' Shea

www.ingramcontent.com/pod-product-compliance
Lightning Source LLC
Chambersburg PA
CBHW022107240626
47153CB00007B/2270